ROMAN FEVER

ROMAN FEVER

Domesticity and Nationalism in Nineteenth-Century American Women's Writing

ANNAMARIA FORMICHELLA ELSDEN

The Ohio State University Press
Columbus

Formichella Elsden, Annamaria, 1964–
Roman fever : domesticity and nationalism in nineteenth-century American women's writing / Annamaria Formichella Elsden.
p. cm.
Includes bibliographical references (p.) and index.
ISBN 0-8142-0946-7 (Cloth : alk. paper) — ISBN 0-8142-5117-X (Paper : alk. paper) — ISBN 0-8142-9030-2 (CD-ROM)
1. American literature—Women authors—History and criticism. 2. Women travelers—United States—Biography—History and criticism. 3. Nationalism and literature—United States—History—19th century. 4. Women and literature—United States—History—19th century. 5. American literature—19th century—History and criticism. 6. Americans—Foreign countries—History—19th century. 7. Travelers' writings, American—History and criticism. 8. Nationalism in literature. 9. Family in literature. 10. Home in literature. I. Title.
PS147 .F67 2004
813'.3099287—dc22

2003025904

Jacket design by Dan O'Dair.
Text design by Jennifer Forsythe.
Type set in Italian Old Style.
Printed by Thomson-Shore, Inc.

The paper used in this publication meets the minimum requirements of the American National Standard for Information Sciences—Permanence of Paper for Printed Library Materials. ANSI Z39.48–1992.

9 8 7 6 5 4 3 2 1

CONTENTS

ACKNOWLEDGMENTS

Without the help of the following kind and generous people, this book would not have been possible. I am indebted to Elizabeth Ammons, Sheila Emerson, Alan Lebowitz, and Lisa MacFarlane for responding to the project in its early versions. My friends Margot Sempreora and Jon Hodge have been both encouraging and insightful throughout the various stages of the writing process. In addition, I owe thanks to my academic assistants, Adam Schenck and Angela Silvey, for their willingness to help prepare the final manuscript. My most tireless, insightful, and supportive reader, Valerie Rohy, deserves more thanks than I can express. I am also grateful to be blessed with a family that has inspired me in many ways. My father instilled in me a love for Italy and excellence while my mother showed by example how to be both strong and kind. Lastly, I must express deep gratitude to my husband and children, who have been patient enough to give me the time and space I needed to complete this study. Darin, Gabriel, and Ariana are the foundation upon which the rest is built.

INTRODUCTION

"A Tale of Import So Divine": New Women in the Old World

Rendering the plight of the nineteenth-century, middle-class woman in graphic terms, Florence Nightingale wrote in 1852 "She is like the Archangel Michael as he stands upon Saint Angelo at Rome. She has an immense provision of wings, which seem as if they would bear her over earth and heaven; but when she tries to use them, she is petrified into stone, her feet are grown into the earth, chained to the bronze pedestal" ("Cassandra" 50). Nightingale's revision of the "ministering angel" stereotype—which she herself has come to epitomize—exposes the gender ideology that constrained nineteenth-century British women and caused Nightingale to lament that "there is perhaps no century where the woman shows so meanly as in this" (50). Her feminist treatise, "Cassandra," develops the pointed question, "Why have women passion, intellect, moral activity—these three—and a place in society where no one of the three can be exercised?" (25). Embodying her question in the image of the petrified angel, whose powerful wings are neutralized by their decorative status, Nightingale knew that to be idolized often meant to be chained to the altar.

At the same time, Nightingale's appropriation of the statue revises the central symbol of Rome's Castel Sant'Angelo in the service of a feminist argument. Both the archangel Michael, biblical victor over Lucifer's dark forces, and Castel Sant'Angelo, a stone fortress connected to the Vatican by a hidden passageway through which popes historically escaped danger, exemplify masculine strength. Indeed, the towering sculpture itself, spreading its bronze wings and sheathing its mighty sword, is formidable, to say the least. Nightingale's adoption and feminization of such a symbol emblematize the kind of revisionary strategy this study explores. The nineteenth-century American women writers I examine, similarly bounded by the ideology of the "angel in the house," manipulate Italy and Italian imagery in their texts, enabling their feminist projects by portraying escape from both domestic boundaries and the stereotype of nineteenth-century femininity.

In *The Bonds of Womanhood,* Nancy Cott argues that in the nineteenth century "the central convention of domesticity was the contrast between the home and the world" (64). This definition was relevant to White, middle-class women on a national as well as a personal level, making the term "domestic" multivalent in my study. In the first part of the nineteenth century, the term as it applied to the home, and specifically to middle-class women, became a powerful signifier; the "'domestic sphere' as woman's pro-per realm" became codified (Cott 11). As early as 1545, however, "domestic" signified "pertaining to one's own country," in contrast to "foreign," a meaning of signal importance in a century that began with the rise of Jacksonian republicanism and closed on the eve of the First World War. A third meaning of "domestic"—referring to a wild creature made tame—also operates in this project, as "living under the care of Man" becomes a source of conflict for late-nineteenth- and early-twentieth-century, middle-class White women *(OED).* Taken collectively, the various significations of "domesticity" collapse the realms of public and private; that is, they suggest the complicated interrelationship between issues of the home and issues of state that characterize selected texts written by nineteenth-century American women about Italy.

Critical studies of both male and female writers and artists have frequently acknowledged the nineteenth-century American fascination with Italian culture, art, and history. Starting with Van Wyck Brooks's 1958 study, *The Dream of Arcadia,* and continuing with Nathalia Wright's *American Novelists in Italy* (1965), Theodore Stebbins's *The Lure of Italy: American Artists and the Italian Experience* (1992), and Leonardo Buonomo's *Backward Glances: Exploring Italy, Reinterpreting America* (1996), twentieth-century scholars have demonstrated Italy's unique and influential position in American arts and letters. Other critics have underscored the American attraction to Italy in more specialized terms: William Vance, for example, examines the Eternal City in his two-volume *America's Rome* (1989), as do a number of contemporary scholars in Robert K. Martin and Leland S. Person's collection *Roman Holidays: American Writers and Artists in Nineteenth-Century Italy* (2002); Jenny Franchot looks at Catholicism's influence on American literary history in *Roads to Rome: The Antebellum Protestant Encounter with Catholicism* (1994). While all of these studies make important contributions, and several have influenced my discussion in significant ways, none specifically examines the impact of Italy on nineteenth-century American *women's* writing.[1]

My study groups six American women whose writings were shaped by their encounters with Italy to argue that we can expand our critical understanding of nineteenth-century American womanhood *and* nationhood by investigating women's attempts to leave behind the domestic, in all the senses of that term.[2] My grouping, admittedly selective, provides a suggestive composite view of how middle-class, White, American women apprehended and represented the Italian land and culture. Their texts form a subgroup of American literature that is both cohesive and divergent, sharing common themes and differing in significant ways from men's texts produced during the same period. From the beginning decades of the nineteenth century, U.S. women not only traveled abroad but also composed texts that interrogated the artistic and political potential of both their gender and their country, concepts that they framed as inextricably linked. The following chapters show how Italy enabled such arguments by affording these women both a removal from and a reencounter with "domesticity" on the levels just now outlined: as a concept of state, as a thematics of the home, and as a tamed status in which wildness has been curtailed.

Certainly, as recent criticism has established, the domestic sphere was central to nineteenth-century American constructions of middle-class womanhood.[3] Yet a number of women were privileged and daring enough to leave home and nation, and the ways they made sense of their travel experiences in writing significantly affect any historical and critical understanding of nineteenth-century American gender roles. As Ann Shapiro reminds us in *Unlikely Heroines,* "If [nineteenth-century literary heroines] are different from the heroes of American literature, they are also surprisingly similar. They do not hunt whales or raft on the Mississippi, but they exhibit the same urge to break with tradition, the same rejection of conventional values, and the same desire for adventure" (4). Passion for adventure can be said to inspire the women writers of this study—Catharine Maria Sedgwick, Margaret Fuller, Harriet Beecher Stowe, Sophia Peabody Hawthorne, Constance Fenimore Woolson, and Edith Wharton—who utilized letters, travel narratives, newspaper columns, novels, and short stories to accommodate the new ideas and sensations that arose during their encounters with Italy.

Beyond its significance as the *Dream of Arcadia* Thomas Cole painted in 1838, Italy held a special charm for the women writers I study. Sophia Hawthorne called Rome the "Empress of the World." Margaret Fuller exclaimed, "City of the Soul! yes, it is *that;* the very dust magnetizes you, and thousand spells have been chaining you in every careless, every murmuring moment. Yes! Rome, however seen, thou must still be adored; and every hour of absence or presence must deepen love with one who has known what it is to repose in thy arms" (238). Even contemporary critic Sandra Gilbert invests Italy with magical power: "[Italy] is a utopian motherland whose glamour transforms all who cross her borders, empowering women, ennobling men, and—most significantly—annihilating national and sexual differences" (198). Examining the particular attraction Italy held for these women travelers reveals as much about nineteenth-century American culture—its investment in art, gender, and nation—as it does about the Italian land itself.

Italy is useful to these women's texts in many ways. Idealized as a golden Arcadia where sensual life could be savored and practicality abandoned, Italy represented a particularly tantalizing form of release to the nineteenth-century American mind. For women travelers, liberated from household chores and from a self defined solely in relation to home and family, Italy offered opportunities for education and contemplation unavailable in a domestic (or domesticated) context. The promise withheld from Isabel Archer in Henry James's *Portrait of a Lady* (1881)—"Italy, as yet imperfectly seen and felt, stretched before her as a land of promise, a land in which love of the beautiful might be comforted by endless knowledge" (207)—is fulfilled, to a degree, for the women of my study, who could be personally and artistically liberated from the patriarchal marriage plot during their travels. These writers' encounters—with Italian art, female Catholic saints, the social position of Italian women, contemporary Italian politics, historical monuments, and ancient Roman mythology—result in self-awareness and an interrogation of American republicanism, in stark contrast to the stifling marriage Isabel Archer endures with Gilbert Osmond. Margaret Fuller's emphatic "Arcadia!—would the name were America" (98) exemplifies the idealistic and reformist agenda found in these women's textual responses to Italy. The fantasy of the paradisiacal sweet life ("la dolce vita"), together with contemporary Italian social conditions, often fueled their discursive efforts to envision a better state at home.

Perhaps the most vexed aspect of Italy for nineteenth-century travelers, men *and* women, was Catholicism. Critic Paul Giles describes "the early nineteenth-century image of Catholicism as a sinister, gothic phenomenon, full of devious monks and dark dungeons" (76). Yet precisely what Americans found offensive about Catholicism—its ornamentation, idolatry, ritual—was also subordinated as feminine and placed in contrast to the more masculine values of Enlightenment Protestantism. This feminization of Catholicism seems to explain, in part, the complex relationship that often developed between American women in Italy and Catholic sights. When Giles writes, describing the dominant, nineteenth-century American perspective that "one traveled to Catholic Europe for a broadening humanist education or for aesthetic frivolity, a temporary flirtation with the exotic 'Scarlet Woman' of Rome" (84), he does not describe the experiences of the women in my study. First, it is doubtful that these women traveled to Italy to flirt with an exotic foreign woman. Second, their texts reveal a far more complicated and often sympathetic view of Catholicism's ideals, if not its practice. Margaret Fuller's commentary on the barrenness of Protestant churches suggests what she and others, like Sophia Hawthorne, celebrated in Catholicism: "How sorrowfully bare is the interior of such a cathedral [the Minster of York], despoiled of the statues, the paintings, and the garlands that belong to the Catholic religion! The eye aches for them. Such a church is ruined by Protestantism; its admirable exterior seems that of a sepulchre; there is no correspondent life within" (83). Such passages suggest how grouping these women's texts can enrich and complicate our understanding of the nineteenth-century American view of Catholicism.

Their work shares common pleasures, like Catholic ornamentation, as well as concerns, like fears about women's condition both abroad and at home. Thus the "fever" of my title signifies both women's enthusiasm for travel (and reform) and the dangerous consequences risked by American women abroad. Many women writers depict a divided Italy, simultaneously enchanting and lethal, lush host to the malaria that emblematized the danger awaiting ambitious or independent women. Harriet Beecher Stowe indicates Italy's dual nature in her novel *Agnes of Sorrento* (1862), observing that "In our day, these lovely places have their dark shadow ever haunting their loveliness: the malaria, like an unseen demon, lies hid in their sweetness" (390). In *Letters from Abroad to Kindred at Home* (1841), Catharine Maria Sedgwick asserts that in Italy, "Nature is, indeed, here a tender restoring nurse" (II:72), while acknowledging later that many must flee the Roman campagna to save themselves from deadly disease. Sophia Peabody Hawthorne describes in *Notes in England and Italy* (1869) "the half-moon" that "shines without the thinnest veil over the dazzle of her radiance," adding wryly, "and this is the atmosphere of the fatal campagna" (540); and Margaret Fuller, in "Dispatch 26" (1849), writes of a "Rome that almost killed me with her cold breath of last winter, yet still with that cold breath whispered a tale of import so divine" (238).[4]

The main character of Constance Fenimore Woolson's "Street of the Hyacinth" (1882), Ettie Macks, explicitly frames the passion and the risk that drew the female artist to Italy: "There comes a time when [artists] have to live on hope and their own pluck more than upon anything tangible that the present has to offer. They have to take that risk. Well, I have taken it; I took it when we left America" (174). The hope of something "more" than "the present has to offer" motivates and unites the literary endeavors of the women discussed here. Despite danger, American women of the middle and upper classes traveled far to hear, and later to write, the "tale of import so divine" that Fuller describes. Historically, men's literature—Nathaniel Hawthorne's *Marble Faun* and James's *Daisy Miller,* for example—has highlighted Rome's (and love's) dangerous power over women. But when the women in this study encountered Italy's whisper for themselves, they heard a more complex narrative within which they were mobile, ambitious, brave, and independent. This is not to say that all six women included here interpret Italy in precisely the same way, telling the same tale six times, yet their texts share themes that emerge when we view this body of writing en masse. Escape from home and country ultimately freed them to expand their discursive territory beyond hearth and romance and to examine issues of a public nature in relation to their private experiences as women. Even Stowe's novel *Agnes of Sorrento,* the most conventional in terms of narrative, uses a fifteenth-century Italian setting to alter the conventional marriage plot and accommodate a political activism that is national in scale.

Taken collectively, the texts I examine undermine simplistic nineteenth-century constructions of womanhood and nationalism. The writing often exhibits a brutal honesty that contrasts with pastoral myths of Italy and reflects the writers' subject positions as women in a patriarchal culture. Texts by American men frequently fantasized an idyllic Italy, as William Vance argues in *America's Rome:* "The Rome they loved was, even more than has been realized, 'no Rome of reality,' but an imaginary place, a Rome of the mind" (II:78). Women writers make use of this fantasy as well, yet they also describe the vulnerability and constraints on mobility they faced in a foreign environment. Sophia Hawthorne could forget neither her immediate surroundings nor her physical body when she was denied access to a painting that her male companion was permitted to see (451). Similarly, Sedgwick's description of the "idle men, who collected about us and stared so unmercifully at the girls that they clung to me" (*Letters from Abroad* II:27) strikingly illustrates how Italy's "reality" pressed in upon women travelers.

Another noteworthy difference in women's texts is their explicit concern with the material conditions of women in the United States and abroad. Encounters with Italian women who are both more and less liberated than their American counterparts provoke comparisons that undercut essentialist notions about womanhood. In Sedgwick's and Fuller's texts, for example, the existence of female professors at the University of Bologna validates their sense of women's power and reinforces hope for the future of American women. In contrast, Fuller invokes domestic violence against Italian women, "the cries of mothers and wives beaten at night by sons and husbands," as evidence for "the ills of Woman's condition and remedies that must be applied" (245–46). Such gender-based observations are characteristic of much women's writing and provoke a variety of responses, yet all the women's texts examined here either make or imply the connection between individual women's lives and the larger political climate of their day. At times transcending boundaries between nations, these nineteenth-century women link Italian and American women's experiences and use both to bolster their arguments for more truly democratic republics.

At other times, however, the texts I examine are clearly invested in national borders. Benedict Anderson's theory of modern nationalism, outlined in *Imagined Communities,* proposes nationalism as a concept that is both historically determined, originating out of changes that occurred in the eighteenth century, and imagined. That is, "because the members of even the smallest nation will never know most of their fellow-members, meet them, or even hear of them" (6), the connection that Americans feel to each other is entirely a product of their own minds. Aided by nationalist propaganda such as the newspaper and the flag, the idea of nation takes root in the individual imagination. Clearly women, as fully half of the nation's population, participate in this construction of imaginary community; simultaneously, their relationship to public affairs has historically been circumscribed.[5] How, then, did women imagine the nation and their relationship to it? Unable to vote, to hold public office, and to fight for their country in the militia, did nineteenth-century women exhibit a sense of themselves as Americans that differed from that of men?

The decades after the Revolution bred anxiety for American nationalism. Although from our contemporary vantage point it seems that the major battles for the nineteenth-century American nation were fought on domestic soil, a significant number of Americans were traveling to Europe, and specifically to Italy, to confront a cultural frontier almost as fraught as the "savage" frontier of the American West. As a newly constituted republic, the nineteenth-century United States sought cultural legitimacy in addition to political actualization. No longer tied to England, the United States needed a literary aesthetic that would validate its nationhood and differentiate it from older European cultures. Emerson's assertion in "Self-Reliance" (1841) that "it is for want of self-culture that the superstition of traveling, whose idols are Italy, England, Egypt, retains its fascination for all educated Americans" betrays an anxiety about American culture from which he sought refuge in his concept of self-reliance (186).

Many travel texts of the period reflect both this fear of inadequacy as well as a sense of political and artistic destiny. Nineteenth-century travelers, men *and* women, who made the pilgrimage to Europe confronted their nationality on many levels, and those who textualized their experiences through journals, letters, and fiction returned incessantly to the subject of political and artistic Americanness. Politically, the nation had already taken on the mission of actualizing humanitarian ideals by becoming a democracy where, in theory, all "men" were created equal and all citizens could achieve prosperity. Yet, as a role model for other emerging democratic states, the United States had to confront failures in the form of slavery, a genocidal policy toward the native population, and restrictions on the rights of women. Artistically, travel writers attempted to compose a distinctly American portrait, aided by what they saw as the sharpened outline of the American traveler against the foreign background and motivated in part by the competition such juxtapositions engendered.[6]

In *Nation and Narration,* Homi Bhabha describes "the political 'rationality' of the nation as a form of narrative" (2). If nation is itself a narrative—if both "lose their origins in the myths of time and only fully realize their horizons in the mind's eye" (1)—what story of American nationalism do the women's texts grouped here tell us? In the late eighteenth and early nineteenth centuries the concept of republican motherhood was available as one way for free women to conceptualize their role in nation formation. Their contribution to a healthy republic was the production of civic-minded children well versed in the components of republican virtue. As Suzanne Gossett and Barbara Ann Bardes argue, such an arrangement provided middle-class women with only an indirect relationship to politics: "[T]he republican mother had to be well-educated and politically aware, although her only participation in political decision-making would be through others—her husband and sons" (16). In contrast to this limited political agency, by the turn into the twentieth century the suffrage movement had gained tremendous strength, with women gaining the vote in 1920. During the period between republican motherhood and women's voting rights, roughly a century, literature was a pivotal space in which women could proclaim their political views to a national audience; indeed, the texts I explore provide detailed examples of how nineteenth-century women imagined and narrated their nationalism.

Building on Anderson's notion of nationalism as imagined, Bhabha's concept of nation and narrative as linked entities, and the work of historians of women in the United States such as Gossett and Bardes, *Roman Fever* reveals how these American women's texts both contribute to and contest men's literary patriotism. Of this gendered nationalism I would highlight two salient aspects. First, American women recognized and manipulated traditional structures that promoted nationalism; their texts utilize the rhetorical strategies and symbolism that male writers often invoke. Second, these women sought to establish connections between their own experiences as women and the "domestic" state as a whole. Women like Stowe "imagined" a republic that reflected the values—like religious devotion and maternal compassion—to which they were committed in their daily lives. I want to emphasize the coexistence of both strategies so as not to imply either that all nineteenth-century, middle-class women's texts participated unproblematically in the master narrative of nationalism, or that all such writing depicted state affairs solely in terms of women's homes. It is important to recognize the combinations of public and private that these women undertook to write.

Ernest Renan's definition of "nation" suggests the synthesis these women's texts attempted. Anticipating Benedict Anderson's work by just under a century, Renan's "What Is a Nation?," a lecture delivered at the Sorbonne, stresses the interiority of nationalism and its roots in the citizen's individual consciousness. The "soul" of a nation, Renan writes, is constituted by two components that reside in the individual: "[O]ne is the possession in common of a rich legacy of memories; the other is present-day consent, the desire to live together, the will to perpetuate the value of the heritage that one has received in an undivided form" (19). The issue, then, for the women in my study was how, as women, to lay claim to this "rich legacy of memories," how to establish their connection to the nation's past, and how to "perpetuate the value of the heritage" in their contemporary contexts. Connections to the nation's past and future could be made through literary productions that promoted women's role in both.

The desire to connect to the past that motivated these nineteenth-century women writers also motivates my project now. Contemporary feminism demands a reevaluation of women's contributions to the American canon; we must acknowledge that women writers were prolific and popular, that they wrote beyond the narrow boundaries still ascribed to them by too much twentieth-century criticism, and that the unified voice of American individualism turns out to be a false construct. I want to emphasize that many women wrote in ways that challenged the status quo and that readers consumed these texts, at times voraciously. We have useful criticism that examines White, American women's relationship to the North American landscape, like Annette Kolodny's *The Land before Her,* yet nineteenth-century White women and their texts were shaped by international influences as well. Italy, viewed by many nineteenth-century Americans as the center of art and culture, drew certain privileged women writers who wanted to see this illustrious history for themselves and to interrogate and fortify their connection to Western culture's past.

My intent in foregrounding some central nationalist texts by women and reconstituting this countertradition in American literature is to promote the aims of materialist feminism, specifically its historicist project. Rosemary Hennessy describes the political imperative of this approach: "Materialist feminists need to insist on one of the strongest features of feminism's legacy—its critique of social totalities like patriarchy and capitalism—without abandoning attention to the differential positioning of women within them" (xii). Hennessy challenges feminist criticism to maintain feminism's strength while acknowledging that "woman" is not a monolithic concept, but a culturally and historically based one, and suggests that "without forfeiting feminism's specificity, materialist feminism fosters the alignment of a feminist standpoint with other political movements" (xviii). The following chapters align feminism with nationalism, with the intention of broadening our perceptions of concepts that continue to be sites of contested meaning in early-twenty-first-century America.

In *Reconstructing Womanhood,* Hazel Carby explains materialist analysis as "interpreting individual texts in relation to the dominant ideological and social formations in which they were produced" (6). My goal is to read America women's Italianate texts by foregrounding historical context in order to present a nonessentialist view of American womanhood *and* nationalism. At the same time, I want to resist a reductive biographical approach, which seems to be applied widely to women authors but much less extensively to men. My intention is neither to speculate on Margaret Fuller's feelings for her lover based on close readings of her dispatches, nor to suggest that the primary influences on her journalism were her romantic affairs. My goal is to read the *texts* as products of and contributions to particular historical circumstances. When I invoke biography, then, it is either as a means of gaining insight into the primary texts, or as a text that itself can be read as a product of a historical age.

It seems critics have read women's writing through a biographical lens due to a tradition of associating women with the home, rather than with schools of thought or mainstream literary traditions or political events. In criticism, we read more about women writers' spinsterhood than we do about most male writers' bachelorhood because men had access to a professional milieu (and a means of self-definition) in which a wife was not required. Women like Sedgwick, on the other hand, were expected to marry as part of their responsibility to the "woman's sphere."[7] Yet she did not marry. She *did* become a published writer; therefore I believe it is imperative to read her texts, and those of the other women included here, as contributions to a national literary moment, rather than as clues to understanding an idiosyncratic personal decision.[8]

My study is a necessary counterpart to critical works that overlook these women entirely or offer them as minor players in the nineteenth-century's major movements. Indeed, Percy Adams's study, *Travel Literature and the Evolution of the Novel* (1983), while it recognizes travel's literary influence, makes no mention of Catharine Maria Sedgwick, Sophia Hawthorne, Margaret Fuller, or Harriet Beecher Stowe, all of whom wrote travel-inflected literature contemporaneously with Nathaniel Hawthorne, Henry James, and William Dean Howells (male writers included in Adams's survey). Likewise, William Stowe's *Going Abroad: European Travel in Nineteenth-Century American Culture* (1994) omits Sedgwick, Sophia Hawthorne, and Constance Fenimore Woolson in favor of the more conventional Henry Adams and Mark Twain. Stowe does offer a chapter on Margaret Fuller, perhaps the most-often-studied woman in my group. And despite its broad subtitle—*American Writers and Artists in Nineteenth-Century Italy*—*Roman Holidays* maintains a relatively narrow focus, with eight essays on Hawthorne and two on James, and only two chapters that depart from those twin icons of the international theme. One of the Hawthorne essays incorporates Fuller, but other women are notably absent from the study. In the most unfortunate cases, then, women's contributions are elided entirely; in other studies they are subordinated to the more canonical male tradition.

As Mary Suzanne Schriber writes in *Telling Travels,* "It is indisputable that during the nineteenth century, American women, the majority of them white and middle class, began to travel abroad in significant numbers for the first time in history" (xi). This phenomenon started in the 1820s, according to Schriber, when increased affordability and accessibility of transportation facilitated women's travel.[9] As Schriber's observation about class and race suggests, the economics of travel contribute to my study's almost exclusively White, middle-class focus. Cultural oppression in the forms of poverty, slavery, and racism barred working-class women and most women of color from access to the Grand Tour. Thus, in the creative tradition I examine, produced by women who sought educational and cultural expansion in Italy, African American women are underrepresented. One notable exception is Edmonia Lewis, whose work I discuss in chapter 4, alongside Sophia Hawthorne's travel narrative. A sculptor of Chippewa and African American ancestry, Lewis sold enough copies of her sculptures to fund a trip to Rome in 1868 and later achieved fame for her exhibition of six works at the 1876 Centennial Exposition in Philadelphia.[10] As for working-class travelers, Constance Fenimore Woolson portrays poor female characters abroad in her exploration of the economics of artistic study, yet Woolson herself came from a middle-class, New England background and cannot be labeled "working class." The critical work of exploring how women of color and the working class imagined nationalism and contributed to the American national narrative remains a fruitful area of study but lies outside the scope of my work. Future studies of these issues, as I hope is true of my project as well, will contribute to a more multifaceted and thorough understanding of nineteenth-century American nationalism than has traditionally been offered by mainstream history.

There are times, of course, when the texts in my study reveal the biases and blindnesses of their age, as my work no doubt does, too. Stereotypes of Italians as childlike, of convents as unnatural and perverse, and of Italian workers as lazy and avaricious appear even in texts that are elsewhere supportive of the Italian people. For me, these moments are the most problematic, the most difficult to reconcile with the writers' humanitarian agendas. Although intent on democratic reform, these writers were blinded by the rhetoric of race that shaped the American perception of southern European countries, including Italy, and insisted that certain foreigners were essentially and temperamentally different from Anglo-Americans—in the case of Italians, passionate, sensual, indolent, and effeminate. This ethnocentrism simultaneously developed from and bolstered nationalist sentiment by promoting the notion that members of a particular nation constituted an identifiable race, a belief that contributed to patriotism's power to unite U.S. citizens against people of other nations. Unfortunately, this rhetoric pervaded the nineteenth century, and, if even reformist writers failed to overcome such biases, we may be less than surprised to see that, at the start of the twenty-first century, violence in the name of race and nation persists. The question that underlies this study but remains ultimately unanswered is, why do certain forms of nationalist bias, which have historically divided the world and engendered such violence, continue to be insurmountable?

My study proceeds chronologically, roughly following the contours of women's travel, which became extensive in the early-nineteenth century. I begin in 1841, with the publication of Sedgwick's *Letters from Abroad to Kindred at Home,* and end with Wharton's 1934 short story "Roman Fever." My discussion thus opens with the rise of Jacksonian republicanism in the first half of the nineteenth century and continues through the first part of the twentieth century, when the modern era revised concepts of womanhood and nationhood. The boundaries of this study mark important historical spans in both Italy and America. In Italy, the nineteenth century witnessed the revolutionary movement known as the *Risorgimento,* the 1861 unification of previously disparate states into one nation, the abolition of the pope's temporal power in 1870, and the rise of the Fascist party in the years after the First World War. These changes, combined with American political and cultural shifts and evolving attitudes toward Italy and the "foreign," produce the rich historical backdrop that informs women's writing of this period. Early in the nineteenth century, as Theodore Stebbins observes, "Almost every nineteenth-century observer contrasted the practicality of modern, utilitarian, materialistic America with the joyfulness, the impracticality of daily life in Italy," but by the beginning of the twentieth, "the myth of Italy as Arcadia, as a place with links to the Golden Age, was finally shattered" (21, 26).

During this historical span, the American women I discuss were removed from their home turf, enmeshed in Italian culture and politics, and liberated from what has been described in criticism as the "pull" of the American land. In much American writing, Christopher Mulvey notes, "A universal, cosmological scheme focused upon America, represented by the great forest, the great valley, or the great prairie, could generate a religious and millennial awe as it excited a personal and patriotic identity" (13). The absence of the "great" American landscape afforded women travelers a different perspective, no doubt aided by a European ideology in which the myth of individualism was not held sacred. Indeed, Joyce Warren argues that in Europe, individualism was "a negative concept connoting selfishness and social anarchy. . . . American republicanism differed from democratic tendencies in other countries, where the emphasis was on collectivism and social unity rather than on individual rights" (*Narcissus* 4). Europe's cultural climate, with its emphasis on community, reinforced women writers' discursive attempts to redefine America based on communal values.

Moving chronologically, my study focuses in chapter 1 on Sedgwick's

Letters from Abroad to Kindred at Home. By manipulating the travel narrative genre, Sedgwick inserted herself into a male literary tradition to address the concerns of nineteenth-century, middle-class American women and other marginalized groups. *Letters* reveals how Sedgwick's experiences in Italy shaped her conception of herself and her nation. Her firsthand encounter with the Austrian occupying forces in northern Italy, for example, and her inquiries about the condition of Italian women ignited and expanded her political activism. Using the travel genre to insist that the rights of others, especially women, must be incorporated into a truly humanitarian republic, Sedgwick's letters from abroad are designed to convince her nation to "bind to its altars its domestic ties and its charities" (II:155).

Part of a similar political project, as chapter 2 explains, Margaret Fuller's *New York Tribune* dispatches (1846–1850) present the Italian Revolution, in which she became actively involved, as a lens through which to view American democracy. I take Fuller's journalism and involvement in an emergent republic as examples of her participation in the construction of nationhood. Her dispatches reveal that not only do issues of state affect how individual women live, but women's activities also contribute to nation building. Ultimately, Fuller reproaches her nation while holding out hope for future American greatness: "I do not deeply distrust my country. She is not dead, but in my time she sleepeth, and the spirit of our fathers flames no more, but lies hid beneath the ashes" (230).

In chapter 3 I examine Harriet Beecher Stowe's 1862 novel *Agnes of Sorrento,* which also promotes a humanitarian and idealistic agenda. A sentimental novel that champions the domestic values of religion, community, and selflessness, *Agnes* reveals the implication of the personal in the political and vice versa. The romantic story of young Agnes intersects a political narrative concerned with the fifteenth-century Italian struggle for religious reform. My reading explores the interpenetration of the two plots, demonstrating how the sensibilities of Agnes make a significant contribution to her suitor's revolutionary agenda. I also examine Stowe's revision of concepts like "home" and "mother" in her projection of an ideal republic, a democracy inspired by a woman's valor.

Chapter 4 deals with Sophia Hawthorne's *Notes in England and Italy* (1869), a text that centers on Hawthorne's encounters with Italian art and celebrates strategies for distributing rare paintings to a wider audience. Hawthorne sees art as a vehicle for emotional and religious advancement, a necessary remedy for contemporary societal ills: "We need more Fra Angelicos to open the doors of Paradise for us" (416). Adding her own (textual) representation to the process, Hawthorne examines copying as a means of encouraging a return to pre-Renaissance values. This chapter also considers the work of two American sculptors working in Rome during the same period, Edmonia Lewis and Harriet Hosmer, whose art shares Hawthorne's feminist ideals: belief in women's potential both to succeed as artists and to serve as noble subjects for great art.

In chapter 5, I examine two short stories by Constance Fenimore Woolson, "'Miss Grief'" (1880) and "The Street of the Hyacinth" (1882), in which the woman artist's Roman studies culminate in a tragic confrontation with male standards. Of the work included in this study, Woolson's indicts the domestic harness most explicitly by invoking the connotation of "domestic" that requires the elimination of wildness or freedom. I am particularly interested in her critique of prescribed feminine sensibility, as well as her exposure of how economics maintained both the nineteenth-century's separate spheres and her characters' domestic confinement.

With chapter 6, my focus shifts to the twentieth century and Edith Wharton's short story, "Roman Fever" (1934). Like Woolson's, this narrative presents domestic values as confining, yet gestures toward a liberation from domestic constraints that corresponds to the more general cultural movement into the modern age. My reading of Wharton's fiction, which serves as a conclusion, emphasizes the story's thematics of change through the understated presence of Fascism, portraying major shifts on both personal and state levels. In this final chapter I consider how twentieth-century historical events redefined domestic themes and concerns, for the nation and the women within it, offering a provisional optimism for the future.

Each of my readings attempts both to foreground women writing beyond domestic boundaries and to counteract dominant stereotypes of American women abroad. In James's *Portrait of a Lady,* for example, Henrietta Stackpole is condemned as unwomanly because of her direct gaze and self-assurance. Ralph Touchett's remark, "if [Henrietta] was not a charming woman she was at least a very good fellow" (84), suggests the risk involved for women whose professional choices emphasized their connection to the public realm. To Isabel's observation that Henrietta "knows a great deal, and I know enough to feel that she is a kind of emanation of the great democracy—of the continent, the country, the nation," Ralph replies, "You like her for patriotic reasons. I am afraid it is on those very grounds that I object to her" (86). Both acknowledge a woman's implication in nationhood, yet Isabel glorifies a woman who serves as an active contributor while Ralph objects to such boldness, preferring the woman who reflects well on her nation by knowing her place and staying home.

At the other end of the spectrum, William Dean Howells's Theodore Colville, in *Indian Summer* (1886), observes of the American women in Florence, "Women of fashion always interested him; he liked them; it diverted him that they should take themselves seriously. Their resolution, their suffering for their ideal, such as it was, their energy in dressing and adorning themselves, the pains they were at to achieve the trivialities they passed their lives in, were perpetually delightful to him" (15). Mainstream, nineteenth-century constructions of White femininity seemed to limit male portrayals of women abroad to two categories: the assertive "feminist," whose forthrightness as a person and an American signify as "masculine," and the hyperfeminine lady, whose superficiality trivializes her as a nonthreatening diversion.

In recovering travel-inflected texts by American women writing about Italy, we discover characters and authors who move beyond these stereotypes. Their concerns involve far more than a preoccupation with personal appearance, and their articulation of political goals does not make them men; rather, their politics and their gender are interdependent. The work of recovery has recently begun on the texts included here, with Schriber's inclusion of selections from Sedgwick's *Letters from Abroad* in her anthology, *Telling Travels;* the publication of Fuller's complete dispatches in *"These Sad but Glorious Days";* and the addition of Woolson's "Miss Grief" to the 2002 *Norton Anthology of American Literature.* Yet Sophia Peabody Hawthorne's work remains unavailable, as does Sedgwick's complete travel narrative, and no study has as yet grouped these texts to highlight the literary tradition they reveal. I hope that the following chapters contribute to the study and recovery of these texts, which have much to say about what it meant to be a middle- or upper-class woman, a writer, and an American in the nineteenth century.

CHAPTER 1

"I Forgot Myself": Nation and Identity in Catharine Maria Sedgwick's Travel Writing

Perhaps Catharine Maria Sedgwick surprised her readers when she wrote, in her 1841 travel narrative, *Letters from Abroad to Kindred at Home*, "I would advise no American to come to Italy who has not strong domestic affections and close domestic ties, or some absorbing and wealthy pursuit at home" (II:193).[1] Perhaps she surprised herself. Certainly, as a writer and activist, Sedgwick is strongly identified with the United States, and more particularly with New England regional history. The idea that she could be permanently seduced by Italy, by the foreign and exotic, might have shocked a reading public that expected from her the domestic, as it applies both to the home and to the homeland; at the very least, her admonishment, one might even say her confession, serves to complicate the current critical understanding of her work.

In 1839 Catharine Maria Sedgwick traveled to Europe with her niece, Kate, and her brother Robert's family, in the hope that the journey would help to hasten Robert's recovery from a stroke he had suffered the year before. Though unsuccessful as a therapy—Robert died the year after they returned to the United States—the trip did provide Sedgwick with the raw material she would later develop, polish, and publish, in 1841, as her two-volume work, *Letters from Abroad to Kindred at Home*. This text, a comprehensive record of the ideas, sensations, and ruminations inspired by her encounters with Europe and its people, consists of a series of letters written to her younger brother, Christopher, who remained in the States during Sedgwick's Grand Tour. Sedgwick's blending of the personal and the political—Benjamin Spencer calls her a "sentimental patriot"—makes her text an important contribution to a genre emerging in

American literature during the first half of the nineteenth century: the travel narrative (202). With her travel account, Sedgwick inserted herself into the twin traditions of the Continental tour and the narratives it produced, both of which had been "culturally coded 'male' " (Buzard 16). Manipulating the genre of the travel narrative to reflect the concerns of a nineteenth-century American woman, *Letters from Abroad* charts the process by which Sedgwick's experiences overseas helped shape her conception of herself and her nation. Through descriptions of European countries, Sedgwick articulates her domestic political agenda—a projection of republicanism as it could, and should, function in the newly formed United States.

The proliferation of travel accounts cataloguing the minutiae of American visits to Europe, which had flooded the market even as early as 1841, led Sedgwick to note apologetically in the preface to *Letters* that she and her traveling companions had "passed over a field so thoroughly reaped that not an ear, scarcely a kernel, remains for the gleaner" (x). To justify adding her own text to the multitude already in print, Sedgwick first asserts that her letters "are published rather with deference to the wishes of others than from any false estimate of their worth" (ix) and then provisionally suggests what this worth might be to a reader who has "had already something too much of churches, statues, and pictures" (x). Her text might offer, Sedgwick writes, "the honesty with which I have recorded my impressions, and . . . the fresh aspect of familiar things to the eye of a denizen of the New World" (ibid.). Despite the fact that many travel writers of the day made similarly hopeful assertions, it is Sedgwick's "fresh" sensibility that produces the unique vision represented in the text.

In the interest of explicating Sedgwick's vision, I want to explore *Letters from Abroad* as both a manifestation of, and a variation on, the increasingly familiar, nineteenth-century, American travel narrative. Sedgwick's text both maintains and breaks out of the limits established by the conventional travel narrative form. In addition, her book continues the political activism that informs her other work, though in a format and through a thematics that allow her to be more explicit about her intentions as a woman, an American, and a nationalist; the text is both representative and unique in the context of Sedgwick's other works, specifically her novel *Hope Leslie* and her journal and letters. My concern, here and throughout this study, is to explore how travel to Italy liberated the American women writers who journeyed there, releasing them from the constraints of their lives and homeland, and enabling as well a specifically discursive freedom.

In considering how travel and travel writing are liberatory, I wish to borrow Christopher Castiglia's claim for the subversive potential of the captivity romance and apply it to the travel narrative, which I argue has similar implications for women. Responding to Nancy Cott's observation that "the central convention of domesticity was the contrast between home and the world" (Cott 64), Castiglia asserts that "the captivity romance deconstructs the 'natural' division between 'home and the world' . . . by giving women a plot outside the house" (Castiglia 13). Clearly travel narrative performs the same function, in the sense that the genre presupposes a woman's removal from the domestic sphere and the constraining influences there. If, as Castiglia claims, paraphrasing Cott, "Industrialization forced women's consignment to a domestic sphere ideologically and physically divorced from the public sphere of commerce and politics" and "religion and sentimentalism also formed the cornerstones of this prison" (5), the trip to Italy and corresponding narrative liberate Sedgwick by releasing her to some degree from the constraints of her home, her religion, and the sentimentalism readers would have expected from her fiction.

It is fitting that 1841, the year Sedgwick published *Letters,* was also the year the American sculptor Horatio Greenough completed his now-famous statue of George Washington. As emblems of a new nation's desire to assert itself, both statue and text have much to say in defense of America's greatness, yet both also betray an anxious need to measure the United States against European standards and accomplishments. Greenough's George Washington depicts the nation's first president in the garb and posture of a Roman god; William Vance notes that "the deification of the virtuous and heroic general and president that characterized much of the first part of the [nineteenth] century culminated in Horatio Greenough's colossal statue of Washington as the Phidian Zeus with a reversed Roman sword in one hand" (I:342). Indeed, Washington's imposing visage and carefully draped toga attempt an anachronistic philosophical synthesis, an example of what Vance calls "explicit attempts to equate American political experience and heroic virtue with Roman precedents" (I:17). Greenough and other artists of his day used Roman history to supply Americans with the extensive and prestigious past the young United States lacked. The legacy of Rome may have served especially well as historical validation for American imperialist policies.

After a visit to Greenough's Roman studio and a viewing of the statue of Washington, Sedgwick applauded the sculptor's accomplishments: "It is something to say for our progress in art that, in forty years from Washington's death, the best statue of him is by his own countryman" (II:291). In further praise of Greenough, Sedgwick's letter describes the qualities evoked by the sculpture as consistent with her own assessment of the originary American patriarch: "The head is noble; expressing, almost to the point of sublimity, wisdom and firmness, with as near an approach to benignity as Washington's face will bear without a sacrifice of verisimilitude; good, not quite benignant" (ibid.). In a gesture that reveals as much about her own artistic sensibility as it does about Greenough's, Sedgwick begins in an idealizing tone, but the urge to glorify soon gives way to the realism, the "verisimilitude," that she values. In contrast to Vance, who uses terms like "deification" and "idealization" to describe Greenough's Washington, Sedgwick's critical appraisal foregrounds what she identifies as the statue's historical accuracy—its portrayal of a man's goodness rather than a god's perfection. Many of her other letters demonstrate a similar progression, shifting from laudatory rhetoric into discursive concessions that reveal fissures in the fantasy of the American republic that so many artists and patriots unproblematically likened to an idealized portrait of Rome.[2]

If *Letters from Abroad* does not extol unequivocally the virtues of her native country, neither can her letters be reduced to a recapitulation in writing of the confident patriotism Greenough sought to carve into marble.[3] As a woman, as a writer, and as a believer in fundamental liberty for all people, Sedgwick presents a more critical view of her nation's progress toward a humanist ideal. Indeed, she makes no exception for her home country when she calls for global change in the early pages of her text. On the first stop of her tour, Portsmouth, Sedgwick praises an Admiral Fleming, who volunteered his yacht to convey her to the Isle of Wight: "Now this was surely the true spirit of courtesy; and when this spirit is infused into international manners may we be called Christian nations, and not till then" (I:19). The admonishment comes early on, then, that "we all"—the United States and other European nations that would define themselves as Christian—have some work to do before they will deserve the name. A truly Christian nation, in Sedgwick's vision, would reflect on a state level the courtesy and kindness Christianity demands from people as individuals. She frames this argument outright when she asks much later in her journey, "When will nations hold themselves bound by the strict rule that governs an upright individual?" (II:182). The ways in which the United States, like other nations, falls short of this ideal are illuminated throughout the letters Sedgwick wrote from abroad. The need for change is great and widespread, yet the enthusiasm of her exhortations to her homeland suggests Sedgwick's hope for America's future; that she wrote and published at all implies a certain faith in herself and in the written word as a vehicle for change.

James Buzard, in his critical survey of nineteenth-century travel, *The*

Beaten Track, describes "separation of the tourist from home" as "a physical fact which since the early nineteenth century has invited interpretation as a psychic liberation from domestic social life and the self defined there" (8). Demonstrating Buzard's observation, Sedgwick writes to her brother Christopher, "You may expect to know my sensations on first seeing Rome. I cannot tell them, my dear C. I do not myself know what they were. I forgot myself" (II:147). Politically and personally, Sedgwick forgets herself in Italy: She attends the opera unescorted, argues an explicitly feminist agenda, and fantasizes about a romantic immersion in the Italian culture that would relieve her from the pragmatism and problems of her homeland. The "psychic liberation" of tourism functions discursively for Sedgwick as license to create a text unlike any she had written before. The signification of "abroad" as "out of one's house or abode" predates the more familiar "out of the home country" definition by almost a century and points to a liberation as meaningful for a nineteenth-century woman as her escape beyond national boundaries. *Letters from Abroad* thus constitutes the textual representation of a woman released from her home and free to construct a new discursive self.

The Nineteenth-Century Travel Narrative

The tradition of the Grand Tour in the nineteenth century, as well as the "gaze" with which European sites were apprehended and described, belonged primarily to young men of financial means. Men traveled in search of the picturesque, a manner of viewing coded male and often associated with a sexualized apprehension of the foreign land, accordingly coded female. Italy proved especially susceptible to this gendered fantasy: "divided and 'backward,' the home of emotion and superstition (Catholicism with pagan shadowings) rather than enlightenment, the Italian nation was the more easily moulded to a stereotypical womanhood" (Buzard 133). Both as a location "providing young men with an opportunity to gain sexual experience and confidence, to sow wild oats," and as a passive landscape receptive to a male gaze, Italy was constructed as an ideal object for young men (ibid., 130). Nineteenth-century *American* men traveled to Europe with an especially anxious imperative to locate the picturesque, due to the generally accepted view that America lacked the picturesque in a fundamental way. As a nation that worshipped practicality, industry, and *usefulness,* America's ideology reflected values opposed to the picturesque's privileging of the aesthetic. Thus male American travelers enjoyed the delights of an almost frivolously beautiful, feminized Italy, confident in the knowledge that prosperity and industry—that is, manliness—awaited them at home once they had taken their fill of Old World culture.[4]

What, then, motivated nineteenth-century American *women* to travel to the Continent? The sexualized "taking" of either a hypereroticized foreign woman or a passive landscape would have been neither available nor desirable to most American women abroad. Nor could they have traveled with the ease and nonchalance that characterized American men in Europe, for they could not rest assured that their domestic political interests were being maintained in their absence, as Sedgwick's *Letters from Abroad* indicates. Women had their own motivations for seeking a temporary release from their homeland, motivations both misunderstood and mocked in a genre that developed in response to the growing number of nineteenth-century women visiting Europe as travel became more systematized and accessible.

In this new narrative mode, male writers lampooned women as novice travelers and produced a stereotype of the American woman abroad that would inform travel literature throughout the nineteenth century: "Confronting the many women and families (and boxes) making their appearances on the Continental tour in the decades after Waterloo . . . was a new narrative model, which I will call the 'family-abroad plot.' A chief function of this model seems to have been to characterize the tour that is directed by a woman as a misuse of the acculturating potential of 'travel,' usually involving an illegitimate attempt to gain status at home" (Buzard 140). That the "misuse of the acculturating potential of 'travel' " might have been a charge leveled with equal accuracy against male travelers—who were certainly more than aware of the cultural capital to be gained through a trip to Europe—goes unsaid in Buzard's text. My point here, though, is to argue that the parodic "family-abroad plot" does not accurately encompass women's impact on travel and travel writing in the nineteenth century. As this section demonstrates, Sedgwick's *Letters from Abroad* not only claims the status of the travel narrative in the conventional, "male" sense of the genre, but also negotiates the almost inevitable charges of "misuse" and "illegitimacy" that accompany a woman's attempt to appropriate and revise a masculine genre. An overview of the constitutive elements of the travel narrative will indicate the extent to which Sedgwick manipulates those elements and, more importantly, the strategies by which she breaks free of them. Hardly an incompetent cultural critic, Sedgwick as narrator proves a sharp observer of the foreign, a commentator able to expose the fractures that weakened American claims to superiority.

Letters from Abroad demonstrates both Sedgwick's awareness of the tradition that preceded her as well as her desire to lay claim to that heritage. Following her prefatory apology for adding another travel narrative to a saturated market, Sedgwick goes right on to elaborate her "impressions" of the Old World, despite her admission that the textual terrain has been "thoroughly reaped." The preface continues with a second apology for "the fragmentary state in which my letters appear," which Sedgwick attributes to her "fear of wearying readers less interested than my own family by prolonged details or prosing reflections, or disgusting them with the egotism of personal experience" (x). What follows her disclaimer is notably not fragmentary, but a clearly shaped whole. Her two apologies are offered, then, not as indicators of the author's insecurities, but as markers of an established travel writing protocol. One discursive technique of many that would have been familiar to her readers, the prefatory apologies indicate Sedgwick's awareness of Italy as a " 'fully scripted' environment" (Buzard 159). The abundance of Italianate texts in existence during the nineteenth century obliged travel writers to apologize for their own narrative efforts and determined that most literate Americans, Sedgwick included, first encountered this foreign land on the printed page. Sedgwick notes this explicitly when she refers to her "earliest ideas of Italy," which she "got from Mrs. Ratcliffe's [*sic*] romances" (II:133). That Radcliffe herself constructed gothic descriptions of Italy without ever visiting that country, relying instead on details gleaned from reading, further underscores the extent to which the text often predated, and therefore predetermined, travelers' firsthand perceptions of Italy.

Just how thoroughly the countryside had become a text is demonstrated by a harrowing experience Sedgwick describes just after invoking her gothic introduction to Italy. In the passage that mentions Radcliffe's work, Sedgwick proceeds to tell about feeling uneasy first by "a savage-looking wretch clothed in sheep-skins" and then by "a ragged, wild-looking man in an adjoining field, who eyed me for an instant, and then came rapidly towards me" (II:134). Ultimately no harm comes to Sedgwick, as the first would-be pursuer soon returns "to the reliable occupation of tending his sheep." The second assailant seems to confirm Sedgwick's suspicions by "immediately retreat[ing]" after she seeks the convenient shelter of a recently arrived carriage. That her party's approach sparks such a hasty retreat reinforces Sedgwick's fears regarding the dastardly plans the "wretch" had in store for a lone female traveler. The evidence is, however, purely circumstantial. The villains have done little more than to appear ragged and to stare overmuch at what must have been an uncommon sight in the hills of their country. The threats Sedgwick perceives seem to arise from the placement of a poor shepherd and a beggar into a landscape already replete with gothic associations gleaned from Radcliffe's novel.[5]

Like a gothic specter, the proliferation of texts about Italy haunted both travelers and travel writers. In general, nineteenth-century Americans visited European sites expecting to discover physical locations that accurately reflected depictions found in literature, periodicals, and the increasingly popular guidebooks.[6] Printed matter often served as the yardstick by which spectators measured a site's value, resulting in an inversion by which "the 'original' becomes itself when the viewer perceives that it suits its representations" (Buzard 196). In case of a discrepancy, often the location itself would be discredited, rather than the representation. Accordingly, when Verona does not live up to the expectations Sedgwick derived from Shakespearean drama—the Capulets' palace is "a gloomy, dark old rack-rent edifice" and Juliet's balcony "half way to heaven"—Sedgwick writes that she is "eager to get away before imagination should lose forever the power of recalling" (II:89).

Travel texts like Sedgwick's sought to transcend the boundaries established by their predecessors even as they worked to maintain those boundaries. Thus *Letters* reproduces certain canonically constitutive aspects of travel narrative while also inventing strategies that break out of the genre's predetermined limits. Yet I want to emphasize an important difference in Sedgwick's work. Traditionally, travel writers challenged established limits in an effort to achieve the same effect—a picturesque representation—that resulted from adhering to those limits.[7] In contrast, Sedgwick's text breaks with tradition when its purpose changes. When her writing becomes political, the escapist devices of travel writing prove inadequate means of expression. At times invested in a conventional depiction of a romanticized Italy, the textual gaze is at other times drawn toward the country's more unsightly details, creating a tension in the text and necessitating a break from convention.

The trope of antidescription, in which travel writers abstained from lengthy descriptions with the assertion that words would not suffice, functions as a strategy for Sedgwick to utilize and manipulate. In keeping with tradition, Sedgwick confesses, "My dear C., you may almost doubt my being in Rome, since I have not yet said one word of the Vatican. . . . The truth is, that from the moment of my visit to Winchester Cathedral, I have felt, as I fancy those do who go to another world, that the sensations resulting from a new state and new manifestations are incommunicable. I cannot convey to you what I have enjoyed, and am enjoying" (II:193). The passage articulates a standard fear of travel writers, that words would not do justice to experience, yet Sedgwick's foregrounding of the self rather than the object viewed shifts discursive weight from the Vatican to the female subject. *She* has entered "a new state"; *her* "new manifestations" are what cannot be communicated. The articulation of a female subjectivity continues in this letter that describes by refusing to describe, when Sedgwick quotes Charlotte Eaton's *Rome in the Nineteenth Century,* claiming to "do [her] readers a favour by transcribing" an expert's description of Raphael's "School of Athens."[8] Sedgwick's commentary after the cited passage, however, reestablishes her own critical authority, claiming that Eaton's text, in its own refusal to describe, has overlooked the painting's central image: "It is strange that the writer of this description, a woman, should have omitted the figure of Aspasia, whose intellectual beauty is so shaded with sadness. . . . She seems to be revolving in her mind a mystery: the capacities of her nature and the degradation of her sex" (II:200). Sedgwick's feminist concerns inspire her description of the painting and her implied criticism of Eaton. By fashioning the discourse of antidescription to suit her needs, Sedgwick assembles a text that progresses from the trope of resistance to political commentary.

As a convention, the refusal to describe reveals a conflict within travel writing: the desire to textualize foreign wonders and the fear that such efforts will fail. Sedgwick's rhetoric often reflects a different conflict: the tension between realistic, political prose and the sentimental, almost transcendent response she has to the sights of Italy. To negotiate this conflict, Sedgwick manipulates standard descriptive techniques. The motif of stillness, for example, which "refers to the ennobling feeling . . . when the traveller is alone to savour a place's poignant or powerful reverberations of beauty, sublimity or significance" (Buzard 177), enables expression of her own emotional responses even as it provides a means of commenting on gender. Aware that her trip to Europe allowed her a solitude unavailable at home, she says of the London theater, "We went unattended—a new experience to me. Necessity has taught women here more independence than with us, and it has its advantages to both parties; the men are saved much bother, and the women gain faculty and freedom" (I:59). Taking issue with the cultural assumption that " 'Change,' 'Escape,' and 'Solitude' . . . were licensed for use only by men" (Buzard 140), Sedgwick's text both lays claim to those values and highlights the extent to which restrictions based on gender were conventions of U.S. culture (notably absent in certain European countries), not timeless and essential.

The stillness motif, with its many aspects, informs this rhapsodic record of Sedgwick's sensations in a Venetian hotel room:

> I am alone, the family all being at the opera, and I have just been standing in the balcony looking at the moon, which is pouring a flood of light through this clear atmosphere down upon the sea. . . . I can look up to the familiar objects in the heavens, and almost forget my distance from you; but the painful sense returns as I bring my eyes to earth, for oh! How different is this earth from ours! There is the splendid Church of San Georgio with her tall campanilla, and Santa Maria della Salute with her cupolas, and here are gondolas gliding out of the little canal into the Guidecca, and others gliding in and out among the vessels that lie at anchor in the harbour. . . . I cannot see the Bridge of Sighs, but it is almost within my touch, so near that I feel the atmosphere that surrounds it, and am glad to be cheered by the lively voices of a merry troop that are passing on to the piazzetta, and, as that sound dies away, to hear the delicious voice of a cavalier in a gondola, who is singing for his own pleasure—and certainly for mine. (II:110)

Alone to savor the sublime moment, Sedgwick describes a connection to her surroundings so strong that she can "feel" the Bridge of Sighs and imagine that the cavalier is singing to her. Equally strong, though, is the bond to her brother at home, a reference that foregrounds Sedgwick's familial responsibilities and highlights her experience of a solitude uncommon to a woman of her day, even a woman traveler. Women who managed to travel abroad in the nineteenth century were likely to have family, children, and servants in tow.[9] Time alone to ponder scenery signified differently for them than for male travelers of the same period, to whom such opportunities would have been more familiar.

The Venetian passage just quoted, where the gondolas' use as transportation is eclipsed by the romantic image of the singing cavalier, displays the motif of nonutility, which, like stillness, constructs a given site as available primarily for a spectator's consumption and minimizes the site's practical value to local inhabitants. Sedgwick's later letters, however, demonstrate a more self-conscious tone as they attack precisely this practice of overlooking or romanticizing the conditions in which Italians lived and through which Americans had the luxury of idly roaming. Of the beggars on the streets of Naples, Sedgwick writes, "while we tourists give volumes to ruins and pictures, the *Lazzaroni* [homeless beggars] are slurred over with a line or a sneer. We forget the wrongs which have brought them to their present abjectness and keep them in it, and quiet our sympathies by reiterating that 'the *Lazzaroni* are the most cheerful people in the world!' and so they are (except, perhaps, our slaves!)" (II:272). The heavy irony of the passage foregrounds the insensitivity of American travelers even as it invokes the specter of an American nation guilty of a more insidious crime. Clearly the effect of such critiques, which surface throughout Sedgwick's text, is to undermine the myth of America as benevolent provider for all. Later in this chapter I return to look at Sedgwick's domestic critique in more detail, but here I want to underscore her awareness of travel writing's complicity in the glamorization of what were often painful living conditions.[10]

Pushed to its extreme, discursive glorification becomes theatricality, whereby writers/travelers fantasize that the landscape and its people compose an elaborate spectacle choreographed solely for their entertainment. Catholic ceremonies, for example, are emptied of spiritual value and become performances: "I must confess that, to a Protestant Puritan, disdaining forms and symbols, and disabused of the mysteries of the Church, the ceremonies appear like a theatrical pageant" (II:45). An emblem of travel writing's worship of the stationary image or artifact, theatricality fades over the course of Sedgwick's narrative, displaced by the narrator's evolving relationship to what she sees. By the time she arrives at the Cathedral of Monza to witness the presentation of the crown of Lombardy (said to contain nails used in Christ's crucifixion), her earlier dismissive tone has given way to self-conscious puzzlement: "[T]hese religious ceremonies, where I am forever vibrating between the humility of conscious ignorance and the pride of superior liberty, are always painful to me" (II:60). Later in the narrative, Sedgwick recalls that on witnessing a vesper service "our little guides dropped on their knees and joined in the service; and so did we in our hearts," then continues more effusively, "How skilfully [*sic*] the Catholics have made many of the offices of their religion to harmonize with the wants and spontaneous feelings of man" (II:143). The narrator's realizations demonstrate an evolution in which the theatricality of the early letters gets destabilized by her experiences and corresponding desire to represent a more mutual relationship between herself and Italy.

Toward a similar end, Sedgwick's text both uses and undermines the trope of "saturation," Buzard's term for depictions of a foreign country's beauty as excessive and, perhaps more importantly, *uninterrupted*. In a significant rupturing of this fantasy, Sedgwick's prose moves from the discourse of saturation to contemplation of precisely the type of detail that travel writing sought to elide: "There is a beautiful pavement, the walls are incrusted with Oriental marbles, the ceiling is painted with frescoes; there are columns of porphyry and lapis lazuli, rich carvings, pictures in mosaic, and splendid monuments; not a square inch is left unembellished. And yet, dear C., I think your eye would turn from all this gorgeousness to the squalid, lean beggar kneeling on the step beside you" (II:219). Two impulses exist concurrently here: the urge to memorialize an almost overwhelming aesthetic experience and the drive to record realistically whatever mars the portrait, either of Italy or of Sedgwick's own country. Under the discursive pretense of mapping her brother's shifting attention, Sedgwick indicates her own sensibility when she moves her textual eye from the church's excessive ornamentation to the nearby evidence of poverty.

At those moments when the reality Sedgwick identifies beneath, or alongside, glamorized Italian exteriors overpowers her picturesque impulses, a hybrid text results. The "fertile beyond description" countryside between Turin and Milan and the "perfection of its husbandry" soon give way to the admission that "the country is too level for picturesque beauty" and, further, that "there are no signs of rural cheerfulness; no look of habitancy. The cultivators live in compact, dirty little villages" (II:29). The existence of squalid conditions eventually pulls Sedgwick's gaze away from the more commonly emphasized, idealized details, creating a tension in the text between the escapist aims of traditional travel writing and the political agenda underlying Sedgwick's work. Indeed, the picturesque tradition precludes the articulation of any specific political agenda. Political change exists in the present, while the tradition of romanticizing the Italian countryside involved, at its root, foregrounding the distant and illustrious Roman past. A writer who referred too insistently to the political present would risk rupturing the picturesque fantasy, causing readers to remember unsavory details about their own domestic lives and interrupting the rhapsodic effect of the travel narrative.

Sedgwick takes precisely this risk when, in narrating her experience of the approach to Milan, she moves from standard travel narrative devices to a harsher realism. At first, the picturesque captivates her: "[W]hat, think you, must have been our sensations when . . . we raised our eyes . . . to God's most beautiful work on earth, to the Alps, bounding one third of a horizon of magnificent extent, every point defined, every outline marked on the clear atmosphere[?]" After culminating with the daring claim, "we were in danger of forgetting our humanity," the picturesque impulse is disrupted by the presence of the Austrian military forces occupying Milan. As the scope of the textual gaze narrows, the political implications expand: "[O]ur sight was overpowered, our field of vision contracted to the rich plains of Lombardy, then to the city under us, to the *piazza del duomo,* and to those detestable loaded and primed Austrian canon, and we became quite conscious that this was *not* the best of all possible worlds!" (II:54). What is so often omitted in picturesque travel narratives that treat the foreign world as a museum is compelling to Sedgwick, a realist and activist who cannot stare dreamily at an alpine backdrop while blatant evidence of tyranny sits under her nose.

Thus beauty and politics, the picturesque tradition and realism coexist in *Letters from Abroad*. Despite William Vance's assertion that Sedgwick is "constantly aware of contrasts and generally of her own country's superiorities in the things that mattered most to her (art not really being one of them)" (II:116), the narrative offers occasions when the artistic, "Italian" impulse challenges the pragmatism associated with America; indeed, a late passage in *Letters* credits artistic representation with the power to compensate for what reality lacks. "We know not what art has done for us," Sedgwick writes after touring the Neapolitan countryside, "till we find it peopling these dreary solitudes with such exquisite forms" (II:265). The emerging realization that America lacks the "exquisite forms" to redeem "dreary solitudes" complicates Sedgwick's patriotism and leads her at times to confess an almost irresistible attraction to Italy.

This attraction is articulated in the text's final paragraph, when Sedgwick confesses, "I do not now wonder at the love of art which astonished me on first coming to the Old World," and claims she has begun "to feel the danger (the existence of which I have but just learned) of forgetting the actual in the painted world" (II:296). What the Italian painted world offers and what the letters as a whole illustrate is a transcendence of self, daily life, and, to some extent, national affiliation. The contrasting attributes of Italy and the United States, established through a variety of images, fascinate Sedgwick, who, hardly confident in "her own country's superiorities in the things that mattered most to her," often wishes her compatriots could adopt some portion of what seems "natural" in Italians.[11] Like *Hope Leslie* (1827), in which Sedgwick claims her "ambition . . . would be fully gratified if, by this work, any of our young countrymen should be stimulated to investigate the early history of their native land" (vii), *Letters from Abroad* aims to move its readers to action. The following section examines the specifics of that action as articulated in *Letters* and Sedgwick's other works.

Sedgwick's Literary Politics

In February 1831, Sedgwick traveled to Washington, D.C., where her itinerary included a visit with President Andrew Jackson. A proponent of individualism and the ideology of the self-made man—Jackson himself worked his way to the presidency from humble beginnings in a South Carolina log cabin—Jackson and his brand of republicanism dominated the national consciousness in the 1800s. Joyce Warren observes that "Andrew Jackson's election in 1829 marked a turning point" in the nation's history "after which it was impossible openly to support" any ideology other than individualism (*The American Narcissus* 5). Two years after his election, Jackson's courteous demeanor impressed Sedgwick, who wrote in her journal, "He received us politely—is simple, gentlemanly, and unaffected in his manners" (*Power* 129). A visit to "the nation's drawing room," however, provoked a more critical observation of the elite crowd gathered there to socialize. Sedgwick notes that "great men and accomplished women fancy they live in a country of equality as well as liberty," then asks pointedly, "do they ever feel their inequality more than on such occasions?" (ibid.). That Sedgwick recognized the conflict between individualism and egalitarianism is as apparent in her published works as in this journal entry. Her desire to see a more humanitarian, truly democratic United States surfaces in the highly popular *Hope Leslie,* whose heroine demonstrates "the personal virtues necessary to the republic" (Gossett and Bardes 19). If the narrative romance of *Hope Leslie* allows Sedgwick to comment on the needs of the republic, the various observations she makes about conventional, European tourist attractions enable *Letters from Abroad* to construct an explicit argument with her country's supposedly democratic ideology.

The politics of Sedgwick's written work intimately connect with her personal experience. In her introduction to *The Power of Her Sympathy: The Autobiography and Journal of Catharine Maria Sedgwick,* Mary Kelley notes Sedgwick's "conception of herself as intertwined with the lives of those whom she cherished" (3). Indeed, Sedgwick describes herself in a letter to William Minot (husband of her niece, Kate) as "so woven into the fabric of others that I seem to have had no separate, individual existence" (ibid.). Contrasting Sedgwick's text with other influential American autobiographies, specifically those of Benjamin Franklin, Ralph Waldo Emerson, and Henry Adams, Kelley points out that while the male writers "presented the self on a trajectory toward autonomy," "Sedgwick's emphasis upon an identity constructed in relation to others located her narrative in an alternative tradition" established by women writers who preceded her (ibid., 5).[12] The epistolary structure of *Letters from Abroad,* its direct addresses to Christopher, as well as its discursive awareness of the family members with whom she traveled, anticipates the interconnectedness Kelley locates in the autobiography (written between 1853 and 1860). In Volume I of *Letters,* Sedgwick bemoans her separation from family in telling terms: "This interruption of communication with those who are bound up in the bundle of life with us, is one of the severest trials of a traveler" (173). By portraying herself as "bound up in [a] bundle" with the others in her family, Sedgwick emphasizes her connection to those she loves.

Politically, this sense of fundamental links binding the self to others manifests itself as a concern for the rights of those who have been underrepresented, or overrun, in the race for progress. In Sedgwick's travel narrative, this includes American slaves and Indians, as well as maligned ethnic groups, particularly Italians. The major cause championed in Sedgwick's work is, of course, the rights of women, specifically their right to be regarded as individuals. As a woman who never married and who supported herself financially through her writing, she offered her own life as well as her literary works as evidence of what she believed women could achieve independently. Her journal entry dated July 16, 1849, advances an "opinion" that is "the result of [her] experience"; she writes, "I would advise every woman who can, by any effort, secure an independent home to have it" (*Power* 156).[13] *Hope Leslie* continues the argument for women's autonomy by depicting an independent heroine, strong and resourceful enough to follow a self-determined path, as well as a secondary character, Esther, who "illustrated a truth which, if more generally received by her sex, might save a vast deal of misery; that marriage is not *essential* to the contentment, the dignity, or the happiness of woman" (292). *Hope Leslie* and Sedgwick's journal contribute to the fight for women's rights by endorsing a home-based, personalized activism. Through the establishment of a financially independent home and/or the decision not to marry, women like Sedgwick could carve for themselves a niche of autonomy and live as examples to others.

Sedgwick's feminism was constrained by historical context, as Suzanne Gossett and Barbara Ann Bardes argue: "In 1827, Sedgwick could not assert that woman are oppressed by their exclusion from the political process, but she designs her plot [in *Hope Leslie*] to drive the reader to this conclusion" (23). Thus in *Hope Leslie,* the argument for women's independence must be insinuated by female characters like Hope and Magawisca, who risk much to remain true to the virtues Sedgwick endorsed, establishing in the process that women can show courage and integrity in the face of adversity. Her female characters act according to their consciences, at times in open defiance of patriarchal codes. "The implicit theme of *Hope Leslie,*" according to Gossett and Bardes, "is that a woman may be driven by her sense of political powerlessness to undertake civil disobedience" (21).

What Sedgwick's early novel does not address directly—the issue of women's political disenfranchisement—finds expression in *Letters from Abroad,* whose overtly political speculations were engendered by her confrontation with, and need to make sense of, women's experiences in foreign cultures. Contemporary European surroundings seemed to give her what American history did not. Ann Douglas argues in *The Feminization of American Culture* that after the early historical novels "Sedgwick evaded rather than subverted American history" (222). In Douglas's view, *Hope Leslie* is an "ambivalent" historical work in which the "high-spirited heroine represents benign feminine anarchy wreaking charming havoc with official records" (ibid.). "By the later 1830s," Douglas argues, "Sedgwick had turned to thinly fictionalized domestic manuals and religious tracts. Her apostasy from history, even from subversive history, was little noted but immensely significant. Unable as a woman to find a perspective from which she could adequately treat the past, she turned her very real talents to a depiction of the pleasures and trials involved in running the modern household, and she took her large feminine following with her" (ibid.). While *Letters from Abroad* may also represent an evasion of the historical American context found in *Hope Leslie* and the other early novels, it hardly evades the project begun in her early work. Rather, the escape to the Old World provides her with a different medium through which to examine her political concerns, one that is hardly synonymous with "the pleasures and trials involved in running the modern household." Quite the contrary, *Letters from Abroad* represents the nineteenth-century American woman well outside her home and removed from household chores. No longer identified by her proximity to the domestic, Sedgwick is free to explore and to narrate women's existence in other arenas.

By offering observations on gender issues that encompass the personal, the political, the economic, and the artistic, *Letters* demonstrates a broad concern for women, both those living in Sedgwick's own country and the European women she sees in her travels. Often her ruminations develop out of comparisons between what she witnesses in Europe and what she remembers from home, as when she notes that in England there were "a great number of single women" and that "English women, married or single, have more leisure and far more opportunity for intellectual cultivation, than with us" (I:107). Frequently, the result of these discursive explorations is the realization that in some respects Europe offers more possibilities to women than the United States, despite U.S. claims of superiority. The text thus levels its criticism against a self-proclaimed democratic nation that persists in relegating women, half its population, to a subordinate status and that destabilizes the essentialism by which proponents of the "cult of true womanhood" justified its power in America.[14]

Sedgwick's realization that a German wife has legal claim to half the joint property in a marriage provokes an extended consideration of both class and gender, articulated in the form of a series of questions, which I quote at length to highlight the progression of Sedgwick's argument:

> [I]t seems to me to be but common justice that a wife should be an equal partner in a concern of which she bears so heavy a part of the burden. Would not the introduction of such a law have a beneficent effect on the labouring classes in the United States? How many women would be stimulated to ingenuity and productive labour if the results of their industry were secured to them? How many women are first wronged and then disheartened by having an inheritance consumed by a husband's vices, or dispersed by his wild speculations? How many, well qualified for respectable branches of business, are deterred from attempting them by the impossibility of securing to themselves and their children the proceeds? How many poor women among the lowest class of labourers have you and I both known, whose daily earnings have been *lawfully* taken from them by their brutal husbands? This is a pretty serious evil, as in that class at least (you will allow me to say) the destructive vices are pretty much monopolized by your sex. (I:223)

The series of questions probes the connections between economic concerns and other issues in American women's lives, specifically the professions they will undertake, their relationship with death (in the form of estate/inheritance procedures), their emotional well-being, and the means by which they can care for their families. A rumination on the rights of a German wife leads to Sedgwick's argument that legalized financial rights for American women could have educational, professional, and familial ramifications.

Once Sedgwick arrives in Italy, her letters investigate women's rights primarily through the lens of artistic and intellectual achievement. The city of Bologna, in fact, receives praise from both Sedgwick and Margaret Fuller (writing some ten years later in a *Tribune* dispatch), as a hotbed of women's intellectual activity. Having visited the "splendid public monuments" of Bologna, Sedgwick remarks that "a pantheon is building for the illustrious" of the Bolognese citizenry; in the meantime, "there is a large apartment filled with their busts" where Sedgwick "noticed a very fine one of a woman who was professor of Greek in the University of Bologna within the present century" (II:130). Indeed, not only can Bologna boast a contemporary role model worthy of Sedgwick's notice, but the ensuing meditation on Bologna's history (incorporated into *Letters* as a footnote) reveals the city's tradition of esteem for women's accomplishments: "It is said that Italy has produced more learned women than any part of Europe, and that Bologna has longest continued to respect and reward the literary acquisitions of women. It was a lady of Bologna who, in the fifteenth century, was so zealous a champion of her sex as to employ her wit and learning to prove the world has been all this while in error, and that it was Adam who tempted Eve" (ibid.). Alluding to, and simultaneously undermining, the biblical myth that justified sexist oppression in Christian communities, Sedgwick's passage also celebrates an academic setting noted for its acceptance of women. At a time in U.S. history when women were virtually excluded from academia—it was not until 1833 that the first U.S. college, Oberlin, began to accept female students—certainly an Italian haven that encouraged women in intellectual pursuits would have commanded Sedgwick's attention.

Italian art also inspired Sedgwick to contemplate the past and future of womankind. In her depiction of Rome, for example, she devotes pages to a discussion of Raphael's sibyls, despite her tendency at other points in the text to resist or refuse descriptions of visual art. The work, which she identified as her favorite picture in all the galleries of Florence and Rome, depicts "the four sibyls, the lay prophetesses who are supposed to have intimated to the world the revelations they had received of the coming of our saviour" (II:167). It is no surprise that such subject matter entices Sedgwick, whose enthusiastic portrayal of the second sibyl, the most striking of the group, suggests the painting's power: "[T]he art that could give such force to such delicate lines is amazing. The face is the most spiritual, and I think the most beautiful, I ever saw. Her whole soul is so intent on the record she is making that it seems as if her pen would cut through the tablet" (ibid.). Sedgwick's emphasis on the sibyl's fervor and strength complicate her acknowledgement of the "delicate lines" and "spiritual" face, indicating the composite characteristics that register, for Sedgwick, a woman's beauty. Despite the power evidenced by female subjects in this painting, however, the artist of the masterpiece is a man. Sedgwick's frustration may be implied by the sibyl's violent intensity, which threatens to drive her pen through stone, as though she represents the woman writer who, like Sedgwick, struggles to break free of constraints on a woman's self-expression.

The sibyls are mentioned again, late in the journey, when Sedgwick makes her most explicit appeal on behalf of women: "If I had to answer all the libels of the scoffers at my sex, or to defend the 'rights of women,' I would appeal to this Psyche, to Raphael's sibyls, to Dante's Beatrice, and to Shakespeare's Portia, Isabella, and Desdemona, to show what the inspired teachers of the world have believed of our faculties and virtues" (II:237). The Psyche of which she speaks here, an ancient statue housed in the Royal Museum of Naples, occasions this contemplation of women's complexity, of the "faculties and virtues" possessed by a sex often denied opportunity to express either in the world outside home and family. In this statue Sedgwick recognizes a depth beyond the superficial beauty often highlighted in artistic representations of women. Although little more than the face and neck remain intact, Sedgwick deems Psyche "the perfection of spiritual beauty and grace. There is something in the hang of the head, and a touch of sadness in the expression, that reminded K. [Sedgwick's niece, Kate] of the angel in Retzsch's game of chess; but the face appeared to me far more powerful and comprehensive" (ibid.). The power and grace of the sculpture demonstrate, for Sedgwick, the balance women can achieve; strength and beauty are blended in the various visual and literary representations catalogued in Sedgwick's narrative, their combination a message to readers who would insist upon women's inferiority.

As a political document, the narrative demonstrates much concern with relationships between men and women and with the power dynamics involved on both personal and political levels. The narrative also embraces relationships among women, portrayed in a romanticized tone that echoes the romance of the Italian environment, yet complicates the myth of Italy as the site of sexual possibility by displacing the familiar overtones of heterosexual possession. Near Perugia, one of the last stops on her European tour, Sedgwick makes the acquaintance of a young woman working at a small village inn. Powerfully drawn toward this "rustic lass" who "skims over the floor as a bird over the surface of the water," Sedgwick admits that she "can scarce write for looking at her" and eventually that she "must ask her name, and something of her history" (II:278). The woman's story is tragic; unable to marry the man she loves for lack of a dowry, young Clotilde, Sedgwick speculates, "will probably end the love-tale in a convent" (II:279). But monetary concerns do not compromise the relationship between the two women, who engage in a flirtatious friendship. Once Sedgwick has "looked at [Clotilde's] gay-coloured woolen scarf becomingly drawn over her bosom and confined at her slender waist," she is moved to "tak[e] hold of her string of corals, and asked if it were not a love token." Clotilde smiles and blushes, as she "at first denied the charge," then "laying her hand affectionately on [Sedgwick's] shoulder," whispers the truth, that she does have a beau. After the confession, however, Sedgwick seems to usurp the suitor's place, as the two women engage in the rituals of courtship. Clotilde gives Sedgwick a letter from her lover; Sedgwick in turn offers "a word of advice," then receives from the girl a bouquet of flowers and "pressed one for memorial of her" in the pages of her journal (II:280).

Sedgwick's text emphasizes the purity of this memory, expressing the wish that the flower pressed in her journal will not "outlast the innocence and loveliness" of her friend. Indeed, when a companion suggests to Sedgwick that Clotilde's story might form the basis of a fiction, Sedgwick refuses to consider it, noting in a footnote that she "preferred preserving the unadorned fact to ingrafting upon it apocryphal additions for the sated appetites of souvenir readers" (ibid.). The epistolary representation of Clotilde's memory—in a nonfictional context that seems to resist, in Sedgwick's estimation at least, the greedy and unsavory world of more commercialized writing—can remain as untarnished as the interaction itself. The sanctity of Sedgwick's relationship with Clotilde depends upon a certain distance from the corrupting influences of greed and power as they operate in the patriarchal world. Another passage late in the text demonstrates a similar impulse to render the world of women in a unique relationship to power economics: "We pedestrians stopped at a farmhouse [near Fiesoli], where we were charmed with rural thrift, cheerfulness, and kindness. The womankind were all engaged, from old age to childhood, either in weaving, spinning, knitting, or braiding straw. There was no misery—no begging" (II:295). The discourse in this utopian passage may be sentimental, but it incorporates practicality as well. The women's "thrift" seems to forestall the ubiquitous begging that characterized so much of Sedgwick's Italian journey. In this rural community, women of all ages work together in harmony, and the text implies that this "women's work" exists in contradistinction to "misery" and "begging."

Like *Hope Leslie,* which offers the heroine and Magawisca as "models for the ideal American" (Kelley, "Legacy Profile," 47), *Letters from Abroad* illustrates the advantages of "womanly" affections and concerns in the establishment of a fair republic. Certain of these virtues are exhibited by Italians in Sedgwick's narrative, in spite of the American tendency to vilify the Italian people. Based on her experience of Italy, Sedgwick asserts that even the pope reveals a generous nature when he "permits the public worship of heretics here in the very heart of his dominion. This is better than the burning of the convent in our land of liberty of conscience and universal toleration!" (II:154).[15] In defense of papal liberality, Sedgwick invokes an infamous example of American intolerance, the burning of the Ursuline convent near Boston in 1834 by an angry mob of protestant bricklayers following the anti-Catholic sermons of Lyman Beecher. Jenny Franchot calls the attack "the most important political event in

Massachusetts prior to . . . the passage of the 1850 Fugitive Slave Law" and argues the riot "signaled the renewal of Anti-Catholicism and provided a model for escalating popular demonstrations against hated popery" (136). Resisting a national tide of ethnic and religious hatred, Sedgwick's text defends the benevolence of Italians against the demonization that flourished despite American claims of "liberty and universal toleration."

The denigration of Italians through widespread American acceptance and perpetuation of ethnic stereotypes offends Sedgwick's sensibilities and compels her to defend the Italian character. After a firsthand introduction to Roman society, she admonishes her brother, "Now, my dear C., if the only Romans we chance to know would be valuable members of society anywhere, is it not a hint to us to take the denunciation of travellers with some allowance, and, at any rate, that we may safely enlarge our charities?" (II:175). By exposing the ethnic prejudices of travelers who preceded her, Sedgwick reminds the reader to resist the sweeping generalizations of travel accounts and adopt instead a charitable and open-minded attitude toward the foreign. Similarly, when she hears the story of an English family, quarantined in a small village due to a cholera epidemic, who were given food and shelter for four months, she alerts her brother, "All their wants were supplied. . . . All this, dear C., among the dishonest, lying, murdering, treacherous Italians! There is some superfluous reviling in this world" (II:176). In an ironic reversal, the text depicts nurturing Italians who are more humane than hypocritical travelers who impose themselves on a foreign people and malign their hosts after the fact.

In keeping with Sedgwick's humanitarian sensibility, the text vehemently opposes injustices in American domestic policies whenever the Italian context calls those policies to Sedgwick's mind. On hearing the story of nomadic brigands who received permission to worship in Rome during holy week only to be betrayed by church emissaries, she recalls U.S. policy toward Native Americans: " 'Ah, for shame!' I exclaimed at the conclusion of the story; 'This is as bad as our treatment of the Indians' " (II:182). The passage levels charges of hypocrisy against an American government that, like the pope whom Americans were so fond of demonizing, promised protection and gave persecution instead; the realization leads Sedgwick to wonder when nations will conduct themselves according to the rules that govern the behavior of Christian individuals. Her answer is an evasion as much as a prescription: "When they are in deed as well as in name Christian nations—and not till then" (ibid.). The circular logic employed here may betray Sedgwick's exasperation with a country that professed to know better, yet continued to practice systematic oppression.

Using similar rhetoric, Sedgwick uses the American slave system to remind potentially self-righteous Americans of their own moral culpability. Italians who submit to Austrian occupation, she writes, are "like the most intelligent and conscientious of our slave-holders (and with far better reason)" in that "they submit to the evil only because they hold it to be irremediable" (II:81). The implication that Italians are more justified than Americans in their acquiescence to evil is embedded in a complex accusation that would lead an American reader through the rhetorical logic into a sense of complicity. With her next question, Sedgwick dismantles excuses for passive acceptance: "[I]s any moral evil irremediable to those who will adopt the axiom of the noble old blind man of Ancona, 'Nothing is impossible to those who fear not death' " (ibid.). These strong words articulate the seriousness with which Sedgwick views her duty to identify and fight injustice, a duty she would insist is shared by all Americans who consider themselves Christian and humanitarian. Within the logic of her text, no Americans are free from blame or the responsibility to fight—with their lives if necessary—against the nation's moral failings.

The travel experiences outlined here had a cumulative effect on Sedgwick's political perspective and on her conceptualization of herself and her native country, as she explains in a letter to her brother: "My dear C., it is worth the trouble of a pilgrimage to the Old World to learn to feel—to *realize* our political blessings and our political exemptions" (II:66). "To realize" here may signify both "to become aware of," as in to recognize something already in existence, as well as "to actualize," in the sense of making real what does not yet exist. Both significations resonate in the context of *Letters* as a whole, and both grew out of an astute American woman's interaction with Italy. Sedgwick realizes the accomplishments of her young country, even as she *wants to realize* its potential, as her text demonstrates through a combination of praise for America's ideals and criticism of oversights and oppressions that must be rectified.

Early in the textual journey Sedgwick asks her brother's forgiveness "for observing some contrasts that may perchance strike you as unpatriotic" (I:28). In the letters that follow she explores these contrasts, exposing in the process an American individualist ideology that postures as egalitarian while in fact granting individual autonomy only to certain individuals. As her observations about women, Indians, African Americans, and Italians indicate, the freedom theoretically offered to all hard-working Americans was reserved for a privileged group. In opposing her country's oppressive practices, however, Sedgwick does not abandon patriotism. Rather she constructs a patriotism of a different kind, a hopeful vision of a future in which her young country realizes its democratic potential. Late in her journey she betrays her idealism by incorporating into a letter the words of an unnamed young traveling companion: Upon reading the Italian poet Count Leopardi, the girl, perhaps Sedgwick's niece, is moved to write, "America rises before us in a halo of light, brightening and brightening" (II:256). The view of America represented in *Letters from Abroad* is enabled by distance and defined by potential, depicted in terms that suggest an ongoing narrative "brightening," rather than a static image already fully developed.

Sedgwick resists the imperative, established in more aggressively "patriotic" precursor texts, to aggrandize her home country at the expense of her European hosts. A contemporary British reviewer of Sedgwick's narrative, writing for *The Eclectic Review* in September 1841, recognizes the tendency in travel writing to malign foreign countries and advises, "It is surely time that the mean spirit of detraction in which many have written should be abandoned." In contrast, he praises Sedgwick as "an intelligent American" who "writes in a spirit perfectly friendly, does full justice to whatever excellencies she noted, yet detects some blemishes to which our self-esteem renders us insensible." Thanking "the instructress, who, by wise counsels conceived in much kindness, puts the means of self-improvement within our reach," the reviewer closes "with a sincere desire that all our tourists, whether American or English, may imitate the spirit in which she has related to her 'kindred at home' what she saw and heard in the Old World" ("Review" 273, 277).

Ultimately, it may be fitting that the land of Catholicism provoked Sedgwick's anti-individualist argument, given Paul Giles's assertion that "in the American imagination, Catholicism has traditionally represented everything that is the antithesis of individual liberty" (99). Perhaps Catholicism and Sedgwick's agenda intersect in their (proclaimed) concern for the well-being of the community. This is not to say that Sedgwick unproblematically embraced Catholicism, or that Catholicism's influences have historically been purely benevolent, but it is only to reemphasize the powerful effect of Sedgwick's encounter with Italian life and to suggest that she found certain aspects of Italian culture both comforting and compelling. So much so, in fact, that she worried over losing herself to the world of Italian art and felt justified in issuing the warning with which this chapter opens. Complicating that admonishment to the would-be American traveler—"I would advise no American to come to Italy who has not strong domestic affections and close domestic ties, or some absorbing and wealthy pursuit at home"—the passage continues, "without these strong bonds to his country he may feel, when he returns there, as one does who attempts to read a treatise on political economy after being lost in the interest of a captivating romance" (II:194). The comparison reveals much about how Sedgwick herself was affected by the months she spent lost in the romantic pages of Italy, which, though they contrasted strikingly with the American treatise she was accustomed to, at the same time facilitated her own contribution to the American political text.

CHAPTER 2

Margaret Fuller's *Tribune* Dispatches and the Nineteenth-Century Body Politic

In many ways Margaret Fuller was an eccentric among her peers, a puzzle who mystified her contemporaries and who continues to elude her critics. Fuller herself questioned her identity in an 1831 diary entry that recalls a childhood moment of perplexity: "How is it that I seem to be this Margaret Fuller? What does it mean? What shall I do about it?" (Von Mehren 6). Henry James framed her as an enigma when he reportedly inquired, "Would she, with her appetite for ideas and her genius for conversation, have struck us but as a formidable bore, one of the worst kind, a culture-seeker without a sense of proportion, or, on the contrary, have affected us as a really attaching, a possibly picturesque New England Corinne?" (Perry Miller xxvii). More recent critics such as Ann Douglas emphasize her appearance, calling her "Emerson's difficult and homely friend" (313). Similarly, Joseph Deiss stresses Fuller's "striking" appearance, noting that "she was nearsighted, and had a mannerism of half closing the lids to see more sharply" (14), while Joel Pfister argues that "Fuller's caustic wit and plain physical appearance made her stunning in a different way," contrasting her impressive demeanor with the "'ordinary' feminine manner" of Beatrice in Hawthorne's "Rappacini's Daughter" (69). And of Fuller's conversations, Perry Miller writes, "Margaret Fuller presided over these bacchanic rites in homemade dresses that her adorers thought to be of Oriental magnificence, and at the climax of each session, when she had reduced the others to awed silence, she would close her eyes in an inspired trance and utter unfathomable words, which they thought emanated from some occult or Delphic wisdom" (xi). Regarding her biography, contemporary readers still wonder, did she and Giovanni Ossoli ever officially marry? Was her refusal to be rescued from the shipwreck off the

New York coast a suicidal gesture? And, despite Fuller's landmark role in American periodical writing, questions persist regarding her place in our literary canon, as evidenced by the title of the introduction to Joan Von Mehren's recent Fuller biography, "Margaret Fuller: Should She Be Famous?"[1]

Although such questions and colorful biographical anecdotes are provocative, they threaten to elide Fuller's historical context and political contributions by representing her primarily as a quirky "personality."[2] Bringing the discussion more firmly back to Fuller's writing is crucial to any understanding of how periodical literature, gender, and nationalism intersect in nineteenth-century America. Fuller's journalism connects meaningfully to the political and social climate in the world around her, and dismissals of her as "peculiar" betray the social censure that has frequently attended women who transgressed the nineteenth century's carefully delineated, gendered spheres. The first American woman to work as a foreign news correspondent, Margaret Fuller wrote thirty-seven dispatches between 1846 and 1850 for publication on the *New-York Daily Tribune*'s front page under the heading "Things and Thoughts in Europe." The majority of her dispatches utilize the Italian *Risorgimento,* a revolutionary movement to establish a popular government in which she became actively involved, as a lens through which to assess American democracy. Read with an awareness of context, the dispatches Horace Greeley contracted Fuller to send home from Europe emerge as a revealing product of and contribution to the nineteenth century's burgeoning nationalistic movements. Not only did newspapers such as the *Tribune* function as a primary means of representing imagined national community, but Fuller's journey to Italy and eventual expatriation also occurred at a historical moment dominated by European struggles for republican government. Like the periodical press within which she worked, Fuller's columns and even her personal life were saturated with issues of both national and international importance.

Though her concerns were clearly global, Fuller's experiences as a woman crucially inform her political agenda. In her dispatches, America's democratic actualization becomes coterminous with a woman's political right to self-actualization and full citizenship. Fuller helped to promote nineteenth-century American nationalism, but her journalism also critiqued gender constraints on American women of the mid-nineteenth century. This complex and apparently paradoxical agenda is reflected in her rhetorical use of body imagery. Fuller writes of the "body" politic in terms that speak for the various bodies that contribute to the nation: individual bodies, of all classes, races, and genders, that compose the national community. She refers to her country as a "huge, over fed, too hastily grown-up body" in need of "soul," and later asserts, "I do not deeply distrust my country. She is not dead, but in my time she sleepeth, and the spirit of our fathers flames no more, but lies hid beneath the ashes. It will not be so long; bodies cannot live when the soul gets too overgrown with gluttony and falsehood" (166, 230).[3] This mapping of human sentience onto geographic space links body politic to body personal, perpetuating the sentimentality of mainstream American patriotism even as it stands outside the dominant tradition to critique the nation on behalf of its downtrodden members. The alignment of the two discourses, nation and gender, suggests a parallel optimism underlying Fuller's conception of both. Recognizing the potential for struggle to liberate the Italian people, she underscores in her columns that awareness and political action can effect similar freedom for American women and other oppressed groups and thereby allow the United States to reclaim its glorious founding principles. Certainly the *Risorgimento* liberated Fuller herself, whose removal from familiar soil and immersion in politics abroad cast her in a powerful role drastically different from the spinsterish eccentricity projected onto her by those at home.

Print Journalism

As a journalist paid in advance for news she sent home, reportedly ten dollars per dispatch, Fuller had a distinctive relationship to her audience and her subjects. Horace Greeley's hiring of her was a historic decision, making her "the first female member of the working press" and affirming her right to step into a patriarchal line: "Greeley had hired her to fill the spot vacated by Albert Brisbane (later filled by George Ripley) and he expected her to report on social conditions as well as lend literary prestige to the paper" (Chevigny 288, 290). A political and patriotic publisher, Greeley "hoped to crowd out the sensational rival penny papers by his commitment to morality, social progress, and the arts" (ibid., 288). Acquiring Fuller's commentary on both political and cultural issues was clearly a significant part of this project. Other nineteenth century women travelers to Italy, like Catharine Maria Sedgwick and Sophia Peabody Hawthorne, told of their experiences in private journals and letters that became public documents years after their return home. In contrast, Fuller wrote and was read en media res, her commentary's value determined by how quickly she could dispatch it. She wrote words for immediate public consumption, without the protestations about the worth of the "private musings" that "friends were forcing her to publish" often found in conventional travel writing. As a reporter, Fuller spoke with a broader cultural sanction derived in part from her association with the *Tribune* and its well-known editor.[4]

Fuller's dispatches demonstrate her awareness of the newspaper's function as the "heart" of the country. As Margaret Lukens notes, the *Tribune*'s "nickname was 'The Great Moral Organ' " (187), suggesting its vital role in the American nation. Fittingly, Fuller wrote of the London newspaper, "As for the Times [*sic*] . . . the blood would tingle many a time to the fingers' ends of the body politic before that solemn organ which claims to represent the heart, would dare to beat in unison" (91). The irregular beat she describes indicates her concern that journalistic dysfunction might threaten a nation's integrity. The periodical press, a continuous and pervasive infusion into the community, could either sustain or infect the national body. An address to Horace Greeley penned in Edinburgh indicates how powerfully Fuller believed in journalism's obligation to nourish the moral life of its readership: "[T]he publisher cannot, if a mere tradesman, be a man of honor. . . . [H]e who, for his sordid aims, circulates poisonous trash amid a great and growing people, and makes it almost impossible for those whom heaven has appointed as its instructors to do their office, are the worst of traitors" (66). Aligning the publisher's powers with those of statesmen and priests, Fuller indicates the centrality of the periodical press even as she demonstrates that the profit motive threatened to taint its higher aims and poison the civic body. Fuller used her columns as a platform from which to edify the predominantly male publishers of her country who might have allowed greed to distract them from their higher calling. She not only recognized the influential power of the periodical press, but she also wielded it with passion.

Fuller's existence as an American abroad, living a life parallel to those of readers in the States, gave her dispatches their relevance and force. In Benedict Anderson's theory of the building of modern nationalism outlined in *Imagined Communities,* the newspaper is significant because it reflects and enables modern conceptions of time and also because its consumption is communal.[5] What Anderson calls "homogenous empty time," the sense that readers shared the same moment with the columnist, created the conceptual framework within which Fuller's audience apprehended her textual and ideological connection to themselves. The idea of time, in relation to the nation and the journalist, reinforces this bond and becomes a central component of Fuller's columns; the news, a timely commodity, is enveloped in temporal allusions. She boasts of making history by completing "the shortest voyage ever made across the Atlantic—

only ten days and sixteen hours from Boston to Liverpool" (39), and each dispatch bears the mark of the transatlantic steamer schedule. One letter, "meant to go by the Great Britain" was delayed; later she was "inevitably prevented from finishing one that was begun for the steamer of 4th November" (62, 78). Her columns documented events as they occurred, a concept quite different from the traditional travel narrative or travel-inflected novel, published after the journey when events had often been resolved. The immediacy of the journalistic dispatch kept domestic readers up to date on fast-breaking developments in transportation as well as specific events occurring in Europe and all the while reminded them that they shared a moment with an entire community of nationals, even (or especially) a compatriot who resided abroad.

In addition to creating an imagined nationalism that temporally bound the foreign correspondent to the domestic reader, this sense of immediacy, of time bearing down on the frantic journalist and injustice transpiring even as the reader sat down to read the front page at breakfast, fueled Fuller's calls for immediate political reform. In one dispatch, for example, Fuller means to translate the mission statement of a progressive Roman journal, but mailing constraints limit what she can accomplish: "I intended to have translated in full the programme, but time fails, and the law of opportunity does not favor, as my 'opportunity' leaves for London this afternoon" (139). In another dispatch, she closes with the frustrated declaration, "Time fails, as usual. The clock strikes, the postbag opens and leaves only time to make the sign of [a star—the symbol she used to close her columns]" (146). Perceiving how thoroughly time pervades her craft, Fuller explicitly incorporates this fact into the discourse itself, offering her awareness of time as a facet of the columns. The effect is to involve her readers in her own sense of urgency, an effect well suited to her political message—the need for immediate U.S. action to alleviate suffering, both at home and abroad.

Her tactic for catalyzing social activism is to target the individual reader. Fuller utilizes her front-page platform to make large-scale political pronouncements about her nation and its people, harsh assessments designed to promote the reader's self-scrutiny. When she writes, for example, "The American, first introduced to some good pictures by the truly great geniuses of the religious period in Art, must, if capable at all of mental approximation to the life therein embodied, be too deeply affected, too full of thoughts, to be in haste to say anything" (112), her description invites readers to measure themselves against the standard established for "the American" who is mentally "capable." Similar challenges pervade the dispatches, allowing Fuller to interpolate a diverse population into a cohesive whole with the term "American" and simultaneously to criticize individual members of that population for failing to live up to her high standards. In a representative gesture, Fuller challenges her readers by making categorical assertions about American tourists in Europe. She begins with a pronouncement that again demands self-reflection from her domestic reader: "The American in Europe, if a thinking mind, can only become more American" (161). Left to determine whether one is "a thinking mind," one then faces Fuller's delineation of the three "species" of American travelers and the task of finding one's place therein. The first type Fuller calls "the servile American—a being utterly shallow, thoughtless, worthless" who "comes abroad to spend his money and indulge his tastes" (162). Second, Fuller names "the conceited American," with an excess of patriotism, who "does not see, not he, that the history of Humanity for many centuries is likely to have produced results it requires some training, some devotion, to appreciate and profit by" and is thus prone to criticize European culture (ibid.). The final choice is clearly the best, a character Fuller calls "the thinking American," open minded enough (like Fuller herself) to "recogniz[e] the immense advantage of being born to a new world and on a virgin soil" and also "anxious to gather and carry back with him all that will bear a new climate and new culture" (163).

The *Tribune* readers, an "estimated circulation of 11,000" (Lukens 187), who faced these rhetorical challenges in their original context, as one facet of the newspaper's front-page collage, would have been reminded of their imagined national community even as they were encouraged by Fuller to take a critical stance regarding their own obligation to that community. The resulting conflict manifests itself in the dispatches as a combination of yearnings for an ideal America and confessions of faults Fuller cannot deny. In Dispatch 18, she opens with the glory of America's destiny, "Thou wert to be the advance-guard of Humanity, the herald of all Progress," but soon arrives at a series of sobering admissions: "Must I not confess in my country to a boundless lust of gain? Must I not confess to the weakest vanity, which bristles and blusters at each foolish taunt of the foreign press . . . ? Must I not confess that there is as yet no antidote cordially adopted that will defend even that great, rich country against the evils that have grown out of the commercial system in the old world?" (165). Greeley established the *Tribune* in 1841, according to Chevigny, "as a paper dedicated first to the elevation of the masses—the reading public generated by the new penny papers—and second to the success of the liberal Whigs" (288). Fuller's critique would have contributed to this project by addressing a range of subgroups within her audience. She combines a challenge to middle-class liberals (those with access to the "foreign press") with attacks on America's capitalist system that would have appealed to the working class (Greeley's "masses"). In the same dispatch, she fuels her argument by adding commentary on current events in the States: "I listen to the same arguments against the emancipation of Italy, that are used against the emancipation of our blacks; the same arguments in favor of the spoliation of Poland as for the conquest of Mexico. I find the cause of tyranny and wrong everywhere the same—and lo! my country the darkest offender" (165). With such accusations, Fuller uses her journalistic platform both to consolidate and to arouse an informed public who could remedy the suffering body politic at home.

Equally worthy of her readers' attention was the revolutionary movement occurring in Italy during Fuller's residence there. As one of America's first foreign correspondents, as a political commentator, as a liaison between American and Italian culture, as a progressive revolutionary who recognized capitalism's moral and social implications, Fuller spoke to and about nineteenth century cultural movements that were changing the face of the globe. She participated in a unique historic confluence that conjoined the forces of technology, capitalism, and revolutionary activity in Europe. As nationalism came to denote an internal sense of moral commitment and connection, rather than merely a reflection of random, external circumstances, her columns promoted the ideal that citizens had the right to determine their allegiance based on the values displayed by their country. Indeed, Fuller's immersion in radical politics and her awareness of the profound changes redefining nationhood led her to reevaluate her commitment to the land of her birth: "My friends write to urge my return; they talk of our country as the land of the Future. It is so, but that spirit which made it all it is of value in my eyes, which gave all of hope with which I can sympathize for that Future, is more alive here [in Italy] at present than in America" (230). Her textual expatriation underscored for readers at home the severity of her disillusionment with the United States, the magnetism of the Italian independence movement, and the obligation of individual citizens to make choices that reflected their moral codes.

Fuller and the *Risorgimento*

When Fuller arrived in Italy in 1847, the various Italian city-states (not yet unified into one nation) were engaged in struggles to oust foreign monarchies, limit the pope's temporal power, and establish a centralized, republican government. The resulting revolutionary activities, collectively known as the *Risorgimento* ("renaissance" or "revival"), lasted throughout Fuller's Italian sojourn and became the central concern of her dispatches and her life.[6] Although ultimately unsuccessful, the Risorgimento paved the way for Italian unification a decade after Fuller's departure, providing the previously fragmented Italian people with national heroes and a common cause. Her dispatches constitute a major textual contribution to this movement, her columns distributing the demands of the Italian revolutionaries—which included, notably, "freedom of the press" (Hearder 201)—to an international audience and keeping Americans apprised of developments in the uprising. In representing the Italian revolution for American consumption, Fuller's dispatches cultivated nationalisms on both sides of the Atlantic. Her reconstitution of American revolutionary history simultaneously revived American patriotism and validated Italy's republican mission.

Part of a mid-nineteenth-century phenomenon in which the nation, as an ideology, became reproducible as a model for emerging nations, Fuller's discourse self-consciously performs the important political/historical work of representing the nation. As Anderson notes, "The close of the era of successful national liberation movements in the Americas coincided rather closely with the onset of the age of nationalism in Europe"; therefore, European movements were "able to work from visible models" (67). Fuller recognized the explosiveness of her political moment and offered the American Revolution as a model for a struggling Italian people. The nationalistic uprisings that characterized the nineteenth century seemed, to Fuller, the inevitable consequence of centuries of corrupt monarchical oppression: "Still Europe toils and struggles with her idea, and, at this moment, all things bode and declare a new outbreak of the fire, to destroy old palaces of crime!" (164). The "idea" that would rid Europe of this evil was, in fact, the idea of republican nationhood already implemented in America, an idea imported into Europe through print culture and adjusted to fit political conditions there. A woman whose homeland fell short of her humanitarian ideals, Fuller embraced the European uprisings with their demands for universal rights, and her dispatches were dedicated to a twin project of fostering the nascent Italian republic and redeeming her homeland's democratic failings.[7]

Repeatedly Fuller reminds her readers of America's recent revolution and its corresponding debt to the world: "Ah! America, with all thy rich boons, thou hast a heavy account to render for the talent given; see in every way that thou be not found wanting" (160–61). To heighten the emotional stakes, she invokes patriotic signs, symbols of the imagined nationalism that Anderson sees as originating in American revolutionary activity (81). Not eternal but historically produced, such symbols become part of nationalist rhetoric when Fuller writes home, "This cause is OURS, above all others; we ought to show that we feel it to be so. . . . Please think of this, some of my friends, who still care for the Eagle, the 4th [of] July, and the old cries of Hope and Honor" (160–61). Fuller uses strategic appeals to sentimental patriotism to enlist the aid of fellow Americans in the ultimate goal of transporting American ideals and experience to Italy. Her project may have been especially challenging, as Brigitte Bailey has pointed out, due to Americans' fear of losing Italy as a site of aesthetic fulfillment: "Supportive of these movements for self-determination [the French and Italian revolutions of 1848], especially since they seemed to follow an American model of iconoclastic republicanism, elite Americans also wanted to preserve Europe as a source of icons and instruction in consolidating national identities through images" (60). Such protestations notwithstanding, Fuller's patriotic dispatches constitute a text of nationhood that affirms the American community even as it offers a model for the emerging European republics. In other words, Fuller's attempt to distill the domestic model for foreign consumption actually *creates* the model nation that would serve as precursor. Enabled by the attributes of the periodical press, she inscribed a version of national identity and ideology that would produce patriotism at home.[8]

Despite Fuller's invocations of an idealized American republicanism, she also laments American shortcomings: "Yet, oh Eagle, whose early flight showed this clear sight of the Sun, how often dost thou near the ground, how show the vulture in these latter days! Thou wert to be the advance-guard of Humanity, the herald of all Progress; how often hast thou betrayed this high commission! Fain would the tongue in clear triumphant accents draw example from thy story. . . . But we must stammer and blush when we speak of many things" (165). Such blemishes as slavery, the Mexican War, greed, and solipsism are Fuller's evidence that America has failed to fulfill its special destiny. This combination of, on the one hand, reminders of America's fortunate history with, on the other, examples of national failures forwards Fuller's agenda by showing Americans their sins and offering a path to redemption. The suggestion is that America will rise anew by sustaining other countries in their struggles for freedom: "Send, dear America, a talisman to thy ambassadors, precious beyond all that boasted gold of California. . . . Hail to my country! May she live a free, a glorious, a loving life, and not perish . . . from the leprosy of selfishness" (284). Thus Fuller constructs an international connection within which America redeems itself by offering itself, as the "blueprint" of which Anderson speaks, to an emerging Italian republic.

By valorizing American destiny, the dispatches contribute to a conceptualization of the nation, despite its historical contingency, as eternal. Anderson argues, "If nation-states are widely conceded to be 'new' and 'historical,' the nations to which they give political expression always loom out of an immemorial past" (11). In other words, "it is the magic of nationalism to turn chance into destiny" (ibid., 12); clearly Fuller's columns contribute to the narrative that recasts historical contingency as fate. Reproaching her rich countrymen "who think that a mess of pottage can satisfy the wants of man," that is, who think the poor are content, she writes, "they have no heart for the idea, for the destiny of our own great nation: how can they feel the spirit that is struggling now in this and others of Europe?" (154). In a later dispatch, she draws a parallel between current political action in Italy and a transhistorical fantasy of American values: "It was the spirit of religion [that infused a Florentine celebration of the National Guard]—such my Country; as welling fresh from some great hearts in thy early hours, won for thee all of value that thou canst call thy own, whose ground-work is the assertion, still sublime though thou hast not been true to it, that all men have equal rights, and that these are *birth*-rights, derived from God alone" (158–59). If democratic rights, offered as the "ground-work" of "all of value" in America, are "derived from God alone," they not only extend into an immemorial past, but they receive sanction from a transhistorical and superhuman power. These associations transform the nation into a mythical/moral entity rather than a historical eventuality. Further, Fuller's use of an inflated discourse likely to conjure up biblical associations—"all of value that thou canst call thy own"—would contribute to a sense of nationalistic worship in her readers.

American destiny translates into international leadership with Fuller's assertion that "the facts of our history, ideal and social, will be grand and of new import," an idea that leads Fuller to speculate that sculpture is the consummate artistic medium for the American. "It is perfectly natural," she argues, "to the American to mold in clay and carve in stone," depicting the artist's vocation as both natural and national. As the passage continues, sculpture becomes an expression of civic pride: "He [the American sculptor] will thus record his best experiences, and these records will adorn the noble structures that must naturally arise for the public uses of our society" (267). The repetition of the word "natural" in her argument is significant. Government buildings become "noble structures" that "naturally arise," losing their utilitarianism as they are transformed into organic manifestations of American art and, thus, American greatness. Art, nationalism, and government are combined in Fuller's vision, all representations of the same agenda that arises "naturally" from American soil.

In a dispatch written two months later, Fuller uses a similar rhetoric to celebrate Roman political strife: "This city [Rome] that has grown, not out of the necessities of commerce nor the luxuries of wealth, but first out of heroism, then out of faith. Swelling domes, roofs softly tinted with yellow moss—what deep meaning, what deep repose, in your faintly seen outline" (285). The city "grows" out of moral ideals, and the nation's buildings symbolize more than mere "commerce." The idea of national destiny is transferred from America to Italy, with Fuller's parallel descriptions of the two republics reinforcing the "rightness" of the Italian revolution for the benefit of an American readership already convinced of its own nation's superiority and leadership role.

In her profound identification with the Italian cause, Fuller betrays a communal perspective that runs counter to Emerson's famous prescription against travel in "Self Reliance": "Let us not rove; let us sit at home with the cause" (180). The assertion not only betrays Emerson's naiveté regarding his own nation's formation, but also negates the value of interaction with other cultures.[9] More applicable to Fuller's experience would have been Thoreau's admonition in *Walden:* "Not until we are lost, in other words, not till we have lost the world, do we begin to find ourselves" (217). Yet Thoreau's discovery of self through isolation and withdrawal contrasts with Fuller's self-realization through travel and interaction with other cultures. The Transcendentalism inscribed by Emerson and Thoreau, in its insistence on solitude and domestic pride (the sovereignty of the individual person as well as the individual nation), maintains a separatist logic that Fuller sought to transcend. She lost both the (familiar) world and the self projected onto her there when she traveled to Italy. Her translocation to Italy ignited in her a camaraderie with the Italian people and an emboldened sense of political agency; in addition, the epistolary nature of her dispatches invited a certain intimacy between herself and her readers. Indeed, the essential character of the newspaper column—an evolving pastiche composed of small pieces produced over time, stylistically flexible enough to encompass a range of discourses and voices—uniquely suited Fuller's vision of a literary and political collective.

Her innovative use of the periodical forum, as well as her political engagement, might be demonstrated by her manipulation of the star imprint with which she closed her dispatches. A shifting symbol that reflects Fuller's self-conception, the star becomes increasingly entwined with the content of the dispatches, representing Fuller's growing involvement in Italian politics. In the early dispatches, the star is tacked on at the end of the columns, unconnected to the commentary itself. Yet after Fuller's arrival in Italy, a year into her trip, she begins to play with the star's signifying possibilities, implicating her signature in her column's contents. She closes Dispatch 15, written from Milan, with the statement, "The clock strikes, the postbag opens and leaves only time to make the sign of [star]" (146), thus situating her mark within the text. Five months later, writing from a Rome bombarded by new developments in the fight for independence, Fuller remarks, "Every day the cloud swells, and the next fortnight is likely to bring important material for the record of [star]" (208). The rhetoric implies Fuller's deepening personal involvement in political events, foregrounding their significance in relation to her. After a tour of the hills outside Rome with Giovanni Ossoli, Fuller's star and self are transformed: "Meanwhile the nightingales sing; every tree and plant is in flower, and the sun and moon shine as if Paradise were already reestablished on earth. I go to one of the villas to dream it is so, beneath the pale light of a [star]" (231). The romantic optimism of this dispatch is heightened by the metamorphosis of Fuller's by now familiar byline into a sentimental symbol. In addition, the journalistic convention of self-naming is appropriated and deployed to express the distinctive sensations of an American woman immersed in a foreign culture.

During the height of the revolution, Fuller incorporates Italian speech into her dispatch and essentially writes herself into the narrative of Italian destiny. Calling out her grief to the Virgin Mary over the revolution's violence, Fuller writes, "Ave Maria Santissima! when thou didst gaze on thy babe with such infinite hope, thou didst not dream that so many ages after blood would be shed and curses in his name. Madonna Addolorata! hadst thou not hoped peace and good will would spring from his bloody woes, couldst thou have borne these hours at the foot of the cross." In the final entreaty, Fuller pens the name that applies to herself: "O Stella! woman's heart of love, send yet a ray of pure light on this troubled deep!" (274). Immediately following this exhortation, Fuller's familiar star is printed. The juxtaposition of the star symbol and the Italian word for star (*stella*) suggests the closeness Fuller felt to Italian traditions at that moment and even casts her as a savior figure for this troubled people. Perhaps the "star" of her journalism would shine a new light onto the revolution she was witnessing. Significantly, the star disappears entirely from Dispatch 34, which reports the defeat of the Roman republic and is the only dispatch without the symbolic sign-off. The relationship of

Fuller and her writing to the Risorgimento, represented by the star, became increasingly intense until the defeat of the movement threatened to erase her discursive self. Indeed she writes in Dispatch 35, "To write from Italy is now become a sorrowful business" and then again in Dispatch 36, "I have begun to write, yet little do I feel inclined" (312, 317).

Despite the Roman republic's ultimate defeat and despite her protests about writing, Fuller continued to post her dispatches and maintained faith in the eventual triumph of republicanism in Europe. Her belief in the United States as a fulfillment of providence rather than a result of historical circumstance, combined with the Italian revolution she witnessed, formed the backbone of her journalism and permitted her to write enthusiastically to her compatriots, "I have also a lurking confidence in what our fathers spoke of so constantly, a providential order of things, by which brute force and selfish enterprises are sometimes set at nought by aid which seems to descend from a higher sphere" (283). Fuller could display such confidence, despite the treachery and setbacks that plagued the Italian revolutionaries, because of her astute long-range understanding of world politics. She accurately predicted that the "struggle may last fifty years, and the earth be watered with the blood and tears of more than one generation, but the result is sure. All Europe, including Great Britain, where the most bitter resistance of all will be made, is to be under Republican Government in the next century" (278).

Woman and the Nation: Body Personal and Body Politic

In the periodical writing Fuller contributed to the *Tribune,* she discovered a politically efficacious way to transcend gender and genre. The columns, in their subject matter and in their extensive distribution to a mixed audience, permitted her to fuse her feelings as a woman and as a writer/patriot. Although the majority of her columns deal with national affairs, she also weaves into her writing stories of individual women. Fuller's second dispatch, for example, describes a woman she met during her travels in Scotland. Calling her "a fine specimen of the noble, intelligent Scotchwoman," Fuller goes on to praise the woman as "an only child, a cherished wife, an adored mother, unspoiled by love in any of these relations, because that love was founded on knowledge" (52). The knowledge underlying this Scottish woman's integrity is explicitly political: "In childhood she had warmly sympathized in the spirit that animated the American revolution, and Washington had been her hero. . . . [S]he had known in the course of her long life many eminent men, knew minutely the history of efforts in that direction, and sympathized now in the triumph of the people over the Corn-Laws, as she had in American victories with as much ardor as when a girl . . ." (52–53). Fuller is clearly smitten with this exemplary woman's ability to combine familial devotion and revolutionary fervor, a mixture that Fuller strove for in her own lifetime and advocated in her writing as a healthier and more respectable option for nineteenth-century women than stereotypical, infantile dependence. In contrast to the sentimental novels that were so popular a form for nineteenth-century American women writers, Fuller makes use of a literary space that permits precisely this fusion—that of the political and emotional self.

Fuller further alludes to her literary values in a passage from a later dispatch written in praise of two European women writers:

> I prize Joanna Baillie and Madame Roland as the best specimens which have been hitherto offered of women of a Spartan, Roman strength and singleness of mind. . . . They are not sentimental; they do not sigh and write of withered flowers of fond affection, and woman's heart born to be misunderstood by the object or objects of her fond, inevitable choice. Love, (the passion,) when spoken of at all by them, seems a thing noble, religious, worthy to be felt. They do not write of it always; they did not think of it always; they saw other things in this great, rich, suffering world . . . nor was all their speech one continued utterance of mere personal experience. It contained things which are good, intellectually, universally. (89)

In the preceding passage and in her journalism itself, Fuller lays claim to the entire "great" world as proper subject matter for women who write. Her theory of women's writing self-consciously positions itself in opposition to the conventions of sentimental novels, especially their exclusive focus on home, love, and the wounded woman. In her ideal, the woman writer recognizes that the personal and the political are codependent, that her private experience can encompass a range of issues, and that her literary output should reflect this diversity. An elastic genre that depended upon many individuals' interpretation and transcription of global events, the newspaper underscored an ideology of inclusion and facilitated Fuller's use of personal experience to promulgate a political message.

In contrast to women who "sigh and write of withered flowers of fond affection," Fuller praises women who combine love with knowledge. The Scottish woman gains respect within the home by bringing her concern with public affairs into the domestic sphere: "Dear to memory will be the sight of her in the beautiful seclusion of her home among the mountains, a picturesque, flower wreathed dwelling, where affection, tranquility and wisdom were the gods of the hearth." Fuller follows this idyllic vision with an impassioned appeal: "Grant us more such women, Time! Grant to men the power to reverence, to seek for such!" (53). The rhetorical devices used in this dispatch illuminate how Fuller manipulates print journalism's power on behalf of women's rights. In this case, the apostrophe to "Time" establishes a lofty and traditional tone, reminiscent of classical rhetoric, yet Fuller uses the distanced voice to make demands of her own historical context. The appeal, "Grant to men the power to reverence," accuses American men, the *Tribune*'s readers, of demonstrating a lack of "power" in their treatment of women. Under the guise of an appeal to the generic concept of "Time," Fuller chastises her country*men*. The classical style would have tempered her demands with a tone of formality and diplomacy by making the accusation less direct, though no less weighty. Such hybrid discourse is characteristic of Fuller's journalistic strategies for promoting her feminist message.

When Fuller discovered powerful European women who exceeded their culture's low expectations of them, she incorporated their stories into her column alongside updates on current events and background on Italy's warring political factions. Fuller describes, for example, "an object which gave [her] pleasure" in Chester, namely an old surveillance tower converted into a museum. What pleases her is that, as the museum relied upon contributions "from all who had derived benefit from Chester," "many women had been busy in filling these magazines for the instruction and the pleasure of their fellow townsmen," with one woman contributing "a fine collection of butterflies, and a ship" (49–50). Putting the women's efforts in context for her *Tribune* readership, she asserts, "I like to see women perceive that there are other ways of doing good beside making clothes for the poor or teaching Sunday school; these are well, if well directed, but there are many other ways, some as sure and surer, and which benefit the giver no less than the receiver" (50). The importance of recognizing women's many and various contributions to the larger culture is made explicit here, as is the potential link between the opportunities for women Fuller observes in European countries and the ideals she envisions for America.

In a later dispatch from London, Fuller initiates what seems a conventional observation about the lack of a "woman's touch" in the London Reform Club: "To me this palace of so many 'single gentlemen rolled into one,' seemed stupidly comfortable in the absence of that elegant arrangement and vivacious atmosphere which only Women can inspire. In the kitchen, indeed, I met them and, on that account, it seemed the pleasantest part of the building—though, even there, they are but the servants of servants" (96). The reflection that women are permitted only in a kitchen, where they must serve men, inspires the caustic rejoinder, "I am not sorry, however, to see men predominant in the cooking department, as I hope to see that and washing transferred to their care in the progress of things, since they are 'the stronger sex' " (ibid.). Fuller's flippant inflection of "stronger" attacks traditional gender divisions, suggesting both that men's physical strength might suit them to manual household labor (rather than intellectual privilege) and also that women have historically been responsible for much of the culture's hardest work.

Yet Fuller's Europe also offers evidence that ancient civilizations conceived of a woman's role differently and thus undermines the essentialism of nineteenth-century gendered spheres. Fuller advises her American readers,

> A woman should love Bologna, for there has the spark of intellect in Woman been cherished with reverent care. Not in former ages only, but in this, Bologna raised a woman who was worthy to the dignitaries of its University, and in their Certosa they proudly show the monument to Clotilda Tambroni, late Greek professor there. . . . In Milan, also, I see in the Ambrosian Library the bust of a female Mathematician. These things make me feel that if the state of Woman in Italy is so depressed, yet a good will toward a better is not wholly wanting. These things, and still more the reverence to the Madonna and innumerable female Saints, who if, like St. Teresa, they had intellect as well as piety, became counselors no less than comforters to the spirits of men. (143)

Fuller offers to her contemporary readership not only a history of respect for women in Bologna, but also by implication a call for similar advancements in her own country's future. Her emphasis on St. Teresa's "intellect and piety" echoes her earlier description of the Scottish woman, suggesting that a woman's spiritual and emotional strength depend upon a solid intellectual foundation.

The worship of female saints, which fascinated many nineteenth-century American women writers in Italy, informs a later dispatch in which Fuller confesses, "[St. Cecilia] and St. Agnes are my favorite saints" (241). The stories of Agnes and Cecilia foreground individuals sacrificing themselves for a higher moral principle, echoing Fuller's repeated emphasis on each citizen's responsibility for national ideals. In Cecilia and Agnes, Fuller selected symbols of bodily invincibility who, having pledged themselves to Christ, died defending their spiritual faith. Agnes, "a special patroness of bodily purity," was persecuted for refusing to marry, then tortured, humiliated, and eventually sent by the governor to a brothel "with liberty to all to abuse her person at pleasure." When young men rushed to take advantage of the thirteen-year-old girl, they "were seized with such awe at the sight of the saint that they durst not approach her" and Agnes remained pure (*Butler's* 133–34).

As a means of demonstrating her piety, Cecilia also refused marital relations. After converting her husband and brother-in-law to Christianity, she was punished by a prefect who ordered her to be "suffocated to death in the bathroom of her own house" (ibid., 403). Despite the fact that "the furnace was fed with seven times its normal amount of fuel," Cecilia lived unharmed for a full day. The soldier sent to decapitate her also found his task daunting; having "struck at her neck three times," he left her for dead but she "lingered three days" (ibid.). Like Agnes, Cecilia devoted herself to a faith that gave her bodily invincibility. These women transcended physical limitations through their devotion to a higher ideal, and both determined their fates by refusing coercion. Certainly such heroic foremothers would have encouraged a woman who dedicated herself to journalism's power and sought to transcend the weaknesses her culture ascribed to her. Further, Fuller used her column to publicly valorize women who had been unjustly abused by patriarchal power—most likely, some of Fuller's readers would have recognized the parallels with her own situation.

Relying upon images of body and disease, Fuller's columns often liken weaknesses within the community to sickness and suggest that national health is maintained either by cure or by prevention. The nation-as-body metaphor was not unusual in American patriotic rhetoric; yet Fuller takes the image of the diseased national body to a provocative extreme by bringing gender into the picture. It is possible to trace the movement from body politic to body personal/feminine over the course of her dispatches. In May 1847, for example, Fuller penned one of her most aggressive social commentaries in response to evidence of poverty and hunger in France: "The more I see of the terrible ills which infests [*sic*] the body politic of Europe, the more indignation I feel at the selfishness or stupidity of those in my own country who oppose an examination of these subjects—such as is animated by the hope of prevention" (119). Later, in Italy, Fuller uses similar terminology to remark on the influence of domestic abuse on her sharpening political/social awareness: "[T]he cries of mothers and wives beaten at night by sons and husbands for their diversion after drinking, as I have repeatedly heard them these past months, the excuse for falsehood, 'I *dare not* tell my husband, he would be ready to kill me,' have sharpened my perception as to the ills of Woman's condition and remedies that must be applied" (245–56). The repetition of words associated with sickness and treatment ("prevention" and "remedies") fortifies the thematic bond between the individual woman and the state. In contrast to a literary tradition that often feminized the American land to accommodate masculine conquest fantasies, Fuller textualized a feminine body politic to reveal the injuries caused by patriarchal insensitivity to women's needs. In marking domestic violence as a social issue and in using her status as a reporter to bring the issue to public attention, Fuller was a pioneer. By presenting injuries to women's bodies as analogous to a sickly political body, she demonstrated the interconnections between woman and nation and between private and public and thereby stressed the state's responsibility to treat the (woman's) body in order to heal itself.

"The Bond of Life"

Fuller's dispatches document an urgent call for action that, though interrupted occasionally by her frustration with America's reluctant politicians, ultimately locates hope in radical reform. Clearly concerned with material conditions and capitalism's implication in societal ills, Fuller was an early advocate of socialism and is credited with helping to introduce Marxist thought to the American people. Chevigny reads an 1845 Fuller *Tribune* column as "among the very earliest notices of Marx and Engels in America" (294). In the dispatches Fuller offers an incisive and unflinching assessment of how capitalist class structure depends upon an oppressed working class. From Glasgow Fuller writes home that "the people are more crowded together and the stamp of squalid, stolid misery and degradation more obvious and appalling" in that city than at any other stop on her European tour (79). She continues, describing "persons, especially women, dressed in dirty, wretched tatters, worse than none, and with an expression of listless, unexpecting woe on their faces, far more tragic than the inscription over the gate of Dante's Inferno" (79).

The image of suffering taints the romance of a castle she visits nearby, where centuries ago "lords and ladies gay danced and sang above [while] prisoners pined and wild beasts starved below" (80). The juxtaposition provokes a sober reminder to her readers that while the maintenance of the ancient castle "at first blush looks like a very barbarous state of things . . . on reflection, one does not find that we have outgrown it in our present so-called state of refined civilization. . . . Still lords and ladies dance and sing above, unknowing or uncaring that the laborers who minister to their luxuries starve or are turned into wild beasts—below. Man need not boast his condition till he can weave his costly tapestry without the side that is kept under looking like that, methinks" (80). Fuller's travels brought her into close contact with the oppression that underlies capitalism and contributed to the fervent, radical tone of her dispatches. Once again, her medium proves to be well suited to her message. In 1848, the year Marx and Engels published *The Communist Manifesto,* Fuller published a dispatch detailing for Americans the very issues the German socialists were investigating in Europe: "To you, people of America, it may perhaps be given to look on and learn in time for a preventive wisdom. You may learn the real meaning of the words FRATERNITY, EQUALITY. . . . You may in time learn to reverence, learn to guard, the true aristocracy of a nation, the only really noble—the LABORING CLASSES" (211). The periodical press permitted such a radical declaration, providing Fuller with a wide audience and encouraging (indeed, demanding) her immediate, uncensored response to events, even though her socialist rhetoric would have seemed radical to American readers who believed that the class structure rewarded merit and that the upper classes *deserved* their status and its attendant privileges.

Fuller herself had grown up in a community infused with elitism, her father bestowing upon her a classical education, her brothers attending Harvard, her early conversational circles comprised of wealthy and educated cosmopolitans from the Boston area; but the encounter with Europe and Italy and with poverty and revolution led her to form new and radical allegiances, accompanied by rebellious declarations. She transcended the national affiliation imposed upon her at birth, expressing throughout the dispatches a closer affinity to Italian culture than to her own. The birth of her son (to an Italian father) seems to have broadened and complicated her sense of national belonging. Fuller collapses her political and maternal connections to Italy tellingly in a letter written to Caroline Sturgis Tappan in December 1849. Describing an afternoon outing with a friend, Fuller writes, "We sat down on a stone seat in the sunny walk to see the people walk by. The Grand Duke and his children, the elegant Austrian officers who will be driven out of Italy when Angelino is a man" (Chevigny 492). The chronology, linking Fuller's son's maturity to the overthrow of the occupying forces, suggests causality; a mother's heightened investment in the establishment of republican government casts Angelino as the hero of the revolution.

With new allegiances came Fuller's endorsement of socialism, as she grew to believe that only radical reform could ease the world's suffering: "Here lie my hopes now. I believed before I came to Europe in what is called Socialism, as the inevitable sequence to the tendencies and wants of the era, but I did not think these vast changes in modes of government, education and daily life, would be effected as rapidly as I now think they will, because they must. The world can no longer stand without them" (320). "Hope" is an important term in this prognosis. Despite the defeat of the Italian revolutionaries and what she saw as America's failures, Fuller's dispatches remain cautiously optimistic. Comparing the Italian zeal for reform with American domestic policy, she asks the barbed question, "And my country, what does she? You have chosen a new President [Zachary Taylor] from a Slave State, representative of the Mexican War" (245). She continues with a prescription for American redemption and sends a hopeful message on behalf of her own sex: "Pray send here a good Ambassador—one that has experience of foreign life, that he may act with good judgment; and, if possible, a man that has knowledge and views which extend beyond the cause of party politics in the United States. . . . Another century, and I might ask to be made Ambassador myself . . . but woman's day has not come yet" (ibid.). In its suggestion that Fuller herself possessed the requisite characteristics to serve as a diplomat and its evocation of an approaching "woman's day," the dispatch offers a feminist hope to American readers.

Fuller offers a larger-scale hope as she closes her final dispatch from Italy, dated January 6, 1850:

> Joy to those born in this day: In America is open to them the easy chance of a noble, peaceful growth, in Europe of a combat grand in its motives, and in its extent beyond what the world ever before so much as dreamed. Joy to them; and joy to those their heralds, who, if their path was desert, their work unfinished, and their heads in the power of a prostituted civilization, to throw as toys at the feet of flushed, triumphant wickedness, yet holy-hearted in unasking love, great and entire in their devotion, fall or fade, happy in the thought that there come after them greater than themselves, who may at last string the harp of the world to full accord, in glory to God in the highest, for peace and love from man to man is become the bond of life. (323)

Although her nation often disappointed its citizens' dreams, Fuller did not ultimately relinquish her faith in American destiny or her reliance on the concept of nation itself. In light of her literary accomplishments and social activism, it is ironic that Perry Miller felt compelled to assert that Fuller "may easily be dismissed as an eccentric, as no true voice of American civilization" (xii). Clearly her discourse, situated at a historical moment of crisis abroad and problematic expansion at home, critiques America's greed even as it participates in constructing that nation as a manifestation of the ideal republic. A "true voice" speaking to the contradictions inherent in her nation's ideology, she was a radical *and* a patriot, working within the emerging, nineteenth-century periodical press and in response to the major nationalistic upheavals around her. Margaret Fuller's columns and commentary blurred the line between public and private affairs as she attempted to supersede, personally and politically, the limitations of her time.

CHAPTER 3

Domesticity and Nationalism in Harriet Beecher Stowe's *Agnes of Sorrento*

[A]nd Sorrento-O Sorrento was beyond picture, beyond poesy, for the greatest Artist had been at work there in a temper beyond the reach of human art.

— MARGARET FULLER, *At Home and Abroad*

Twelve years after Fuller's tragic return from Europe, Harriet Beecher Stowe published her novel *Agnes of Sorrento* (1862), with a preface that reads, "The story was a child of love in its infancy, and its flowery Italian cradle rocked it with an indulgent welcome." Although Stowe's prefatory remark echoes the by-now familiar thematics of domesticity that inform much of her work, this chapter explores the complications that the flowery Italian cradle suggests.[1] The centrality of the home in Stowe's fiction, especially *Uncle Tom's Cabin,* has been well established in recent criticism. Gillian Brown, in her essay "Getting in the Kitchen with Dinah: Domestic Politics in *Uncle Tom's Cabin,*" locates Stowe's domesticity quite particularly in the novel's depiction of the kitchen, a space that stands as a symbol of women's sphere of influence. "The call to the mothers of America for the abolition of slavery," Brown argues, is rendered urgent through the textualization of "the chaos in Dinah's kitchen"; that space will be clean and orderly, the argument goes, once some national housekeeping has taken place (16). Similarly, Dorothy Berkson asserts in "Millennial Politics and the Feminine Fiction of Harriet Beecher Stowe" that "the kitchens in Stowe's New England novels are the symbolic center for . . . domestically ideal communities" (250). Located north or south of the Mason-Dixon line, Stowe's fiction typically explores a domesticity defined by its location in America and in the home. In contrast, *Agnes of Sorrento,* like the phrase "flowery Italian cradle," takes Stowe's domesticity out of the kitchen and out of the country.

Published serially in the *Atlantic Monthly* from May 1861 until April 1862, *Agnes* is noteworthy, in the words of one critic, as Stowe's "only historical novel and the only one not set in America" (Nathalia Wright 90). Serialized a year after the publication of Hawthorne's *Marble Faun,* Stowe's text constituted one of the earliest international novels, a genre that would become central as the nineteenth century progressed and American literature continued to define, and refine, itself. Yet, despite its unique position in the Stowe canon and its role in establishing the international novel as a prominent American literary tradition, scant critical attention has been paid *Agnes,* beyond a short plot summary buried in a comprehensive list of Stowe's fiction or an occasional disparaging aside such as Van Wyck Brooks's characterization of it as Stowe's "weak little novel" (130). Echoing Brooks's deprecation, William Vance describes Stowe's "little discourses" as "merely self-congratulatory recitations of what everyone knows to be true" (*America's Rome* II:23). Even Joan Hedrick, though she recognizes its importance in popularizing the inter national theme, damns the novel with faint praise as "no more unreadable today than Hawthorne's *Marble Faun,*" which "shares with it a lush Italian setting, a virginal young heroine, and a brooding atmosphere of Catholicism and decadence." Hedrick's next sentence levels a stronger criticism: "None of this is likely to appeal to contemporary readers." The book's weaknesses, Hedrick points out, "owe much to [its] picaresque mode of composition," in which Stowe wove into the fictional story the observations of Italy she had jotted down in her travel diary (292). Likewise, feminist critic Nina Baym highlights the novel's failures when she notes, "There are immense technical problems involved in portraying an unearthly character in an earthly form within the confines of a realistic novel, and in my view Stowe did not surmount them" (234).[2]

Stowe offered her own reductive gloss on *Agnes of Sorrento,* composed following a visit to Italy with her family in the winter of 1859–1860, when she described it to her editor and traveling companion, James T. Fields, as "a spontaneous tribute to the exceeding loveliness and beauty of all things there" (290). Her prefatory letter seems to undermine further the "seriousness" of the novel's construction: "All dates shall give way to the fortunes of our story, and our lovers shall have the benefit of fairy land, and whoso wants history will not find it here, except to our making, and as it suits our purpose." However, precisely what these critical assessments offer as evidence of the novel's simplicity or weakness—its enjambment of the mystical and the earthly, its emotive celebration of the beauty of the Italian landscape, its narrative distance from the contemporary American lives of its audience, its collagelike juxtaposition of Stowe's travel experience and the romantic plot—I propose as the crucial aspects that make this fiction complex, historically suggestive, and worthy of closer reading. The intricacies of the text both mirror and produce the conflicted relationship with her own country that compelled Stowe to use a foreign setting for her story.

The novel eludes categorization in a particular genre, as critics demonstrate. Called a historical novel by Nathalia Wright, a realistic (though unsuccessful) novel by Baym, a "romance" by Brooks, and a "historical romance" by Jenny Franchot, Stowe's fiction incorporates various literary traditions as it straddles the two modes said to dominate the nineteenth-century American artist's experience of Italy. William Vance describes the first mode as "that of romantic classicism," which "had begun in 1760 with the arrival in Rome of the young artist Benjamin West" and "had reached its climax in 1860 with the publication of *The Marble Faun.*" "The second phase," Vance asserts, "coincided with the realistic movement in American literature and art." Significantly, Vance identifies the inauguration of this second, realistic phase with the arrival in Genoa of the American steamship *Quaker City,* which had completed "the first organized cruise ever made from America to Europe" ("Seeing Italy" 94). The ship delivered its cargo of tourists, including Mark Twain, to the Italian shore on July 4, 1867, seven years after the climax of romantic classicism identified by Vance. The chronology leaves Stowe's *Agnes* in the ambiguous space between romance and realism. This space proves fertile to a novel that blends an almost mythical storyline with explicit calls for contemporary political action. The juxtaposition of the myth of Italy and "realistic" references to nineteenth-century American dilemmas produces the argument Stowe undertakes with her contemporaries regarding the benevolence of U.S. nationalism.

To claim that Stowe's fiction champions domesticity is not to break new critical ground. What I argue here, however, is that *Agnes of Sorrento,* by exporting its thematics, constructs a domesticity unique in Stowe's work and thus challenges the patriarchal ideas of nationalism that dominated America during the second half of the nineteenth century. The challenge posed by Stowe's nondomestic domesticity develops from the combinations and contrasts that occur in the text, combinations that critics have pointed out—often as flaws—but, I would claim, have neglected to interrogate. Stowe's "child of love," begun abroad as diversionary entertainment for a traveling party detained by a storm, is born from the relocation of a nineteenth-century American woman's sensibility to the historical and cultural context of fifteenth-century Italy. My reading explores the significance of Stowe's narrative translocation by examining the way Italy resonates in *Agnes* and by viewing the historical context through the lens of Benedict Anderson's theory of nationalism. Ultimately, the narrative articulates a particular form of resistant nationalism that questions the values of nineteenth-century American nationalism through its deliteralization of the terms "home" and "mother." It may be useful to explicate the complexities of Stowe's child of love before moving on to an examination of the ways in which the "flowery Italian cradle" enabled the novel's maturation into a sophisticated cultural critique.

Domestic Fiction: "The Child of Love"

Why is *Agnes of Sorrento* so consistently either dismissed as trivial or overlooked entirely? Ann Douglas omits the novel in her list of Stowe's works published before 1871 ("Feminine Sentimentalism" 235). Dorothy Berkson, in her construction of a compelling argument about women as priests in Stowe's fiction, writes that Mary Scudder of *The Minister's Wooing* "is Stowe's only virginal, innocent, female priest who is allowed to live" (251). What of poor Agnes? A more virginal, innocent, and priestly character is difficult to imagine. And Agnes survives quite capably, despite narrative obstacles, effectively preaching throughout the novel. I believe Agnes is neglected because of her foreignness; critics are uncertain about how to interpret this devout young Catholic of late-fifteenth-century Italy. My purpose in the first part of this chapter is to rescue *Agnes* from relative obscurity and to examine the text as an intriguing manifestation of Stowe's domestic concerns. The second and third parts of the chapter examine in more detail the way domesticity gets complicated by the distant historical and geographic location.

The term "domestic" encompasses a wealth of meanings; indeed, its complexity produces the reading I undertake here. Most useful to me initially is the definition that Joyce Warren offers in her essay "Canons and Canon Fodder." As one of five categories of nineteenth-century women's textual resistance that Warren identifies, domestic novels "question the self-orientation of American individualism" through their deployment of certain signal narrative themes: "Religious earnestness, the insistence upon selflessness for men as well as for women, and the concept of an empowering force that could enable the powerless to challenge the power of the established order" (5, 10). The character of Agnes, a "sweet image of purity and faith" (121) who has the power to save disillusioned and bitter souls, clearly epitomizes the central, "feminine" characteristics championed in domestic fiction.

The religious earnestness of the fifteen-year-old, Italian peasant girl Agnes is the novel's central and most pervasive theme. Possessor of "a face as you sometimes see painted in those wayside shrines of sunny Italy," with a "high forehead, whose serious arch, like that of a cathedral-door, spoke of thought and prayer" (8), young Agnes shines throughout the text as a beacon of spiritual integrity. The narrative trajectory follows her as she confronts a world, and specifically a papacy, where greed and self-interest often eclipse the traditional Christian values on which she has been raised and in which she so unproblematically trusts. Sheltered by her grandmother from knowledge of the world outside the small town of Sorrento and the convent located nearby, Agnes has "grown up with an unworldly and spiritual character"; "a poetic mist," we are told, "enveloped all her outward perceptions" (36). Her confrontation with evil (embodied in the knavish Pope Alexander VI) results from complications in her developing relationship with Agostino Sarelli, a cavalier whom she loves despite her knowledge that he has been excommunicated. In order to resolve her conflicting desires, Agnes must discover through a pilgrimage to Rome that the pope is not the all-loving father she believed him to be, thereby shedding her childhood naiveté and moving into womanhood possessed of a more worldly and mature faith.

Agnes's spiritual devotion echoes the Christian piety of Eva in *Uncle Tom's Cabin,* a character read as an embodiment of "the feminine Christ" (Ammons, "Mother-Savior" 164) yet who also displays characteristics associated with Eve and Mary. As an Italian girl, raised in a land where Mary-worship almost eclipses devotion to Christ, Agnes can be more explicitly and insistently depicted as a reincarnation of the Madonna than the American Eva who preceded her: Agnes's "delicate face was framed," a representative passage tells us, "with its tremulous and spiritual expression most resembling in its sweet plaintive purity some of the Madonna faces of Fra' Angelico" (25).[3] The novel exploits this likeness to Mary as Stowe constructs a utopian, feminized community. Like Eva, the pure and sheltered Agnes must navigate a sinful world in which Christians have lost sight of the true tenets of their faith. Yet whereas Eva must die in the American setting of *Uncle Tom's Cabin* "to demonstrate that there is no life for a pure, Christlike spirit in the corrupt plantation economy the book attacks" (Ammons, "Mother-Savior" 157), Agnes survives her confrontation with the forces of depravity, triumphing at the end of the novel as "a princess of the house of Sarelli . . . whose sanctity of life and manners was held to go back to the traditions of primitive Christianity" (412). In this revision of the conflict between purity and corruption, Stowe has constructed a setting where pure faith both survives and nourishes others. The Italian location and historical context enable the establishment of this spiritually nurturing home, for a host of reasons that I examine in detail later.

Not a "weak" trait desirable only in women, Agnes's selflessness pervades the novel as a virtue for all to emulate. The exhortation to men to share in domestic values is embodied in the character of Brother Antonio—an inspired artist, monk, and brother of Agnes's grandmother Elsie. Born of the novel's celebration of the religious artist's vocation, Brother Antonio exudes kindness, love, and an unwavering confidence in the goodness of God. "Happy!—child, am I not?" he exclaims to Agnes. "Holy Mother, am I not? Do I not walk the earth in a dream of bliss, and see the footsteps of my Most Blessed Lord and his dear Mother on every rock and hill?" (103). In a significant step toward her final moral and personal victory, Agnes recognizes the contrast between her loving uncle's optimistic faith and the oppressive scare tactics of the church pastor: "She pondered the dark warnings of Father Francesco, and then thought of the cheerful, fervent piety of her old uncle. How warm, how tender, how life-giving had been his presence always!" (398). The novel celebrates the maternal through Brother Antonio, whose "tender" and "life-giving" presence enables him to be an effective Christian influence, while the cold, authoritarian approach of Father Francesco cripples him as a minister.[4]

Father Francesco's coldness is also significant as it illustrates the curative power of Agnes's religious earnestness and selflessness. Agnes walks with saintlike security through a landscape peopled with doubters like this discouraged priest. Victim of "a melancholy deep as the grave" (44), he pursues his spiritual calling only to discover "how utterly powerless and inert any mortal man is to inspire others with his own insights and convictions" (43). Notably, the mortal *woman* Agnes effortlessly wields the power Father Francesco has futilely sought. In contrast to the priest's "most fervent exhortations" (44), which are ineffective, the "clear, sweet tones of Agnes" (ibid.) enact a dramatic change in Father Francesco:

> Since his acquaintance with Agnes, without his knowing exactly why, thoughts of the Divine Love had floated into his soul, filling it with a golden cloud like that which of old rested over the mercy-seat in that sacred inner-temple where the priest was admitted alone. He became more affable and tender, more tolerant to the erring, more fond of little children; would stop sometimes to lay his hand on the head of a child, or to raise one up who

> lay overthrown in the street. The song of little birds and the voices of animal life became to him full of tenderness; and his prayers by the sick and dying seemed to have a melting power, such as he had never known before. It was spring in his soul,—soft, Italian spring,—such as brings out the musky breath of the cyclamen, and the faint, tender perfume of the primrose. (47)

Agnes inspires the metamorphosis of Father Francesco into a maternal, and thereby effective, preacher, his soul blossoming like the Italian landscape consistently figured in the novel as nurturing. "Such is the wonderful power of human sympathy," Stowe's narrator observes (45). Young Agnes, a "powerless" girl without education, political influence, or money, saves an important member of the church hierarchy from the darkness of self-absorption. The light of human community represents an alternative—and more redemptive—value system to that advocated by the male theocracy.

This challenge to patriarchal power is the backbone of Stowe's narrative. Although rooted in the home and women's sphere, the values espoused in Stowe's domesticity—community, selflessness, religious devotion—exert a broader influence. Not only does Agnes inspire Agostino Sarelli's personal salvation—he says of her promise to love him, "that promise has brought me from utter despair to love of life. Nay, since you told me that, I have been able to pray once more; the whole world seems changed for me" (164)—but through her intervention, Sarelli meets and joins forces with Brother Antonio and eventually Girolamo Savonarola, leader of a major religious revival and movement of protest against Pope Alexander VI.[5] Like Stowe's *Uncle Tom's Cabin, Agnes of Sorrento* reverses traditional gender roles; Agnes rebels against the constraints placed on her sex by undertaking a pilgrimage to Rome for the twin purposes of saving Sarelli's soul and escaping an unappealing marriage her grandmother has arranged.[6] Further, the Christian ethos of Agnes—reflected in the ideology of Brother Antonio and Savonarola—demonstrates to the militant Sarelli the value of selflessness as a means of protest:

> "Even you could fight, Agnes," said the knight, "to save your religion from disgrace."
>
> "No," said she, "but," she added, with gathering firmness, "I could die. I should be glad to die with and for the holy men who would save the honor of the true faith. I should like to go to Florence with my uncle. If he dies for his religion, I should like to die with him."
>
> "Ah, live to teach it to me!" said the knight. (398)

And she does. Domestic values thus serve not only to shift the emphasis of the forces of rebellion from violent combat to self-sacrifice, but also to provide a common bond by which various factions are brought together in the fight against papal corruption. The moral lesson and the political bond, the text makes clear, originate in Agnes and her devout spirituality.

Though the resolution of the novel depends upon the marriage of Agnes and Agostino, the text does not promote romance as a woman's sole means of personal fulfillment. The figure of Agnes's dead mother hovers about the periphery of the narrative like an eerie specter, a reminder of the menace romantic love can pose for women. The favorite of a princess, Agnes's mother had the misfortune of loving, trusting, and marrying the princess's brother, who, at the slightest hint of a scandal, turned his back on his young family and denied the marriage outright. This betrayal both silenced and crippled "the once beautiful and gay Isella," who left Rome with her mother, Elsie, as a "poor, bedrabbled, broken-winged song-bird" that "soon panted and fluttered her little life away" (31). In a notably cynical passage, Stowe's narrative voice explicates the tragedy of Agnes's mother: "Of course, the rose of love, having gone through all its stages of bud and blossom into full flower, must next begin to drop its leaves. Of course. Who ever heard of an immortal rose?" (30). The rose's transience emblematizes the instability of romantic love; once the petals have fallen, an ambitious man will act "as a well-instructed young nobleman should, who understands the great difference there is between the tears of a duchess and those of low-born women" (31). Earthly, carnal love should not be trusted, as the sage narrator reminds us, and as Agnes's grandmother Elsie realizes: "This child *should be happy;* the rocks on which her mother was wrecked she should never strike upon,—they were all marked on Elsie's chart. Love had been the root of all poor Isella's troubles,—and Agnes should never know love" (32). Significantly, the final union between Agnes and Agostino grows out of a spiritual foundation and reformist goals rather than a blinding passion; theirs is "a marriage bond . . . that was indeed a sacrament, and that bound together two pure and loyal souls who gave life and courage to each other in all holy purposes and heroic deeds" (49). Ever present is the imperative that Agnes not repeat her mother's mistakes and be misguided by romantic love.

The image of the child of love, a description of both Agnes and the text itself, foregrounds the novel's concern with domestic values founded upon religious devotion and communal goals. The phrase, of course, resonates in another way, as a description of the bastard child resulting from an illicit sexual union. Agnes complicates this distinction as she is both legitimate (in the eyes of the reader and narrator, who are privy to the details of her history) and illegitimate (in the eyes of her community, which will not know of her parents' secret marriage until very late in the novel, if ever). A clandestine marriage blurs the boundaries of legitimacy, which are predicated on public knowledge and/or public record. A child is legitimate not when her parents are married, but when everyone *knows* that her parents are married. In Stowe's novel, the public does not know Agnes's patriarchal heritage, but what the public can know about her, and about any child, is the identity of her mother. The figure of the mother is central to the novel, and Agnes's murky paternity only highlights her definitive connection to her family's matriarchal side. In this sense, she is a "child of maternal love," a name that empowers, rather than belittles, her. Yet what does it mean to apply the "child of love" label to the novel itself? How is the text a bastard?

To answer this question I begin by turning to the man who has been named the father of American literature, Ralph Waldo Emerson, and his 1841 essay, "Self-Reliance." Arguing for American self-sufficiency and against the growing trend of international travel, Emerson insists, "Let a man then know his worth, and keep things under his feet. Let him not peep or steal, or skulk up and down with an air of a charity boy, a bastard, or an interloper, in the world which exists for him" (175). This admonishment functions as a continuation and an application of an argument begun in the previous paragraph, with the assertion "Every true man is a cause, a country, and an age." A man who knows this, who understands his self-sufficiency, will not move with uncertainty, in the manner of charity boy, bastard, or interloper. Significantly, the term "interloper"—and I am reading the three terms as equivalent, each displacement a substitution—arises again a short time later in the essay, when Emerson describes the wise traveler as one who "visits cities and men like a sovereign and not like an interloper or a valet" (186). He makes this concession grudgingly. Ideally, Americans would not travel at all: "It is for want of self-culture that the superstition of travelling, whose idols are Italy, England, Egypt, retains its fascination for all educated Americans" (ibid.). Both of these moments in the essay posit an opposition between a self-assured possession of one's physical space and a timid deference to the external world. A bastard is, in Emersonian logic, one who doesn't belong, who lacks (or doesn't aggressively claim) entitlement, specifically the entitlement to the North American continent that comes with status as an Anglo-American male.

The answer to my question, then, may lie in the fact that there are no Americans in Stowe's novel. Though critics in the nineteenth century debated whether American literature should, as Emerson insisted, spring from American soil or whether, as Henry James asserted later in the century, "It is not necessary that the scene of an American work of imagination should be laid in America. It is enough that it represent our character and manners either at home or abroad" (Perosa 18), the common denominator remained that, clearly, an American novel should portray an American sensibility somewhere. Stowe's novel not only omits the American characters who populated so many other American works in the international genre; it also precludes the very possibility of an American, as it takes place more than a hundred years before colonial settlements began to form on what would become the American mainland. The text could be said to be a bastard, then, to the extent that it denies or at least obscures its American paternity.

In constructing the text around a foreign location and historical context, however, Stowe leaves for herself no space within the storyline to articulate her concerns as a nineteenth-century American woman. Her agenda must be voiced, instead, by a narrator who "keeps maternal company with her readers and guides them to a clearer understanding of this communal Christian life" (Franchot 251). Through this narrator, Stowe offers elaborate commentary on plot events and creates a dialogic text whose varied impulses encompass the complex web of sentiments that composes Stowe's relationship to nineteenth-century American nationalism. The gap formed between the story's plotline and the sensibility of the narrator provides an interesting space within which to interrogate the intersection of narrative and nationalism, which I pursue in the last section of this chapter. First, I shift my attention to the lush Italian landscape Stowe chose as a setting for her novel.

The "Flowery Italian Cradle"

In *Uncle Tom's Cabin,* Gillian Brown argues, "Stowe seeks to reform American society not by employing domestic values but by reforming them" (18). This reform is necessary, according to Brown, due to "domesticity's applicability to both slave and capitalist economies," a fact "which causes Stowe's uneasiness about the virtues of domesticity as a replacement economy" (23). Stowe's text "explicitly thematiz[es] the intimacy and congress between economic and domestic endeavors, between market and kitchen systems" and argues for a domesticity not implicated in the transactions of the male marketplace (18). I would suggest that *Agnes of Sorrento* furthers this project of reformation through its narrative translocation. Not only does the story take place in the late-fifteenth century, thereby freeing its author from her misgivings about the capitalist marketplace in America (and the concomitant slave trade that sustained it), but the Italian landscape also replaces the kitchen as the site of community and domestic interaction. *Agnes* posits a new domesticity, free of the fetters of American capitalism, through its mapping of the domestic themes central to Stowe's fiction onto the Italian countryside.

Sorrento itself, "guarded on all sides by a barrier of mountains which defend it from bleak winds and serve to it the purposes of a garden," with its "groves of oranges and lemons" and "almost fabulous coincidence of fruitage with flowers," is an Edenic home that makes interior shelter unnecessary (15). Indeed, the town's drawing room is located on the bridge to the mainland, described as "a favorite lounging place for the inhabitants" where "at evening a motley assemblage may be seen lolling over its moss-grown sides,—men with their picturesque knit caps of scarlet or brown falling gracefully on one shoulder, and women with their shining black hair" (16). From its opening pages, the novel makes much of the nourishing, hospitable Italian land. The action throughout takes place almost entirely outdoors, in an exterior world depicted as more protective than the enclosure found inside: "Nothing can be more striking, in common Italian life, than the contrast between out-doors and in-doors. Without, all is fragrant and radiant; within, mouldy, dark, and damp. Except in the well-kept palaces of the great, houses in Italy are more like dens than habitations, and a sight of them is a sufficient reason to the mind of any inquirer, why their vivacious and handsome inhabitants spend their lives principally in the open air" (88). In Sorrento's temperate climate, the outdoors can be figured as nurturing, in contrast to the harsh exterior elements of Stowe's native New England.

Stowe explicitly compared warm Italy with the cold United States in a letter to her editor. Working in 1861 on both *Agnes* and *The Pearl of Orr's Island* (a novel set in Maine), Stowe wrote, "I wrote my Maine story with a shiver, and come back to this [*Agnes of Sorrento*] as to a flowery home where I love to rest" (Fetterley 111). This imagery echoes Stowe's prefatory comments as well as this passage from the novel, in which she sings the praises of Sorrento: "[U]nder these kindly skies, a native courtesy and gentleness of manner make themselves felt. It would seem as if humanity, rocked in this flowery cradle, and soothed by so many daily caresses and appliances of nursing Nature, grew up with all that is kindliest on the outward,—not repressed and beat in, as under the inclement atmosphere and stormy skies of the North" (16). The recurring images of the "flowery cradle" and "flowery home" that project domestic signifiers onto the landscape demand insistently that the reader bridge a certain presupposed distinction between indoors and out, private and public space. In *Agnes,* cradle and home denote sites of comfort, locatable even—or, in Italy, especially—outside the walls that traditionally mark domestic space. Ann Romines, for example, defines domestic rituals as "rituals performed in a house, a constructed shelter, which derive meaning from the protection and confinement a house can provide" (12). Clearly a different notion of domesticity informs Stowe's project in *Agnes.* Confinement, either of the personal or national type, is not what Stowe advocates. Like the shivery confines of Maine, interior space in the novel is bleak, while Italy's exterior landscapes provide warmth and sustenance.

Such a view of Italy was not shared by all nineteenth-century Americans who visited and wrote there. In Hawthorne's *Marble Faun* (1860), for example, the Italian land is depicted as an oppressive force; if you visit Rome with a troubled heart, the narrator warns the reader, "all the ponderous gloom of the Roman Past will pile itself upon that spot, and crush you down as with the heaped-up marble and granite, the earth mounds, and multitudinous bricks of its material decay" (294). For Hawthorne and other Americans (such as James eighteen years later in *Daisy Miller*), the legacy of the Roman Empire rises up from the Italian land itself, a weight from the past that burdens the present. Hawthorne's American character, Kenyon, notes that the Italian sky "was soft and bright, but not so gorgeous as [he] had seen it, a thousand times, in America" (194); for Stowe, on the other hand, the Italian land provides a beauty not available to her in her native country.

In addition to blurring the boundaries of the home, *Agnes* utilizes an expanded signification of "motherhood." The depiction of Sorrento's natural forces as mother—the "daily caresses and appliances of nursing Nature"—gives way later in the text to the looming maternal presence of the Eternal City:

> Then, as now, Rome was an enchantress of mighty and wonderful power, with her damp, and mud, and mould, her ill-fed, ill-housed populace, her ruins of old glory rising dim and ghostly amid her palaces of today. With all her awful secrets . . . still Rome had that strange, bewildering charm of melancholy grandeur and glory which made all hearts cleave to her, and eyes and feet turn longingly towards her from the ends of the earth. Great souls and pious yearned for her as for a mother, and could not be quieted till they had kissed the dust of her streets. . . . Even the mighty spirit of Luther yearned for the breast of this great unknown mother, and came humbly thither to seek the repose which he found afterwards in Jesus.
> (361–62)

Just as Stowe deliteralizes home, so "mother" here signifies a nurturing presence represented as a geographical location. This broadened signification of "mother" arises also in the story of the cavalier Sarelli, whose breach with his faith the text figures repeatedly as a severed connection to his mother; indeed, the two become indistinguishable, with Sarelli "yearning towards the grave of his mother, yearning towards the legends of saints and angels with which she had lulled his cradle slumbers and sanctified his childhood's pillow" (118). The parallel syntax aligns "mother" and "the legends of angels and saints," as the mother's capacity to comfort inheres in her articulation of religious doctrine; similarly, Catholicism exerts its influence over him to the extent that it informs his memory of his lost mother. As the novel goes on to emphasize, Agostino can no more entirely relinquish his attachment to the church than erase his connection to his mother.

The Catholic tradition serves Stowe well here, as worship of the Virgin Mary lends itself easily to the text's inscription of a universal mother, abundant enough to tend the flowery cradle, and a potentially healing maternal presence lacking in the church patriarchy.[7] Struggling with her desires for Sarelli and resisting the imperative to confess to Father Francesco, Agnes reflects, "If only I could confess to my Mother Theresa, that would be easier. We have a mother in heaven to hear us; why should we not have a mother on earth?" (168). It is worth noting that Hawthorne's Hilda voices a similar concern in *The Marble Faun:* " 'Ah,' thought Hilda to herself, 'why should there not be a woman to listen to the prayers of women, a mother in heaven for all motherless girls like me?' " (251). This invocation of an idealized maternal power is undermined in Hawthorne's novel, however, by Kenyon's earlier ruminations on the qualities desirable in a leader. Upon seeing a statue of Marcus Aurelius on Rome's Capitoline Hill, Miriam exclaims, "Oh, if there were but one such man as this! . . . One such man in an age, and one in all the world; then how speedily would the strife, wickedness, and sorrow of us poor creatures be relieved. We would come to him with our griefs, whatever they might be—even a poor frail woman burdened with her heavy heart—and lay them at his feet, and never need to take them up again. The rightful king would see to all." Kenyon's response is to mock Miriam: " 'What an idea of the regal office and duty!' said Kenyon, with a smile. 'It is a woman's idea of the whole matter to perfection' " (125). The giving of succor and comfort is hardly "regal" to Kenyon, who sees nurturing and authority as antithetical.

That Miriam's fantasy is "a woman's idea to perfection" is reinforced by the way gender functions in Stowe's depictions of authority figures.

Agnes's search for personal salvation can be conceptualized as a movement from the father to the mother, as she must learn to mistrust the church patriarchs (the pope and Father Francesco) and to trust in herself, her maternal uncle, and her spiritual connection to the Madonna. In contrast to an idealized church that "is a tender mother to all her erring children" (158), as Brother Antonio advises her, Agnes confronts for herself "the defilement and impurity of what she had ignorantly adored in holy places" (397), the Rome of Pope Alexander VI, where she goes in search of a "great and benignant father" (369). Far from a paternal protector, Pope Alexander VI reveals his lecherous nature when he instructs his henchmen to abduct Agnes and smuggle her to his "impure den" (393), the depravity of which is so unspeakable as to prevent Stowe from textualizing what transpires there. We know only that Agostino follows and rescues Agnes, that he takes her "pale and fainting" (392) from the pope's clutches, and that afterward Agostino marks "a flash from her eye, and an heroic expression on her face," the result of a "revelation [that] seemed to have wrought a change in her whole nature" (397). Alexander VI, a figure in the annals of Catholicism who exemplifies some of the worst abuses of theological and masculine power, elected "as a result of the most corrupt election in papal history" (Hearder 120), stands at one end of a gendered spectrum operating in Stowe's novel, providing her with an extreme of masculine corruption in the church against which to measure the purity and good faith of the providers of salvation—women or those men who display feminine values.

Along with homage to Mary, the worship of female saints contributes to Stowe's revision of the domesticity inaugurated in *Uncle Tom's Cabin*. In that novel, Gillian Brown argues, "the fact that Stowe retains the name of the male God throughout her matriarchal design suggests that her imagination of a feminized world still requires the sanction of male authority" (38). In contrast, *Agnes of Sorrento* selectively uses Catholic traditions to undercut the need for male authority. The gendered spectrum that places the evil pope and the benevolent Mary at opposite ends also operates in Stowe's depiction of laudable, sainted women who triumphed spiritually despite the oppressive influence of the male clergy. In a passage that questions the Catholic sacrament of confession, with its potential to corrupt a man given "the divine right to unlock the most secret chambers of the soul" even as it threatens the penitent, who must expose herself, the narrative voice reflects, "In reading the lives of those ethereally made and moulded women who have come down to our day canonized as saints in the Roman Catholic communion, one too frequently gets the impression of most regal natures, gifted with all the most divine elements of humanity, but subjected to a constant unnatural pressure from the ceaseless scrutiny and ungenial pertinacity of some inferior and uncomprehending person invested with the authority of a Spiritual Director" (142–43). The novel offers female saints as role models not only insofar as they led devout lives, but also to the extent that they survived (even triumphed over) male inquisitors who sought to overpower them. Stowe's selective valorization of the Catholic church involves a celebration of the matrifocal traditions that flourished alongside, and in spite of, the corrupt male bureaucracy.

Other American writers, like Hawthorne, peopled their novels with American expatriates whose relationship to the Catholic church tended to be antagonistic; American characters could be Protestant, whereas Stowe's Italians could not. In *The Marble Faun* Hawthorne makes it clear that Hilda remains uncontaminated by the menace of Catholicism: Hilda protests to Miriam, "You must not call me a Catholic. A Christian girl—even a daughter of the Puritans—may surely pay honor to the idea of divine Womanhood, without giving up the faith of her forefathers" (46). Significantly, the attention Hilda pays to the Madonna cannot displace the primary connection she retains to a patriarchal tradition, "the faith of her forefathers." Such disclaimers on the part of American characters abroad were necessary in an era when American visitors to Rome, like James Jackson Jarves, were asserting that while "Catholicism provided a pageant from the past of enormous political interest . . . politically and intellectually it was repugnant to all progressive values" (Vance, *America's Rome* II:3). In his discussion of nineteenth-century American travel writing, critic Jeffrey Alan Melton notes that "no religion offered a more assailable target than Catholicism. Writers who were catering to a mostly Protestant readership, took many opportunities to denigrate the Catholic Church while touring through Europe" (216). Melton underscores Jarves's assertion when he claims that for nineteenth-century readers "the [Catholic] church was an institutional evil—anti-democratic, anti-American" (217). And in a telling hierarchization, Emerson listed in his journal in August 1847 "The Superstitions of our Age." His first entry is "The fear of Catholicism" (481).

Despite this tradition of anxiety about Catholicism, Stowe's narrative presents an all-Catholic cast of characters. Perhaps the use of a temporally distant setting for the narrative made Stowe's selective endorsement of certain Catholic practices more palatable to a U.S. audience. In passages that champion the fifteenth-century Italian reformer, Girolamo Savonarola, Stowe anticipates the coming of Luther and the advent of Protestantism, thereby mitigating the threat of what her readers could perceive as a spiritual defection. As Jenny Franchot points out, antebellum American depictions of Italian Catholicism tended to demonize it as "Whore of Babylon" and "partly legitimized Catholicism's status at home as national menace and potential contaminant" (xxiii).[8] Stowe puts a Protestant spin on early Catholicism through her regression in time and her emphasis on Savonarola as a precursor of later Christian reformers.

Even in looking forward to Luther, however, Stowe's narrative undermines its own celebration of Protestantism's redemptive power. Stowe must go back in order to go forward, always relegating Luther only to the position of a star shining hopefully in the future, where his promise can remain forever untested and unbounded, and in so doing constructs a Catholic landscape that reaffirms certain aspects of faith that are absent from the Protestantism of nineteenth-century America. In the words of one critic, Stowe may have regarded the Catholic church as "a virtually ideal religious tradition. Unsatisfied by the bareness and severity of Puritanism, she was strongly attracted by the elaborate and colorful ceremonies, the liturgical music, and the hagiolatry of Roman Catholicism" (Nathalia Wright 89). Certainly, in its construction of an ideal community, the narrative makes extensive use of discourses associated with the Catholic tradition, especially the histories of saints and the Virgin Mary.

The novel's recurring imagery of saints suggests the centrality in Stowe's idealized landscape of one of Catholicism's fundamental beliefs: faith in a community of the living and the dead, a bond between humans on earth and saints in heaven who remain available for petitions or intercessions on behalf of troubled souls. At a historical moment when Protestantism seemed ill equipped to stem the tide of division and conflict that threatened to inundate the United States, the novel's "fictional reconstruction of a lost Catholic past for an American Civil War readership" (Franchot 248) provided not only an escape into a distant and mystical past, far from the bloody battle over slavery, but also a model for a religious community in which bonds across time and space create a continuity that transcends earthly frictions.[9] "The great truth, that God is not the God of the dead, but of the living," Stowe's narrator reminds us, is conveyed through "the saints of the Church Triumphant, having become one with Christ as he is one with the Father," whose "presence often overshadowed the walks of daily life with a cloud of healing and protecting sweetness" (273). In contrast to a fifteenth-century Italy, where "the Church visible and invisible were in close, loving, and constant sympathy,—still loving, praying, and watching together" (83), the individualism of Protestantism mirrored the individualism of American ideology, both of which ultimately fail in Stowe's text as models for salvation or personal fulfillment.

Also, the construction of the flowery Italian home and cradle facilitates Stowe's expanded view of home and mother in a more obvious sense, as an expatriate gesture. That an American would locate her home so insistently in a foreign land challenges simplistic notions of where and how bonds of loyalty develop. Further, the Italian landscape, with its history of use as a symbolic and mystical place in American literature, enables Stowe's portrayal of an idealized, "domestic" community precisely because of its status as the "non-domestic," the unusual and foreign.[10] In her prefatory letter Stowe insists "that this story is a mere dream land, that it neither assumes nor will have responsibility for historical accuracy." A powerful pastoral symbol in much nineteenth-century American art and literature, Italy invokes a lost, idealized past and reinforces the novel's utopian, romantic tone. This romanticizing tendency, reflected in works like *The Marble Faun* and Thomas Cole's famous painting, "The Dream of Arcadia" (1838), makes use of a "myth of Italy as Arcadia, as a place with links to a golden age" (Stebbins 26). Discursive representations of Italy more invested in mythology and mystery than in historical realism reflect the view, suggested by Brooks, that "for many Americans, visiting Italy, the whole country was like a stage, while the Italians seemed to them like actors playing parts in some poetic dream" (51). In contrast, nineteenth-century America had become too practical, too concerned with the mundane. Hawthorne reacts against this practicality in *The Marble Faun,* noting in his preface that "Italy . . . was chiefly valuable to [the author] as affording a sort of poetic or fairy precinct, where actualities would not be so terribly insisted upon as they are, and must needs be, in America" (vi). Like other American artists of her time who "contrasted the practicality of modern, utilitarian, materialistic America with the joyfulness, the impracticality of daily life in Italy" (Stebbins 21), Stowe inserts her novel into a tradition of fantasizing the Italian land, thus gaining access to a dreamland in which to locate her dream land and furthering her project of domestic deliteralization.

Acknowledging the fantastical possibilities with which the Italian setting abounds, Judith Fetterley asks, "Did Stowe find it easy to write *Agnes* and did she privilege this twin [over *The Pearl of Orr's Island*] precisely because she constructed it as exempt from the requirements of truth?" (111). I would argue that more is at stake here than ease of composition. Freedom from the requirements of "truth" operates in Stowe's favor by serving her political project, as we see on those occasions when the underlying political agenda ruptures the novel's romantic surface. The use of a composite tense to describe the novel's genesis suggests this combination of the political and the fantastic. In a scenic gorge, the author and her traveling companions come upon two figures who will become the Agnes and Elsie of the novel. For this traveling party, "fresh from strolls and rambles around ancient Sorrento," Stowe writes in her preface, "the whole golden scene receded centuries back, and [we] saw them in a vision as they might and must have been in other days." While "might" resonates as a verb of dreamland, suggesting the fancy with which she could compose her tale, "must" invokes the inevitable, indeed a political imperative. Often depicted as a golden scene wherein fantasy rules, Sorrento exists on the pages of Stowe's novel also as another kind of dream, one projected onto the landscape by a nineteenth-century American woman in the process of self-definition. The narrator sometimes recedes to let the fictional characters perform, and at other moments she returns to remind the reader that places such as Sorrento existed as a contemporary fantasy against which nineteenth-century American travelers could construct their sense of national belonging.

Nationalism

Though she published her novel in 1862, Stowe situated the story in the late-fifteenth century, effectively distancing the narrative from pragmatic, capitalist nineteenth-century America. In fact, the exact year in which the story takes place remains a conspicuous absence, hinted at but not revealed in the third paragraph, which reads, "Whoever passed beneath this old arched gateway, thus saint-guarded, in the year of our Lord's grace——, might have seen under its shadow, sitting opposite to a stand of golden oranges, the little Agnes" (7). The text thus offers Agnes to ground the story, obfuscates the precise historical moment, and creates a mystical environment in which the narrative can unfold. Clues to the story's exact temporal location must be gleaned from Stowe's historical references, though she carefully points out in her preface that historical accuracy is not her goal: "[W]hoso wants history will not find it here, except to our making, and as it suits our purpose" (vi). Temporal ambiguity facilitates Stowe's rhapsodic portrayals of Sorrento, a land with fields "so starred and enamelled with flowers that they might have served as the type for those Elysian realms sung by ancient poets" (15). Her description evokes a sense of community and timelessness, producing a landscape upon which ancient Greek poets, fifteenth-century peasants, and Stowe herself have stood to admire the flora. The passage offers the song, rather than the actual place, as the important invocation; Sorrento is significant less for its physical attributes than for its ability to inspire poetic representations. As such, ancient Sorrento functions as the dream space upon which Stowe can project her fantasies of ideal community, free from the constraints of contemporary historicity.

Protestations notwithstanding, Stowe does make use of significant personages and events from Italian history that enable the reader to locate the story in or around the years 1497 and 1498, during which time the Florentine monk Girolamo Savonarola was excommunicated by Pope Alexander VI and eventually executed (Procacci 123).[11] A resonant figure for Italians of the mid-nineteenth century who were engaged in a struggle for unification under a centralized, republican government, Savonarola functions in Stowe's text as a prototype of Luther, a figure for the individual's struggle against corruption. Describing him as "an Italian Luther," Stowe's narrative voice praises Savonarola as "the poet and prophet of the Italian religious world of his day . . . pouring through all the members of the order [at the Convent of San Marco in Florence] the fire of his own impassioned nature, and seeking to lead them back to the fervors of more primitive and evangelical ages" (98). In the fight against corruption, Savonarola, like Stowe, wields his art as a weapon: "He inspired the pencils of artists, guided the councils of statesmen, and, a poet himself, was an inspiration to poets" (ibid.). And his art, like Stowe's, calls for the return to an originary and more communal Christianity.

In the service of this political project, historical distance serves another purpose in Stowe's narrative. Benedict Anderson's theory of the formation of nationhood provides a useful perspective on the effects of the historical translocation. Anderson identifies the religious community (along with the dynastic realm), rather than the nation, as the dominant imaginative construct of the eras prior to the eighteenth century, a construct distinct from and prior to modern conceptions of nationalism.[12] The two constructs perform a similar function, that of creating community, and Anderson places them on a timeline in which nationalism takes the place of religion as the site of continuity during the eighteenth century (11).

For Stowe's contemporaries in 1862, the nation had come to dominate the American imagination, and this preoccupation, not surprisingly, often found literary expression. With the Civil War as a catalyst for nationalist reevaluations, Benjamin Spencer points out, "After the beginning of hostilities, of course, most American writers of an analytical temper turned from a consideration of the character of the national literature to the graver and more elemental issue of the national structure: Union or Confederacy" (290). The nineteenth-century's confrontation with the concept of a divided nation was mirrored in a national literature that relied on boundaries: In 1856 William Gilmore Simms wrote, "To be national in literature, one must need be sectional. . . . [H]e who shall depict one section faithfully, has made his proper and sufficient contribution to the great work of national illustration" (quoted in Perosa 40). For nineteenth-century American authors, the project was to create a literature somehow representative of "the nation."

In contrast, Stowe's novel returns to an era free of the preoccupation with nationhood, a time when one conceptualized allegiance primarily in terms of religious affiliation. In mapping Anderson's formulation onto Stowe's text, it is useful to differentiate the imaginative constructs of nation and religious community in terms of structure. The idea of the nation relies on boundaries carefully constructed and policed at the perimeter, whereas religious communities were conceptualized based on a central and divine power: Anderson notes that in the religious community "fundamental conceptions about social groups were centripetal and hierarchical, rather than boundary-oriented and horizontal" (15). Anderson's formulation echoes the deliteralized domestic spaces of Stowe's narrative. If domestic space is often conceptualized as bounded at some periphery, much as the modern nation defines itself, Stowe's dissolution of domestic boundaries can be read as resonating on a national level. This dismantling of national (domestic) boundaries in the service of imagining a global community contributes to the revisionist project that we see in the novel's return to an era dominated by the imaginative construct of the religious community. Read in terms of Stowe's domestic thematics, this model, tethered at the center, reinscribes the centripetal force of the mother. Maternal power underpins Stowe's utopian vision of an idealized Christian community, held together from the center, and thereby potentially all inclusive, rather than walled in at the perimeter.

Stowe's attempts to distance her story from its nineteenth-century American audience represent one-half of a divided impulse in the narrative. She systematically ruptures her depiction of a prenationalistic time and virtually Edenic place with overt signals to readers that serve as both reminders and enablers of imagined, nineteenth-century American nationalism. The narrator describes, for example, a crucifixion by Fra' Angelico that, in the novel's narrative time, can reveal the glorious unity of Christ's church: "The face upon the cross, with its majestic patience, seemed to shed a blessing down on the company of saints of all ages who were grouped by their representative men at the foot" (291).[13] The commentary then shifts suddenly to the nineteenth century, as the narrator asserts rather cynically, "In our day such pictures are visited by tourists with red guide-books in their hands, who survey them in the intervals of casual conversation" (ibid.). This narrative aside both delineates a recognizable contemporary group (bound together by phrases such as "our day" and "tourists") and indicts this group's superficiality. Fifteenth-century values, including the notion of a pure, spiritual connection to the visual image, provide a critique of "tourism" and the distance from "true experience" it implies, a distance that only isolates Americans from each other and from the Christian community. Stowe's text invokes tourists and the specter of American nationhood and juxtaposes against them the simplicity and power revealed in early Christian art's depictions of "the unity of the Church Universal" (ibid.).[14]

Like the early Christian artists who provided visual bonds to structure an imagined religious community, Stowe attempts to unite her readers through her art. Anderson points to the novel as the genre that "provided the technical means for 're-presenting' the kind of imagined community that is the nation" (25). Fiction enables imagined nationalism, and Stowe "conjures up the imagined community" through inclusive language—referring to, for example, "the wave of a great religious impulse—which in our times would have been called a revival" (41)—and allusions to popular American figures: "The angels and celestial beings of these grave old painters are as different from the fat little pink Cupids or lovely laughing children of Titian and Correggio as are the sermons of President Edwards from the love-songs of Tom Moore" (284). Not only does her text effect a kind of interpellation, a call to the readers that constructs them as contemporary American subjects, but it also takes for granted a common base of shared experience and values, as when Stowe projects her reader onto the Italian terrain: "[T]he present traveler at Sorrento may remember standing on this bridge and looking down the gloomy depths of the gorge" (16). This assumption of shared values and past experience creates nationalism and as a narrative gesture privileges homogeneity and disregards ruptures or variations among the members of the group.

Yet this confidence in the shared values of Stowe's fellow nationals is both constructed and deconstructed in the novel. The mapping of contemporary American crises against a paradisiacal backdrop foregrounds the shortcomings of modern nationalism, questions the existence of a homogenous group that can be called "Americans," and proposes the possibility of a more humanitarian society through the return to a prenationalistic context that is nurturing, Christian, and communal. Not surprisingly, criticism identifies veiled references in the novel to the central conflict of Stowe's era, the Civil War. The novel repeatedly posits a north/south opposition, with the north, either of Italy or Europe, depicted as rational and the south associated with a heightened emotionalism: "[T]he Northern mind of Europe is entirely unfitted to read and appreciate the psychological religious phenomena of Southern races. The temperament which in our modern days has been called the mediistic, and which with us is only exceptional, is more or less a race-peculiarity of Southern climates" (113). Critics offer this passage and others as evidence of a neat north/south parallelism that can be imported back to U.S. soil: Nathalia Wright refers to "an echo of the nineteenth-century American sectional conflict over slavery in the contrast established between the voluptuous south of Italy and the north, with its reforming impulse" (93). Franchot asserts that Agnes "offers an expatriate justification for American northern assertions of superiority over the American South . . . and its enslaved population of African Americans" (247). In the wake of *Uncle Tom's Cabin* and a literary tradition that has more than established Stowe's commitment to the abolitionist cause, these readings may be as unavoidable as they are compelling, yet I think they are misguided in their reductive tendencies.

One need only continue reading Stowe's paragraph to discover the novel's conflicted position on the north/south dichotomy: "The Southern saints and religious artists were seers, men and women of that peculiar fineness and delicacy of temperament which made them especially apt to receive and project outward the truths of the spiritual life; they were in that state of 'divine madness' which is favorable to the most intense conception of the poet and artist, and something of this influence descended through all the channels of the people" (113). What the novel advocates is not a simple reaffirmation of faith in the "Northern mind," but rather the recovery of at least a measure of the "Southern" passion with which early Christian artists communicated their spirituality. In a formulation that places the male/rational/Northern (Anglo) in opposition to female/emotional/Southern (Mediterranean), Stowe reminds us that "Certain English writers, looking entirely from a worldly and philosophical standpoint, are utterly at a loss to account for the power which certain Italian women of obscure birth [namely, saints] came to exercise in the councils of nations merely by the force of a mystical piety" (ibid.). This passage alludes to mysterious powers more effective than those of enlightened rationalism—powers that arise from a feminized devotion to Christianity—which can both contend with ancient patriarchal assemblies and puzzle contemporary writers. The reader, like Agnes, can partake of this southern, feminine mysticism and thus "feel the dissolving of all earthly things, and the pressing nearer and nearer of the great cloud of witnesses who ever surround the humblest member of Christ's mystical body" (112). North/south opposition informs the text, but its complexities prohibit reducing the novel to a simple indictment of all things southern or reading it as a reinscription of the regional conflict of the U.S. Civil War.

To fuel Stowe's argument for the establishment of a broader and more benevolent community, the novel makes explicit use of other fractures in nineteenth-century American ideology, namely U.S. worship of individualism and male treatment of women. In contrast to such political divisions, Agnes voices a belief system that transcends earthly boundaries: "For her faith taught her to believe in an infinite struggle of intercession in which all the Church Visible and Invisible were together engaged, and which bound them in living bonds of sympathy to an interceding Redeemer, so that there was no want or woe of human life that had not somewhere its sympathetic heart, and its never-ceasing prayer before the throne of Eternal Love." The narrator intercedes in this passage to contrast Christian ties, radiating from a loving and sympathetic maternal center, with the contemporary (and limited) perspective of nineteenth-century Americans: "Whatever may be thought of the actual truth of this belief [the union of the Church Visible and Invisible], it certainly was far more consoling than the intense individualism of modern philosophy which places every soul alone in its life-battle,—scarce ever giving it a God to lean upon" (141). The individualism at the heart of the American rhetoric of republicanism is antithetical to the maternal, Christian community that the novel constructs as ideal. The nationalist ideology that produced James Fenimore Cooper's call, earlier in the century, for a "manly, independent literature" (quoted in Spencer 78)—a formulation that denies the ties that bind this "man" to others even as it refutes connections between the United States and other nations—is critiqued in Stowe's novelistic world as an "intense individualism" that isolates and handicaps those who would worship it.

Idealized depictions of community combine in Stowe's text with criticisms of American individualism, functioning much like Stowe's other discursive syntheses: the blending of the practical and the emotive, the Protestant and the Catholic, the American and the European. The text does not endorse any one term in these binaries but rather advocates the dismantling of such distinctions and incorporates values on both sides of the dividing line. Within the novel's logic, the closest approximation to an ideal community combines traditions and can be found only at a great historical, geographical, and theological distance from the nineteenth-century United States: "No institution in modern Europe had a more established reputation in all these respects than the convent of San Marco in

Florence. In its best days, it was as near an approach to an ideal community, associated to unite religion, beauty, and utility, as ever has existed on earth" (97). The recipe is explicit. The utility of Protestantism, echoed in the novel's description of the Italian Elsie as "being as decided a utilitarian as any old Yankee female born in the granite hills of New Hampshire" (98), united with the "exceeding loveliness" of Sorrento, the surrounding Italian countryside, and the passion of early Christian artists, can create a balance that acknowledges and satisfies the needs of the many, perhaps especially the needs of women.

In positing the convent as an ideal space, a building "consecrated by a religion recognized alike by all parties" that "afforded to misfortune the only inviolable asylum," Stowe's narrator articulates a contemporary imperative to establish a secular space reflecting similar domestic values: "If the destiny of woman is a problem that calls for grave attention even in our enlightened times, and if she is too often a sufferer from the inevitable movements of society, what must have been her position and needs in those ruder ages, unless the genius of Christianity had opened refuges for her weakness, made inviolable by the awful sanctions of religion?" (64). Notably, although such homogeneity is antithetical to American individualism, it is the "religion recognized alike by all" that enables the sanctuary found in the convent. In contrast, the enlightened culture of nineteenth-century America accepts, even perpetuates, a sexism that endangers women. The danger that "calls for grave attention" in Stowe's novel gets dismissed by male authors of her day; "In ninety-nine cases out of a hundred," the narrative voice in *The Marble Faun* confidently asserts, "the apprehensiveness of women is quite gratuitous. Even as matters now stand, they are really safer in perilous situations and emergencies than men; and might still be more so, if they trusted themselves more confidingly to the chivalry of manhood" (Hawthorne 279). In fact, trust in chivalry endangers the women in Stowe's novel, leading them to abandonment, abduction, and death. *Agnes* calls readers to attend to this danger by inscribing reminders of contemporary injustice alongside backward projections of a Christian utopia.

Agnes of Sorrento explicitly defines the ideal community as one that blends religion, beauty, and utility. This community, structured around a maternal center, transcends modern boundaries that divide nation from nation. In Stowe's text, the model for such a community must be found in a past religious era; contemporary nationhood, like contemporary religion, is barren and restrictive. The retreat to a distant historical moment permits Stowe's idealization of Christianity because it maintains the romantic tone that would remind readers that her utopian community is not founded upon the Christianity of contemporary life. As the daughter of a Calvinist minister whose anti-Catholic sermons provoked a convent burning, Stowe would have understood the risks involved in valorizing any powerful, patriarchal institution. The romanticized recreation of a four-hundred-year-old, imaginative construct gave Stowe the freedom to create what was lacking in nineteenth-century America: a broader, more inclusive, more maternal religious model, a Christianity based on domestic values, with the potential to embrace the world. In *Agnes,* her project for reformation could become global in scale: "No nation imagines itself coterminous with mankind. The most messianic nationalists do not dream of a day when all the members of the human race will join their nation in the way that it was possible, in certain epochs for, say, Christians to dream of a wholly Christian planet" (Anderson 7).[15] In fifteenth-century Italy, a prenationalistic time and place as well as a mythic fantasyland, Stowe discovered the raw materials onto which she could project her political agenda for nineteenth-century America. Through a fusion of the mythical and the pragmatic, the novel constructs an ideal Christian community that does not foreground national boundaries between peoples but instead offers its readers an expanded vision of domesticity, founded on Christian values and structured around the central precept of maternal love.

CHAPTER 4

"How Can I Write Down the Flowers?": Representation and Copying in Sophia Peabody Hawthorne's *Notes in England and Italy*

Critical attention paid to Sophia Peabody Hawthorne focuses almost exclusively on her influence, both direct and indirect, on the writings of her husband, Nathaniel. Readings of her life, letters, journals, and paintings become critical treasure hunts seeking references, however obscure, to Nathaniel's activities, health, state of mind, social engagements, and literary productivity. In his introduction to Sophia's 1862 diary, Thomas Woodson confesses, "it is natural that one's first curiosity about this diary should be for what it tells us about Nathaniel Hawthorne's life and writing" (282). When Sophia's 1861 diary does not yield the desired references, the same critic concedes, "Since her husband's role here must disappoint the student of American culture, we may see Sophia's sister, Elizabeth Palmer Peabody . . . as the star performer of the diary" (3). Under this logic of selective valorization, readings of Sophia Hawthorne's writing conspire to make anyone except Sophia herself the object of critical study.[1]

Similarly, criticism that places Sophia herself under scrutiny investigates her life primarily as a means of prying open Nathaniel's literary works. For example, she is often crited with serving as the model and impetus for specific female characters in the novels. Thus Claire Badaracco can assert that Sophia is "best known in this century for the omissions in her 1868 edition of Hawthorne's *Notebooks*, and as the model for Hilda in *The Marble Faun*" (92).[2] Elsewhere Sophia is read as a force inflecting Nathaniel's work in general: Joyce Warren notes that "Hawthorne's recognition of and respect for Sophia as an independent person and his simultaneous preference for gentle femininity in a wife help to explain why in his fiction he balanced his independent women characters with gentle dove-maidens" (*American Narcissus* 208). Representing a critical extreme, Edwin Hoyt's investigation of the Peabody family's influence in New England confuses art and life long enough to state outright that "Sophia was the central female character in *The Marble Faun*" (180). Perhaps analysis of a wife as a literary influence will inevitably collapse text and life, but Hawthorne criticism seems especially prone to hyperbole and sentimentality.[3] What is most shocking is that this Sophia—otherworldly, peripheral yet omnipresent, an almost impossible phantasm with capabilities surpassing Nathaniel's—has been constructed in a body of criticism that seldom considers her own creative work as a painter and a writer.

Emphasis on Sophia as either an editor or a catalyst for another's creative work continues a legacy of silencing begun during her marriage. Nathaniel recognized her talents, copying "sixteen passages from the second and third volumes of Sophia's Cuba Journal into his first American Notebook" (Badaracco 98). In a characteristic act of modesty perhaps abetted by a husband who sought to stifle her voice, Sophia excised those passages from her 1868 edition of his papers. Furthermore, as Joyce Warren observes, "although Sophia apparently only censored Hawthorne's letters to her, he completely destroyed all of hers to him." Warren postulates that "her letters revealed an unreserve that Hawthorne did not believe should ever be witnessed by anyone but her husband" (*American Narcissus* 208). Certainly this anecdote suggests Nathaniel Hawthorne's belief in the nineteenth-century American logic of gendered spheres, which permitted him to determine how much of himself to bare to the public while demanding that Sophia remain entirely hidden. Well known for his protest against what he called a "damned mob of scribbling women," Nathaniel refused to allow his wife to publish her written work. As Edwin Miller writes, "Although Hawthorne acknowledged the superiority of Sophia's accounts of England and Italy to his own, he did not want her to become a female scribbler: he preferred silent women and no competition." Miller adds posthumous insult to injury by continuing, "He had nothing to fear from Sophia, who knew what every woman knows, or should know, the vulnerabilities of her husband" (202).

Despite Nathaniel's proscriptions, more than fifteen years after the letter burning, Sophia stepped out into the public's gaze, acknowledging in the act of publishing *Notes in England and Italy* her desire to reveal herself to a readership even as she described, in her preface, "the pain it has cost me to appear before the public." The rhetoric suggests Sophia's intimate connection to her written work and the harrowing self-disclosure involved in the bold act of publication. Still, she published *Notes in England and Italy* in 1869, and Gloria Erlich indicates some of Sophia Hawthorne's conflicted feelings about publishing: "Although [Sophia] was a capable writer as well as artist, she accepted during [Nathaniel's] lifetime his prohibition against publication by females. Only after his death and pressed by financial need did she publish some of her travel notes" (101). I would suggest that more was at stake for Sophia than monetary gain. Her compulsion to compose privately during her husband's lifetime indicates the active, though submerged, desire to communicate with an audience that surfaced after his death with the book publication.

A series of journal entries composed in Europe, *Notes in England and Italy* articulates a creative agenda that Sophia Hawthorne nourished privately for years and ultimately sought to display. Through her travel narrative, Sophia argues for the profound communicative potential of visual art and insists that by returning to a certain honesty of intention and expression, artists can and must redeem a historical context that lacks spirituality. In addition, gender is a crucial concern within Sophia's aesthetics, as her text emphasizes women's role in the creative process. Interestingly, two American sculptors working in Rome during the same time period—Harriet Hosmer and Edmonia Lewis—seemed to share Sophia's ideals: to demonstrate the potential of strong women to work as artists and to serve as the subject matter for great art. The sculptures of Hosmer and Lewis provide a provocative counterpoint to Sophia's literary art.

The confrontation with Italy and Italian art marked a pivotal shift in the work of both Hawthornes, as Carol Hanbery MacKay suggests: "I submit that from the time of their Italian sojourn to their respective deaths, Sophia and Nathaniel Hawthorne were preoccupied with copying and with its values and limitations" (114). What is surprising here is not the grandness of the claim—the idea that Sophia was obsessed with copying is both useful and pronounced—but rather that the critic makes this assertion without having read, or making reference to, the very text that developed out of Sophia's Italian journey. By collapsing as it does the rhetoric surrounding Sophia's editorship of Nathaniel's notebooks, her training as a painter, and her representation of the Italian art world, the concept of copying becomes more complex in Sophia's work than critics may have realized.

In my reading of *Notes in England and Italy,* I see a similar binary logic operating both in the subordination of Sophia's work to Nathaniel's and in the subordination of copying to "original" production. I am interested in the complexities of copying as they arise in *Notes* and in copying as a shifting value and useful vehicle in Sophia's struggle to represent and communicate a woman's artistic vision. Not surprisingly, "the trope of crossing borders—often forbidden borders—into new territory," located by Karen

Lawrence in British women's travel experiences, thematically inflects Sophia's travel writing and resonates on a broader level in the fact that she published her work at all (19). Crossing various borders that constrained nineteenth-century, American women artists, *Notes* asserts Sophia's right to criticize, create, and publish. Often challenging the prevailing opinions of noted authorities, the text assumes bold critical stances on the artworks Sophia visited, studied, and reproduced and interrogates the traditionally accepted hierarchies of male/female, original/copy, image/text to facilitate Sophia's expression of her theories about artistic representation.

An artist's response to an "artistic" land, *Notes* negotiates the process of representation in terms of a shifting relationship between word and image. The tensions involved in translating the visual to the verbal resulted in Sophia's exclamation, "How can I write down the flowers?"—a question that betrays uncertainty even as it articulates power and the desire to assert that power (299–300). Her text searches for an effective representational medium, a way to "copy" what she sees on her travels and transmit it to readers at home. Visual arts are often championed in *Notes,* yet the act of publishing a verbal text, rather than the drawings an artist of Sophia's accomplishments might have produced, seems to undermine the hierarchy Sophia argues explicitly. This tension between visual and verbal media ultimately creates a complex discourse that interrogates the value system inherent in nineteenth-century (male) standards of artistic expression.

Sophia's Vision

Notes in England and Italy opens, like many nineteenth-century travel narratives, with a disclaimer: "I think it necessary to say that these 'Notes,' written twelve years ago, were never meant for publication; but solely for my own reference, and for a means of recalling to my friends what had especially interested me abroad. Many of these friends have repeatedly urged me to print them, from a too particular estimate of their value; and I have steadily resisted the suggestion, until now, when I reluctantly yield."[4] Despite protestations about her text's "value," by the time Sophia undertook her European tour she had substantial training in art, and her *Notes* reveal a sophisticated artistic sensibility. The European tour was no casual trip for Sophia Hawthorne, nor was the publication of her *Notes* a haphazard endeavor. In fact, as Nathalia Wright claims, most likely Sophia herself instigated the Hawthorne family's sojourn to Italy so that she might study firsthand the masters she had encountered as reproductions during her days as an art student (138). Unarguably, the Italian people and countryside would make a unique imprint on Nathaniel's fiction, but for Sophia, as Thomas Woodson argues, "Italy's treasures of art represented a chance for the fulfillment of a lifetime's dream of study and appreciation" (*The French and Italian Notebooks* 904). Although remembered as the copyist who transcribed her husband's notebooks, she consistently made time for her own text even as she negotiated a hectic editing schedule. Woodson notes that "Mrs. Hawthorne's journal for 1869 reveals that she completed copying Hawthorne's English notebooks in June, and that she spent a month in July and August making her own Italian journal ready for Putnam. . . . After reading proof of her own book in October, she recorded on November 1: 'I began to copy my husband's Continental journals' " (ibid., 922). The journal suggests the chaotic publishing schedule Sophia was obliged to adhere to, as well as a persistent dedication to her own work.

Despite the centrality of Sophia Hawthorne's Italian text in her own life, references to *Notes* are conspicuously absent from contemporary criticism. Occasionally a critic will invoke the text briefly and dismissively, at times even replicating the nineteenth-century cultural logic of separate spheres, as in Edwin Miller's assertion that "her descriptions constitute a rather prosaic and impersonal travelogue, too self-conscious to do justice to herself or her subject matter. When Sophia was writing about the home, she was at her best" (202). According to Miller, Sophia's text suffers from being too "impersonal," a characteristic that might have surprised a reader (or critic) expecting the sentimentality typically associated with nineteenth-century women's writing. Yet one wonders how an "impersonal" text can be criticized also for its "self-consciousness." Sophia is both not there and too much there, caught again in the binary trap that represents her position throughout contemporary criticism. Her text is equally "not there" in the work of Carol Hanbery MacKay, who writes that "despite [Sophia's] opposition to women's rights and her outward compliance with Hawthorne's proscriptions for women, she may well have unconsciously rebelled against her husband's restrictions on female creativity" (115), a statement that seeks to liberate Sophia's creativity but comes dangerously close to stifling it, eliding as it does a very *conscious* rebellion in the form of a published book.

Critics tend to be equally dismissive of Sophia's work as a visual artist. The extent of her artistic reputation is suggested in an 1836 letter she received from her sister, Elizabeth Palmer Peabody, which mentions several of Sophia's paintings in progress and refers to potential purchasers and organized exhibitions of her work. In a footnote to this letter, Bruce Ronda offers further evidence of Sophia's artistic ability: "Washington Allston encouraged [Sophia's] art, which had turned primarily to copying. By the end of the decade, Sophia had a studio with a friend, Mary Newhall, while Elizabeth, as this letter suggests, was at work selling her copies" (155). In fact, it was Allston, the well-known American artist, who encouraged Sophia to make an artistic pilgrimage to Europe for the purposes of studying and copying masterpieces (Valenti 6). During her lifetime, Sophia produced paintings that continue to be displayed in public and private locations; indeed her body of work has prompted Patricia Valenti to assert that "Sophia should be considered among the earliest serious female painters in America" (2).[5]

Nevertheless, Edwin Haviland Miller has declared that "Sophia was an amateur painter of somewhat limited talents, although she was praised on one occasion by Washington Allston" (199). One wonders, exactly how many occasions of praise from a renowned artist demonstrate true talent? Further, the fact that Sophia sold her copies of well-known paintings argues against Miller's use of the term "amateur." A similar dismissal occurs when critic Gloria Erlich, describing the illustration Sophia created for Nathaniel's story "The Gentle Boy," argues, "Like Hilda of *The Marble Faun,* [Sophia] accepted the role of interpretive copyist rather than the assertive one of original creator" (101). Beneath the dismissive tone of such criticism lies a misapprehension of copying's significance. A process central to Sophia's literary and visual art, copying is deemed subordinate by many critics in a binary logic that seems to replicate the historical subordination of women to men. The "interpretive copyist" of Erlich's logic is a feminized substitute for the more "assertive" (and masculine) "original creator." Thus male/female corresponds to original/copy, primary/secondary in a hierarchical relationship that places higher value on the first term. Later in the chapter I discuss copying in more detail, but I wish here to highlight how references to copying contribute to a general critical subordination of Sophia's work.

The European tour that inspired Sophia's *Notes* began in 1857, following Nathaniel's tenure as American consul in Liverpool. The Italian section of her travel narrative includes entries dated between February and October 1858, during which time she toured Italy with her husband, three children, and their governess, moving from Rome to Florence and back again to Rome. In 1860 the Hawthornes returned to the States, and nine years later Sophia published the lengthy manuscript that *is,* to borrow Miller's term, "impersonal," in the sense that it downplays details about Sophia's private life. Yet these same pages document what is intensely personal—though not as the term has been traditionally applied to women—to Sophia, her developing and individualized aesthetic sensibility. Having taken root during the artistic training of her youth, this sensibility flourished in the rich soil of Italy. "How my vision grows!" she exclaims on viewing the Roman forum early in her journey, and her text goes on to explicate that vision. The visual perspective afforded by Italy and the freedom to create outside of domestic boundaries will allow Sophia's artist's eyes to see America's future through the Italian past.

Unlike other nineteenth-century travel narratives, Catharine Maria Sedgwick's, for example, which guide the would-be visitor through the intricacies of Italian daily life, Sophia Hawthorne's *Notes* take the reader on a journey through both famous and lesser-known museums, villas, and churches in search of memorable works of art, primarily those of the Great Masters of the Renaissance. Overwhelmed by the multitude of worthy stimuli, she declares early in her travels, "I looked with all my eyes at every side. I wished to be Argus, so as to see all round at once, and not lose anything behind while I was gazing before, or on one hand while looking on the other" (182). We might understand the text as Sophia's attempt to unfold this Argus-view for herself and the reader, as her thoroughness of detail registers more than would meet the casual tourist's gaze. Sophia's detailed prose seeks to render, recreate, and *increase* the visual intensity of Italian art so that her audience might appreciate its value.

Constructing a worthy representation of her vision constitutes the central problem of Sophia's text. Her desire to communicate what she sees both energizes and confounds her, produces the published *Notes* as well as the oft-expressed frustration that words cannot communicate visual images. Ultimately, she seeks to achieve her goal by combining media: At times she alludes to sketches that may have been included in her personal journal but did not appear in the published version. Sophia's narration of attempts to sketch the works that most impress her indicates the discovery that grows out of artistic connection. In the following passage, for example, both drawing and writing inform Sophia's encounter with a Dürer painting in Rome's Barberini Palace: "I think this Jew was the father of Judas Iscariot. Eccolo! only I cannot get so much wickedness, malice, and meanness into my sketch as are in the original" (210).[6] The Italian interjection, meaning "there he is," demonstrates the immediacy of her visual experience and may signify, on the one hand, that she is writing even as she sees and recognizes a figure in the painting; on the other hand, "there he is" may refer to her own sketch, suggesting that she has succeeded in capturing his essence in her drawing, even as she admits to falling short of exact reproduction. In both cases the creative act of making a copy, a re-representation either in writing or drawing, facilitates understanding the original. Such passages underscore the intimate relationship between representation and "copying," complicating the critical perspective that would valorize original over copy. The cultural value ascribed to originals and copies, as well as the variable worth of "false" and "true" copies, informs *Notes in England and Italy* and preoccupied Sophia during her artistic career.[7]

Using verbal copies of drawings, *Notes* attempts to convey Sophia's intense response to certain Italian artifacts and, therefore, faces the challenge of compensating for a shift in medium. Aware of the difficulties, Sophia declares, "I am trying to render into words what Titian's pencil alone can manifest" (269). Yet she persists, and, to inscribe visual impressions rhetorically, she constructs long meditations on painting after painting that combine descriptions of her response as viewer with often minute catalogues of a painting's component parts. The two techniques work together to emphasize the capacity of visual artwork to affect its audience. Here, for example, is a response to Domenichino's *Martyrdom of St. Sebastian:* "This is unlike any martyrdom I have seen, for Domenichino has succeeded in making the triumph over pain complete, and instead of the distressing horror, I felt only a peace which passes all understanding. The longer I looked, the more profoundly I was affected by the sublimity of the sacrifice" (205). Her language indicates art's emotional impact and the transmissive nature of the viewing experience. Not only does the martyr's serenity become Sophia's own inner peace, but also the act of looking produces and increases the profound effect. The apprehension and serenity, not located entirely within the artwork itself, are created by the subjectivity that encounters them, a subjectivity willing to look long and eager to convince others to follow her example.

Intertwined with descriptions of emotional reactions, Sophia will use close readings of a painting's composition, as though to map out the vision for her readers and thus explicate the work's effectiveness. The details of Domenichino's *Martyrdom,* for instance, occupy more than two pages in *Notes,* with Sophia leading the reader around the fresco like a director manipulating a camera: "Executioners are drawing up the form of St. Sebastian, with ropes, on a cross. On the right, a soldier is dashing by upon a horse, and shakes a truncheon at the saint as he goes. Before the cross, kneeling on the ground, is a woman, turning her face toward the horse-man. Another woman and a child, both with hands extended in fear and horror, crouch in one corner. A man with bow and arrows stoops on the other side, raising his head to speak to a soldier, who is bending down to him." Proceeding much as an artist would, Sophia sketches with broad strokes to indicate the overall composition, then goes back to fill in details: "The woman, kneeling in the centre—her face in profile—is beautiful, a rich mass of sunny tresses gathered beneath a turban, and her neck and shoulders exquisitely painted" (204). Somehow Domenichino's soldier, saint, and tresses exist in a mysterious relationship that produces the "peace which passes all understanding." Patricia Valenti summarizes Sophia's aesthetic thus: Sophia "regarded pictures as an almost magical, definitely spiritual artistic medium which could capture ineluctable qualities of a subject's psyche that eluded verbalization" (15).

The text investigates the mystery of art's magical power, despite the daunting task of explaining what seems to exist, by definition, beyond language. Through catalogues of details and emotions, Sophia's prose strives to textualize her response to Italy's paintings and to demonstrate the potentially global ramifications. After contemplating a *Madonna and Child* by Fra Angelico, she writes, "the child such a glorified innocence as was never portrayed before. He sits upon the Virgin's knee, and looks straight out of the picture, with a face that might make the world sweet and holy, if it were often enough contemplated" (314). The prescription for worldly redemption reveals a two-fold assumption: First, where other forces (government, organized religion, charitable organizations) have failed, a painting can heal. Second, the painted face can exercise its redemptive power only when observed. Again, the work of art is pivotal in Sophia's vision, but equally so the act of looking, an act she is free to perform and endorse as a nineteenth-century woman on tour. Furthermore, as author of a text that reproduces the fresco and thereby increases the number of times it will be encountered, Sophia becomes part of an artistic chain of representation that would "make the world sweet and holy."

Later in the narrative, Sophia's looking becomes more daring, taking on a romantic valence. Implicit in her championing of beauty is an assumed correlation between an aesthetically pleasing image and integrity within. Sophia takes this exterior/interior correspondence quite seriously during an intimate, emotional encounter with, interestingly, another representation of St. Sebastian. Describing the face of Perugino's martyr as "so attractive and winning in its princely state, that in my heart I pronounced him the ideal cavalier, the gentlest, the bravest, the truest" (323), Sophia demonstrates a keen desire to look at a figure and discover his moral status. As the passage continues, she adopts the stance and rhetoric of a lover, claiming that "it afflicted me so much to know that I should never see him again, that I gazed with a trembling eagerness, and took no time to glance at the other saints" (323). Oddly sexualized, the act of looking becomes the compulsion that binds Sophia to Sebastian in an exclusive union; the effect is physical, the "trembling eagerness" enough to make her forswear others and devote herself entirely to her "ideal cavalier." In this passage, the passionate nature of art and spectatorship far exceeds what is suggested in more "polite," mainstream depictions of Americans strolling casually through foreign museums.

Berating herself for not sketching this godlike figure, Sophia confesses that the painting depicts a divine beauty more intense than she had thought possible, "and such as a Co-Raphaelite or a Pre-Raphaelite only could have delineated" (323). Here she reinforces another of the narrative's major lamentations: that truly great art passed with Raphael. In contrast to the nineteenth-century world around her, Sophia idealizes a certain austerity within which Renaissance artists created: "With what wonderful devoutness these ancient masters painted! They pray, they adore God, they deny themselves, they live gloriously,—all with their pencil. They painted religiously, and there is an expression in the faces and figures nowhere else found, excepting in Raphael, who imbibed so deeply the spirit of those men, and who was their last expression" (309). The lost art the text bemoans reflects Sophia's fantasy of a bygone era, precapitalist and simple, when artists worked for the love of God rather than for money or worldly praise. "If painters now were holy men," she speculates, "and dedicated their genius to heaven, perhaps angels and cherubs would still live to their imagination, and so to our eyes, through their pencils. But what watery, theatrical, unspiritual, impossible angels we have now-a-days" (328). With a litany of complaints against the apathy of nineteenth-century American culture, Sophia remains cynical about the changes termed "progress" in the age of industrial and capitalist growth: "Remote antiquity might teach us a great deal, though we brag so perpetually about our improvements" (428). What empowers Renaissance art for Sophia is its ability to render possible, or real, a sense of the spiritual. Both artistically and culturally, Sophia sees nineteenth-century America as inhospitable to her angels.

Among the so-called improvements of nineteenth-century America would have been the Protestant rejection of ornamentation and what was perceived as Catholicism's misguided tendency toward idolatry. Thus Sophia risks censure with her implied criticism of the starkness of Protestant churches when she writes, following a visit to the chapel in the Florentine Palazzo Vecchio:

> What a pity it is that any wall should remain a dead blank when they might all blaze with glory in this way, and wake the soul by touch of art divine! Must we not go back to this adornment again, since it arose from the demand of the soul, and the soul demands it still? What were colors made for, if not to use for the worship of God, and the culture of the spirit? Are we more devout for bare walls? Are we less spiritually-minded when the plain plaster gives place to rainbow-winged angels, holding dulcimer, cithern, and harp, praising God—their faces refulgent with His light? We need more Fra Angelicos to open the doors of Paradise for us, and to crowd blank

> space with seraphim and cherubim—also Ghirlandaios and Michel Angelos to reveal the sublime brows and forms of Prophets, Sibyls, Saints, and Martyrs whenever we lift up our eyes. (416)

The passage demonstrates Sophia's willingness to challenge popular opinion, to question a value upon which her homeland's nationalism had been founded. In opposition to American utilitarianism, Sophia's aesthetics demand color and ornamentation, which she sees as deriving from the spiritual realm and offering salvation. The artist (perhaps Sophia herself) who would "open the doors of Paradise" with such rich texture could guide viewers to redemption through the power of visual imagery.

In contrast to this artistic fantasy, *Notes* voices Sophia's concern that nineteenth-century progress and industrialization menace the creative process and interfere with a spectator's apprehension of art. Specifically, the text attacks the modern tendency, in life and in art, to examine the world too carefully and invasively. It is this painful and misguided attention to detail that Sophia "shrunk from in the galleries of England" when viewing modern paintings. Hypersensitive attention to detail in painted works is, in Sophia's aesthetics, both inhuman and unrealistic: "[I]n the living subject, Nature contrives to avoid this shocking bareness—but the prying modern artist seems to take magnifying glasses to the human face, as well as to the landscape—and bring to view what is veiled from common sight" (312). On the other hand, "the holy artists," by whose work Sophia is smitten during her Italian travels, "did not think it incumbent upon their truth and sincerity to paint every hair on the skin, or the rough ferocity of the weather-beaten, sunburnt complexion" (ibid.). What mechanical instruments bring, unnaturally, into view is not truth in Sophia Hawthorne's artistic vision. Not discoverable by camera or microscope, truth resides in the intensity, integrity, unity, and beauty of a spiritually inspired work and demands appreciation of the whole rather than individual parts. Not invasively investigative, great art is comprehensive, like Guido's *Archangel*, which inspired her to write, "A perfect work is a unit of Truth, and all truth is one" (258). Indeed, Guido's *Archangel* speaks volumes to Sophia, who notes, "The whole destiny and history of man in relation to the Deity can be read in this picture" (ibid.).

Contemporary paintings displayed in England, on the other hand, had no such power and claimed Pre-Raphaelite status erroneously according to Sophia. "What is called preraphaelite painting in England is not like this," she declares, indicating Italian Pre Raphaelite art: "Expression without beauty, to be sure, we see in modern English pictures, called by this name; but all the religion is left out, all the holy fervor, sincerity, and simplicity.

Perhaps I should not say the sincerity is left out; but the simplicity is—the single thought—the unselfish aim" (312). The critic who takes on the Pre-Raphaelite brotherhood reveals an equally courageous conviction when she writes of Andrea del Sarto's *Madonna of the Sack,* "It has a certain free and flowing style; but even before being injured by time, I do not see how it could ever have been a great picture. I cannot discover Andrea del Sarto's merits" (447). Though a willing student, Sophia does not simply accept the entire legacy of the Great Masters but interrogates each work to determine how it fits into her own aesthetic philosophy. Her objection to del Sarto's painting reinforces the aesthetics that have been emerging throughout the text. Although Mary has a face that is "round and full," it remains "without any divine expression." Sophia can find nothing to say about Joseph other than that he "is seated on a sack, with a book," and the infant Christ receives no specific description at all (446). What is missing from this picture is emotional intensity. A successful artwork, according to Sophia's understanding and vision, foregrounds a certain emotional realism in which the subjects express, unmistakably, the feeling that would realistically arise in a given situation.

When William Vance refers to an "individualizing realism" that impressed Sophia and other American travelers who viewed ancient Roman portraits, he identifies an aesthetic that enabled viewers of sculpted busts to appreciate figures in Roman history as individuals, rather than "reducible to a common type" (*America's Rome* I:186). Taking this phenomenon to an extreme, Sophia records that the realism of certain Roman sculptures convinced her that she had actually met the subjects depicted: "I have now seen Octavianus face to face, and also Marcus Aurelius. . . . I shall go and become acquainted with all these potentates" (225). I call Sophia's realism a spiritual or sentimental realism, which is to say she praises a representation that is not photographic but that demonstrates the artist's (and later the viewer's) empathy with the subject's emotional state. Her own artistic efforts share this communicative aim, and she denounces those painters who fall short of her criteria for greatness.

In like manner Sophia offers her criticism of a central figure in American letters, Ralph Waldo Emerson. In his influential essay, "Self-Reliance," Emerson writes, "It is for want of self-culture that the superstition of Travelling, whose idols are Italy, England, Egypt, retains its fascination for all educated Americans." Opposing the American penchant for the European Tour, Emerson insists, "The soul is no traveller; the wise man stays at home" (186). Apparently reflecting on this well-known assertion, Sophia betrays a scornful attitude toward what she perceives as narrow-mindedness: "How could the wise and great Mr. E. say such a preposterous thing as that it was just as well *not* to travel! and that each man has Europe in him, or something to that effect? No, indeed; it would be better if every man could look upon these wonders of genius, and grow thereby. . . . It was mere transcendental nonsense—such a remark" (326). Again we see Sophia's emphasis on looking and the metamorphosis that can result. In addition, this particular celebration of the power of Italy's artistic heritage performs the corresponding work of dismantling the American myth of self-culture espoused by Emerson.

Taken cumulatively, the entries in Sophia's *Notes* articulate an individualized perspective, one that may subvert reader expectations regarding nineteenth-century women's writing. A traveler in an age that relegated women to the home, Sophia took the further step of writing about the artistic rather than the domestic aspects of her experience abroad. She published despite her husband's proscriptive decree. Her text interrogates hierarchies of representation and champions an ornate style that contrasted with nineteenth-century American ideals of simplicity and practicality in art and religion. Sophia Hawthorne made substantial use of what Mary Suzanne Schriber calls in *Telling Travels* "the commodiousness and elasticity of the genre" (xxv), appropriating the travel narrative like other nineteenth-century women to offer a unique vision and argue for humanitarian ideals.

Copying

A collage made up of household chores ("I sewed till near five"), familial responsibilities ("I made up a portfolio of Julian's productions to send to Salem"), educational outings ("We heard a lecture on history from Mr. Sanborn in the schoolroom"), and the trials of getting to town to shop and pay bills ("The wind blew very hard & very cold[.] We had to walk backwards"), Sophia Hawthorne's journal for 1862 indicates she led a busy life. Daily duties notwithstanding, however, her entry for January 12, 1862, reads, "I copied Raphael's angel all day." Two years after her return from Italy, she still made time for her art amidst domestic routines, and copying continued to figure as a significant component of that art. The influence of Italy stayed with her, as she "read Arnold's Rome," "read Ellery's Rome," and on a June 11 visit to Dorchester, "talked Rome all the evening." Similarly she maintained her concern with reproduction as production and the efforts—"All day I copied the angel for Una"—that would extend the power of the great works she had seen and add her artistic hand to the continuum.

Copying had been a fundamental component of Sophia's education. As an art student, she was often encouraged by her mentors to copy the work of Renaissance painters canonized as the "Masters." In her relationship with the painter Chester Harding, copying became a mark of privilege and an indicator of her talents. After a visit to his studio, Sophia recorded in her journal this compliment: Harding "said I should copy his portrait of Allston which he would not suffer any body else in Boston to do" (Valenti 4). Even as she moved past apprenticeships into her own career, copies continued to occupy much of her creative time, enabling her to gain mastery over different techniques, contributing to her artistic reputation, and earning her an income. Furthermore, the process of reproducing masculine models informed American women's education in general during the nineteenth century. Claire Badaracco explains, "Sophia belonged to that last generation of the women of pre-industrial American society who were not admitted to public schools, but who had access to the schoolrooms only in the evening or summer, when the boys were resting or playing. Within that tradition, where girls were educated in front parlors, "reading" was commonly understood to mean *elocution,* "composition" was *making copies,* and "writing" was primarily an exercise in journals and copy-books" (96, Badaracco's emphasis). Both as a method of learning and, more importantly for my argument, as a means of *expression,* many nineteenth-century American women would have found copying a familiar activity in their academic and creative lives.

For a twentieth-century reader (or critic), copying often registers as derivative and culturally suspect, more often associated with popular (or "low") art than high art. Witness the generally contemptuous attitude displayed by many listeners toward rap music, a genre dependent on "sampling" melodies from precursor songs. In a similar vein, Patricia Valenti argues, "The flawlessness of [Sophia's] copies could have provided her with a comfortable living, but she aspired with the intensity and seriousness of a professional to surpass the status of an amateur or copyist to become a painter of original canvasses" (1). The rhetoric aligns the terms "amateur" and "copyist," as though only an "original" painter qualifies as a professional. Yet Sophia *was* a professional who successfully sold her copies of famous paintings and even supported her husband: "The $150.00 that Sophia had saved from the sale of her decorative arts kept the family afloat while Hawthorne wrote *The Scarlet Letter*" (15–16). And readers of either century might ask, what is "original"? Certainly the works of Raphael and Michelangelo, dependent upon the Bible and on prior representations, cannot claim absolute originality of subject matter. How many Madonnas have been painted in the history of visual art, each one considered original if executed by a well-known and, more often than not, male artist? Sophia's life and text complicate the distinction between original and copy and the relative value ascribed to each.[8]

Demonstrating a synthesis similar to that of rap music in our own time, the copying Sophia Hawthorne praises (and produces) in her text results in a hybrid expression. Artistic copies repeat compositions even as they must necessarily constitute new creations. No copy made by the hand of a visual artist can be an exact duplicate. MacKay points out that "a painted copy can approach but never reach exact duplication of the original, whereas a written copy can be literally precise" (113), and we may say that within the gap between original and copy lies the space where Sophia expresses her creativity. A written copy *can* be literally precise, yet many of Sophia's copies of Nathaniel's journals were not, demonstrating her insertion of her own sensibility into the composition process.[9] Similarly, in *Notes* Sophia's written copies of *painted* originals cannot be exact duplications. As a translating copyist, Sophia must interpret to bridge the gaps between media and inevitably grafts her artistic vision onto the reproduction.

Sophia's background in copying prepared her for what she encountered in Italy. Home of the artwork so many copyists sought to reproduce, Italian locales often presented the traveler with the double spectacle recorded time and again in Sophia's narrative: the original artwork displayed alongside the seated figure of a copyist before an easel. The reproduction in process would create a visual doubling, the juxtaposition suggesting a contrast that rarely goes unremarked by Sophia, whose keen observational powers demand that she assess the relative merits of both representations. Her pronouncements are particular and unqualified, as in her appraisal of "the artist who was copying [Guido's *Archangel*]" who "had entirely missed the face and the attitude, but had succeeded pretty well with the right foot and limb" (258). To make matters more complicated, the burgeoning nineteenth-century tourist trade had inspired and fueled the business by which Italy offered reproductions of itself for purchase. "Picture shops all over Rome displayed a panoply of copies of the Old Masters" (MacKay 105), and capitalism promised to make even distant history into a commodity that tourists could buy and bring home. Sophia demonstrates a suspicion of mass-produced, commercial copies when she writes of Guido's *Beatrice Cenci:* "And now we sat down before Beatrice Cenci! at last, at last! after so many years' hoping and wishing. This is a masterpiece which baffles words. No copy, engraved or in oils, gives the remotest idea of it. It is all over Rome, in every picture dealer's shop, of every size; besides being engraved" (212). Into a context saturated with imposters, Sophia Hawthorne's text offers a critical lesson in the recognition and appreciation of truly powerful representations, whether copy or original.

Arguing that many copies fall short of reproducing the original and that ideally the world's people would visit Italy's redemptive art and see the difference for themselves, a pragmatic Sophia Hawthorne nonetheless recognized the obvious obstacles. Not only would travel be impractical or even impossible for many, but also the artworks in question were fragile, already damaged by the passage of time. Acknowledging both the transitory nature of paintings and their power to enhance her life, Sophia claims to "live better for even pale Giottos, and the whole quaint, devout old band, in any stage of ruin" (405). Yet even an idealist had to realize that the stages of ruin were progressive. The works of the Great Masters were disintegrating, a dire circumstance when coupled with another point underlying *Notes:* that the Renaissance artists Sophia idolized would never come again. *Notes* makes clear that copying could perform the necessary cultural work of facilitating study and transmitting a spirituality Sophia describes as lacking in her historical moment. This fantasy of copyists circulating artistic reproductions suggests Sophia's democratizing desire to make universally available the cultural treasures historically reserved for the privileged.

Significantly, MacKay locates a similar faith in the possibility of an ideal copyist in Nathaniel Hawthorne's *Marble Faun,* embodied in the character of Hilda, an artist who "recreates the spirit that animated the artist in the first place, and the result is necessarily perfect" (95). In Nathaniel's text, the copyist experiences a creative fervor almost identical to that which inspired the earlier artist. From this perspective, constructing the ideal copy both requires and, in so doing, enables a higher artistic understanding: "Hawthorne's underlying aesthetic theory asserts that the artistic value lies in perfect comprehension of an original, however, not slavish or exact copying" (ibid.). Thus an inspired copy might not be exact but could be an instrument of understanding. In the work of both Hawthornes we find the implication that if the copyist is herself an inspired artist, a copy can be a true work of art.

Although littered with references to copyists who fail miserably, Sophia's travel account holds out faith in the possibility of an inspired copyist, a second coming of the great Renaissance artists who would spread the inimitable wealth of ancient art: "Oh, where are the artists to draw these departing glories, that they may be engraved for a never-ending inspiration to all present and future time! Can this child-like, unconscious grandeur ever be found again in art?" (405–6). The text articulates a more profound belief in the coming of a capable copyist than in the birth of a new Raphael, a hope that opens a space within which Sophia herself can operate as an artist. Hinting that occasionally a copy artist meets her exacting standards, she describes a "young artist" in Perugia who manages to copy a Perugino "with the utmost fidelity." "He, and others as accomplished and faithful,"

Sophia proposes, "should be commissioned to save in imperishable lines the vanishing masterpieces of fresco-painting" (320–21). The wishful word "imperishable" betrays her desire to see past art eternally available for consumption by fortunate spectators but overlooks the inevitable tendency of all such representations—even good copies—to decay over time. Less fragile than canvas and paint, the written word of Sophia's text may be her attempt to transcend time's destructive power and offer to a reading public the "lines" that will not fade.

Birds of a Feather

The decade that saw the publication of *Notes* also saw the arrival in Italy of an American woman, Edmonia Lewis, who had funded her own trip abroad to study classical sculpture. Daughter of a Chippewa mother and an African American father, Lewis was unique even among the unusual group of American women artists who lived and worked in Rome during the middle of the nineteenth century. The group was noteworthy enough to attract the attention of Henry James, who called them "that strange sisterhood of American 'lady sculptors' who at one time settled upon the seven hills in a white, marmorean flock."[10] It is not surprising that Sophia Hawthorne's travels took her to the studio of the group's most famous sculptor, Harriet Hosmer, and that Sophia, a visual artist herself, felt a strong and immediate connection to her. Hosmer's sculptures, like those of Edmonia Lewis, often depict strong, impressive women and extol those virtues that Sophia praises when she describes representations of women in *Notes*. Indeed, her description of Hosmer in *Notes* conveys a feminine strength and suggests why Sophia found the young sculptor so compelling: "Her action was as bright, sprightly, and vivid as that of a bird: a small figure, round face, and tiny features, except large eyes; hair short, and curling up round a black velvet cap, planted directly upon the middle of her head, instead of jauntily on one side, as is usual with artists; her hands thrust into the pockets of a close-fitting cloth jacket—a collar and cravat like a young man's—and a snowy plaited chemisette, like a shirt-bosom" (265). The physical attributes catalogued here forecast Sophia's description of her hostess's personality later in the passage. "I liked her at once," Sophia writes, "she was so frank and cheerful, independent, honest, and sincere—wide awake, energetic, yet not ungentle" (ibid.). Displaying those qualities Sophia praises in Hosmer, the work of all three women artists—Hawthorne, Hosmer, and Lewis—shares a common creative agenda despite the disparities of class and race among them. Not only do they all lay claim to women's right to artistic expression and to an education in the world's most prestigious artistic classroom, but all three also use their talents to create works of art that illustrate women in positions of strength.

Having faced prejudice at Oberlin College in an incident that prevented her from graduating, Edmonia Lewis took the steps necessary to secure passage to Europe. In 1862 she was accused of poisoning two white classmates and consequently beaten by a mob; by 1863 legal charges against her had been dismissed, but she was "not permitted to register for her final semester" at Oberlin (Burgard 4). Undaunted, Lewis moved to Boston to practice her art, creating there her famous bust of Colonel Robert Gould Shaw, of which she sold so many plaster copies she was able to fund her own trip to Italy. Such an ambitious journey necessarily resulted from the adversity faced by a woman artist of mixed racial heritage in the nineteenth-century United States; not only had racism denied her a degree from Oberlin, but as a woman she would have been refused admission, like her colleague Harriet Hosmer, to the anatomy classes male artists attended for the purposes of studying the human body. Travel to Italy liberated Lewis, as it had many of her white contemporaries, albeit from a more complex set of constraining forces. The voyage overseas helped Lewis to escape domestic servitude, like her white peers, and also American racism.

Lewis explored classical sculpture in Rome, where not surprisingly her creations synthesized her experiences and interrogated the forces that shaped her life. While there she sculpted *Forever Free (The Morning of Liberty)*, a work that fuses contemporary subject matter (the abolition of slavery) with a neoclassical style. Significantly, the piece uses a male and a female figure, the male "derived from the famous Hellenistic sculpture of *Laocoon* in the Vatican Museums" and the female taken from a contemporary political model: "a nineteenth-century abolitionist emblem that proclaimed 'Am I not a woman and a sister?' " (Burgard 6).[11] Lewis's juxtaposition challenges the values of dominant, homogeneous, neoclassical aesthetics. As Burgard notes, "*Forever Free* highlights the disparity between America's emulation of Greco-Roman ideals and the realities of slavery in both the ancient world and in the United States" (ibid.). His analysis is useful, but I think it is equally important to call attention to the statue's feminist implications. The question, "Am I not a sister?" might have been asked with equal urgency of Black men and of White women, as the latter group's burgeoning women's rights movement overlooked for the most part the political needs of Black American women.[12]

This reading is supported by Lewis's emphasis on women (of all races) in her sculptures as well as her relationship to the "flock" in Rome, specifically to its leader. Well known for their challenges to conventional Victorian gender roles, Hosmer and Charlotte Cushman, an actress who advanced Hosmer's career by bringing her to Italy, "served as role models for Lewis, who emulated not only outward attributes such as their unconventional (and often male) attire, but also their independent artistic personae" (Burgard 5). A community of women gathered around Harriet Hosmer—who was "the first woman to support herself as a professional sculptor in the nineteenth century" (ibid.)—would have helped to give Lewis confidence in her nontraditional lifestyle and ambitions, as well as serving as a resource for artistic technique and guidance.[13] Hosmer's biographer, Dolly Sherwood, refers to the growing number of women sculptors in Rome at the start of the 1860s "who looked to [Hosmer] as their leader and the prime example of acceptance and success" of a woman artist (194).

Hosmer's body of work, like Lewis's, argues for female strength by incorporating representations of women whose historical significance is undeniable. Said to have created her "finest works . . . in the first decade after her arrival in Rome," Hosmer returned repeatedly to the theme of women's strength, specifically the endurance of women "suffering from male oppression" (Rubinstein 43, 37). The first major sculptures of her Roman period, for example, represent the mythical Daphne and Medusa, both depicted as graceful and stoic in the face of male persecution. Her later and most acclaimed works include a depiction of a reclining Beatrice Cenci, imprisoned for killing her incestuous father yet dignified and peaceful in her recumbent position, and a resolute Zenobia, queen of Palmyra, manacled yet noble as she marches through Rome. The thematic bond that links these female subjects is their display of stoicism despite attempts by male forces to undermine their individual agency. Hosmer's depiction of female figures was, according to Charlotte Streifer Rubinstein, "very different from that of her male colleagues—stressing the intellect, character, and strength of her heroine instead of presenting a delectable victim whose eroticism is thinly disguised by allegorical or religious content" (41). Working in opposition to the convention of using the female as ornamental body, Hosmer's statues depict subjects with complex histories and emotional valences, demanding that a viewer interpret the subject on a deeper level than that typically accorded to decorative female figures.

Hosmer must have felt a kinship with these historical women, having been herself the victim of animosity from male peers. A pioneer woman in the Roman art world, Hosmer transgressed boundaries with an ease that apparently threatened male artists, who manufactured false accusations to undermine her credibility. Jealous colleagues spread the rumor through gossip and published articles that Hosmer's work was being executed by the Italian workmen she employed as assistants in her studio. A famous photograph documents her unique position: Dressed in a shirt and tie, Hosmer stands in the center of her Roman studio surrounded by more than twenty male assistants. Perhaps unsettled by this inversion of traditional roles, her accusers revealed a double standard underlying nineteenth-century art culture: Hosmer was damned for a practice, hiring Italian marble cutters, that signified success for male sculptors. This accusation exposes the cultural anxiety produced by a woman whose artistic accomplishments rivaled those of male counterparts and whose status allowed her to manipulate the conventions of gender.[14] Despite such discrimination, resentment, and opposition, Hosmer maintained one of the largest and most frequently visited studios in Rome and went on to become one of America's best-known expatriate artists.

Like Lewis and Hosmer, Sophia Hawthorne emphasizes in *Notes* artistic representations of strong women. A Domenichino painting of the Garden of Eden leads Sophia to describe Adam as "pitiful" and "unmanly," while "Eve is kneeling, and turns to the Creator with a much more dignified and respectable gesture of concern" (211). Inverting the standard hierarchy, Sophia's description asserts feminine strength in precisely the context, the postlapsarian garden, so often cited as the origin of woman's weakness. Here as elsewhere, Sophia emphasizes women as subjects rather than objects. Her aesthetic praises works that endow the depicted women with emotion that is believable and respectful. Her text also indicates that the line between the praiseworthy, respectful painting and the exploitative representation is easily transgressed. Of Raphael's *Fornarina* and a copyist she observed near the painting Sophia writes, "She is beautiful and lovable, spirited, warm, tender, and strong, glowing with Italian sunshine in perfect bloom. Of this wonderful picture the copyist was making a vulgar woman" (352).

Sophia Hawthorne's text emphasizes women's issues that are, as Warren writes, "portrayed as positive and are redefined from a new perspective, where they are not seen as trifles at all but as important instances of human involvement and moral power" ("Introduction" 7). In Sophia's art criticism, the feelings of women rendered in well-known historical or mythical contexts (annunciations, crucifixions, depositions) are important; the sympathetic responses of female spectators who, like Sophia herself, can *recognize* the validity of the subject's expression are equally significant. Thus women's perceptions not only become worthy subjects of serious art, but they also measure a work's greatness. Based on these criteria, Sophia makes distinctions with confidence between works that register as emotionally true and those that fail.

The successful portrait of a woman conveys a depth of feeling suitable to the experience, as demonstrated by the Madonna in Perugino's

Deposition: "The grief of all the bereaved mothers since Eve is concentrated in hers. She turns her head aside, for she cannot look at her crucified Son, and she does not care to look at anything else, so that her gaze is impersonal. She is conscious of the heavy weight of the beloved form; but she cannot weep more. Her grief is deeper than tears now, and she asks for no sympathy and wishes to hear no word" (380). This complex interpretation of a woman's painted visage is typical of *Notes;* the paintings Sophia lauds often provoke lengthy narrative contemplations. On the other hand, Titian's Magdalen elicits only curt contempt: "I do thoroughly detest the picture. Such a woman would be incapable of repentance. She is coarse and earthly in every fibre of her frame, and in every recess of her mind" (392). Convinced that "it is a portrait," and "sorry that Titian knew such a person and contemplated her so minutely," Sophia attacks what she sees as the misguided artistic practice of using favorite models for compositions without adequate reflection on whether the model is appropriate to the historical context (ibid.). Sophia, like Hosmer and Lewis, demands a deeper truth and harmony from art, a sense of veracity determined by her own experiences as a woman. She can concede that Titian's Magdalen is "painted so well" even as she protests the woman's depravity and asks of the finished piece, "How could it have been done?" (ibid.).

Removing the Veil

In the later pages of the travel narrative, Sophia reveals a fantasy of cleaning the cities she visits. Although this theme may be a reinscription of a familiar American preoccupation with the squalid (and stereotyped) aspects of the Italian land and people, it is significant in my reading as an indicator of how Sophia's journey and the process of textualizing it affected her. The desire to clean suggests hope for the future and posits, however provisionally, Sophia as the instrument of change. The cleaning metaphor first arises during her visit to Florence from a meditation on the fall of ancient Rome, in which Sophia proposes a common cause that accounts for every empire's fall: "It is the lack of love, of St. Peter's charity, which is the difficulty." As the passage continues, moving closer to home, America and Sophia herself become implicated: "Cannot a nation be based on [St. Peter's charity] and live forever? America might try it, but has made no sign yet. Italy, however, is not dead—only faint, and Italy alone is thoroughly civilized through and through, since immemorial ages. This I deeply feel, now that I am here; but something has soiled it. In its cities, especially, I have an irrepressible desire to wash them clean, and make them comfortable and fresh. I wish to have every stone scoured" (493). She becomes virtually obsessed with the notion of cleaning Italy, confessing a month later, "I wish I could cease to speak on this subject" (539). Not only does the housecleaning metaphor suggest a domestic sensibility, similar to that championed by Stowe in *Agnes of Sorrento,* in which the values of women and the home can be instituted in the political realm to redeem the larger culture, it also reproduces Sophia's emphasis on the visual. The stain of a debased society and its cruelty to its own people are rendered as visible dirt. Remove the ugliness you can see, by this logic, and you effectively wipe out the evils within.

Yet a later passage complicates a too-conventional reading of the housekeeping thematics, when Sophia describes a method of cleansing that operates outside the traditionally demarcated nineteenth-century woman's sphere. In a particularly lyrical passage that I would argue is the climactic scene of the narrative, not only does Sophia realize art's power to dissolve the grime of daily life, but she also revels in the opportunity to create (clean) publicly. Stopping in Bolsena on her way to Rome, she acquires the unabashed adoration of an audience and, like Harriet Hosmer encircled by her workmen, is centralized both spatially and emotionally as a redemptive force:

> After lunch we went out to sketch. I was soon beset with interested spectators—men, women, boys, girls, and babies in arms, all trying to look over my book. They were more nasty than I can by any means tell, with foulness inherited from the Romans probably, and at any rate very ancient. I could scarcely breathe such an atmosphere as they created, and armies of fleas attacked me besides. Yet, so potent is the human soul, that this beggarly crowd of Italians gave an impression of refinement and civilization, very old and settled civilization, by their manners and bearing. They were quiet and gentle and exceedingly courteous. They spoke in whispers and were deeply interested in my work, from an innate love of art, woven into their members and being. Their glorious eyes (which were clean) shone with delight at every line I drew which they recognized as true. I sketched the castle and the town beneath it, and they called by mellifluous names each house and wall. I told them I liked their castle very much, and they repeated to each other with pride that I said so. How infinitely pathetic and wonderful that they should enjoy their old stones for their beauty, when they have them instead of bread and raiment—only stones! (527)

In this powerful scene, one of the last recorded in her narrative, Sophia becomes the consummate artist, "shining" the eyes of her onlookers with every line she draws. Her art achieves "truth," as evidenced by the discerning eyes of the villagers, and Sophia establishes a common bond with a people she idealizes as civilized, refined, and innately enamored of art. She is successful as an artist at the same moment that she is able to reach out to a community in need. Indeed, her art *is* the agent of social change. Here her aesthetic argument conjoins the private and the public in a glorious union.

In the clean, shining eyes of these village people Sophia finds a kinship, a common love of art that seems to arise from the land itself. The "old and settled civilization" washes away surface dirt and gives the people an air of "refinement." Compare this depiction of a national character to Sophia's indictment of her own countrymen, whose behavior in St. Peter's cathedral seems to justify the worst stereotypes of the arrogant American abroad: "It was necessary to discontinue the custom [of displaying holy treasures], because the Americans and English behaved so indecorously during the ceremony—walking about, laughing and talking aloud, much to the horror of the devout worshippers, and certainly very much to the discredit of the manners and decency of both Protestant nations. I have no patience with them, because I should have seen [the ceremony] tonight, if they had shown proper respect to the faith of the Romans" (285). In the pages of *Notes,* a camaraderie develops between Sophia and a people who respect art, whereas the contemptuous behavior of her fellow Americans causes her to distance herself from them and to enforce this distance by using the term "them" to describe American travelers.

Although Sophia ends *Notes* with a familiar refrain—an allusion to some mysterious power Rome holds over those who visit—she also offers the unfamiliar, insinuating that she possesses the very knowledge that has eluded her predecessors.[15] Upon returning to Rome after three months in Florence, she contemplates the Eternal City's attraction, observing that "here I both feel how it all was, and, strange to say, I am also magnetized with the power that hovers invisibly in this air." The "power that hovers invisibly" provokes her to pose a question, then to answer it for herself but withhold the solution from the reader: "What, then, is this Rome that will hold sway over mankind, whether or no, in past or present time? I have an idea, but it is folded up in a veil, and I cannot take this moment to answer my question" (544). To the reader's loss, Sophia never divulges the answer, and *Notes* ends shortly after this suggestive visual metaphor. The text is "suddenly interrupted by illness" (549), specifically the illness of the Hawthornes' fifteen-year-old daughter, Una, who suffered from several severe bouts of malaria, the "Roman fever" noted by travel writers as a deadly blemish on an otherwise paradisiacal landscape.

As Sophia never returns to lift the veil, we are left to solve the mystery based on the closing image and the pages that precede it. I propose that the veil itself, rather than what it covers, is the answer. By leaving the veil unopened, Sophia points toward the representation—the veil in which she envelops her Italian experience in order to share it with her readers—rather than the experience itself. For Sophia Hawthorne, *Notes in England and Italy* suggests, the mysterious entity that transcends time and lures travelers of all ages to Rome is art, the inspired representations that apprentices travel far to copy and that all people might seek to understand and to emulate. What can come of such a pilgrimage is emblematized by the narrative itself. *Notes* documents the evolution of an empowered, American woman, inspired by Italian art to give voice to her aesthetic argument, to challenge her country and the world, and to present herself as the artist she wanted to be.

CHAPTER 5

"Closing Her Lips with Gentle Hand": Domesticated Artists in Constance Fenimore Woolson's "'Miss Grief'" and "The Street of the Hyacinth"

Not that poor Aaronna's poems were evil: they were simply unrestrained, large, vast, like the skies or the wind. Isabel was bounded on all sides, like a violet in a garden bed. And I liked her so. ("'Miss Grief'")

Constance Fenimore Woolson's Roman stories do not celebrate domesticity. Unlike Stowe and Sophia Hawthorne, Woolson finds no comfort in the nineteenth-century's established woman's sphere. Moreover, unlike Sedgwick and Fuller, she finds no cause for celebrating her nation's promise. In Woolson's stories, domesticity signifies most insistently as a tamed or limited state, constraining the female characters in her stories who struggle to break out of home and nation and into artistic independence. Indeed, her stories expose the cultural mythology at work behind the separate spheres imperative, demonstrating how thoroughly implicated the masculine sphere is in every aspect of a woman's life. Gender *roles* are clearly distinct in Woolson's work, but the spheres are fundamentally interconnected, with the patriarchy determining the limits of both. In her fiction the male marketplace enforces the limitations placed on women, while Italy—idealized in Stowe's and Hawthorne's texts—comes to signify a similar "business" of oppression. No longer a nurturing mother, the Rome of Woolson's stories embodies the patriarchy itself, a formidable state to which women artists are compelled to migrate but from which no successful escape can be made.

The speaker in my epigraph, the male critic who narrates Woolson's "'Miss Grief,'" articulates the central conflict plaguing the artist-heroines of Woolson's Roman stories; under a cultural logic of gendered spheres, women's professional decisions consign them either to the male or to the female domain. To seek independent expression is to be masculine; to accept a more dependent role as a domestic partner is consistent with social constructions of femininity.[1] The heroines of Woolson's Roman stories are women who desire the freedom to express themselves artistically, possessors of a transgressive ambition criticized by male authorities as wild, unpredictable, unruly, and uncivilized. The conservative choice for women is represented by Isabel, associated with the home and the controlled garden, the interior and ordered spaces of late-nineteenth-century domesticity. Despite attempts to negotiate an existence between the two extremes, the main characters of Woolson's stories are ultimately unable to occupy both sides of the binary, to be women and to be productive, free artists.

Two short stories by Woolson, "'Miss Grief'" (1880) and "The Street of the Hyacinth" (1882), take as their subject the woman artist whose pilgrimage to Rome results in a tragic confrontation with male aesthetic standards.[2] As a woman confronting the patriarchal artistic standards that marginalized or silenced her, Woolson constructed stories that expose the conflict and violence that inhabit three significations of "domestic." One applies to the home, specifically to the sphere accorded to nineteenth-century American women; a second is "pertaining to one's own country" in contrast to "foreign"; and the third and most important relates to a wild creature that has been tamed. Hardly the locus of warmth and salvation championed in nineteenth-century "separate spheres" rhetoric, the dark and ugly house in "The Street of the Hyacinth" is symbolically demolished at the end of the story as a "modern accretion" that "disfigure[s]" the nearby Pantheon (208). Similarly, Aaronna struggles throughout "'Miss Grief'" to conceal her humble lodgings from the wealthy narrator, only to have him ultimately track her down to "the most wretched quarters of the city, the abode of poverty, crowded and unclean" (266). As the stories make clear, the elitism of the male-dominated marketplace in art and literature relegates women artists to squalid conditions. The stories reveal economic class as an underpinning of gendered separatism.

Similarly, the Italian setting is deromanticized in these stories, exposed as a site whose meaning is determined by class and circumstance. For nineteenth-century America, Italy had become overdetermined, a nexus of artistic distinction and a golden land offering an idyllic life. As Raymond Noel observes tellingly in "The Street of the Hyacinth," "He had once said himself that the air was so soft and historic that nothing broke [in Rome]—not even hearts" (193). Noel speaks from a position of privilege—based on gender and economic status—and misinformation. As the story demonstrates, hearts do break in Rome, and especially in Rome (insofar as Rome embodies patriarchal power); the heroine's artistic passion is destroyed when classical, patriarchal standards, identified with Roman art, exclude her from the creative world. In their examination of the experiences of women artists, the stories expose the ties among travel, gender, class, and art.

Third, Woolson's short stories set in Rome explicitly critique the "domestic" harness that obliterates wildness or freedom, thereby destroying women's artistic expression. For her main characters, domestication cripples self-actualization and creative voice. In "The Street of the Hyacinth," Ettie Macks suffers for her creative independence, compelled by the story's end to give up her dream and perform the jobs her culture has deemed suitable for a woman. In "'Miss Grief,'" Aaronna Moncrief, like her manuscripts, dies and is buried. The tragic consequences of her female characters' confrontations with the men they seek out as guides suggest Woolson's conflicted feelings about mentorship. The stories critique male standards of artistic excellence by asking, what does it mean to have talent? And who decides? Indeed, Woolson's stories suggest that patriarchal artistic standards and the domestication of women are inseparable, that male success depends to a certain extent on the silencing of the "wild," "unrestrained" woman's voice. Such subjugation cripples her artist characters, who cannot be whole when denied their creative selves. Although Woolson indicts both the prescribed feminine sensibility and the rigid artistic standards that grew out of the nineteenth-century's construction of gender roles, ultimately, like her artistic heroines, she finds no way to synthesize her desires, no "home."

A Woman's Place

There *are* houses in Woolson's stories, structures that shelter her women artists as they struggle to navigate a world hostile to their ambitions. But the stories do not give us *homes,* in the nineteenth-century's idealized sense. According to Nancy Cott, the nineteenth-century home "was 'an oasis in the desert,' a 'sanctuary' where 'sympathy, honor, virtue are assembled,' where 'disinterested love is ready to sacrifice everything at the altar of affection' " (64). In Cott's argument, the sanctuary offered by the home depends upon its separation from "the cunning, treachery, and competition of the marketplace" (69). Aaronna Moncrief, the heroine of "'Miss Grief,'" and Ethelinda Faith Macks, in "The Street of the Hyacinth," inhabit austere domestic spaces that oppose the typical, sentimental conceptions of the home as a nurturing haven whose maintenance dominates a woman's time. Woolson's women have other constructions on their minds: artworks that can compete in the male-dominated art world. Their creative endeavors occupy them totally, leaving them little time to notice or bemoan squalid living conditions. Yet, as the stories make clear, the austerity within which Aaronna and Ettie live does not result from their inattention to domestic details; rather it arises from a gendered system that relegates women to a financially subordinate status. Once the fiction of the home's distinctness from the competitive marketplace is exposed, the houses lose their idealized status.

In "'Miss Grief,'" the story that was published first but seems to push the theme of the woman artist further, domestic spaces are alluded to tangentially. The central narrative action concerns Aaronna's efforts to solicit the unnamed narrator's help with her writing career. Referring to a drama she has written, Aaronna tells the narrator, a successful literary critic, "You will read it. Look at this room; look at yourself; look at all you have" (254). As the plot develops, the comforts of the narrator's living quarters—which include a fireplace, rich foods, fine wines, and a manservant who attends to all—are offered in striking contrast to Aaronna's poverty. Dubbed "Miss Grief" by the insensitive and flippant narrator, who judges the artist by her threadbare clothes, Aaronna attempts to keep her abode a secret, insisting on coming to him whenever they meet, but is found out when she becomes too ill to leave her bed. The narrator encounters Aaronna's companion in the street, discovers Aaronna's sickly condition, and offers to take the distraught old woman home: "Her shabby skirt was soon beside me, and, following her directions, the driver turned toward one of the most wretched quarters of the city, the abode of poverty, crowded and unclean. Here, in a large bare chamber up many flights of stairs, I found Miss Grief" (266).

In a belated effort to save her life, the narrator uses his financial resources to embellish Aaronna's apartment. Although "the wine, fruit, flowers and candles I had ordered made the bare place for the time being bright and fragrant," the gesture is not enough to cure the stricken artist, who confesses on her deathbed her reasons for seeking the narrator's assistance: " 'Did you wonder why I came to you? It was the contrast. You were young—strong—rich—praised—loved—successful: all that I was not. I wanted to look at you—and, imagine how it would feel. You had success—but I had the greater power' " (267, 268). The fruit and flowers cannot sustain Aaronna because they cannot compensate for the greater nourishment she has lacked as an artist. The narrator's complicity in this artistic starvation is both acknowledged and perpetuated after Aaronna's death, when he locks up her manuscripts and reads them occasionally "as a memento of my good fortune, for which I should continually give thanks. The want of one grain made all her work void, and that one grain was given to me. She, with the greater power, failed—I, with the less, succeeded" (269). The story leaves the reader to ponder the nature of the "one grain," a nourishment that may signify wealth or masculinity, two forces that are indistinguishable in the story.

A similar pattern gets worked out in "The Street of the Hyacinth," as Woolson again constructs a male critic, Raymond Noel, and a young female apprentice, Ettie Macks, who travels to Rome specifically to seek his guidance. The house in this story is a more prominent symbol, likened explicitly to the main character herself. Indeed, the successive transformations of the house mirror the stages of Ettie's professional development (or regression) until at the end of the story their fates are inextricable. The house's location on the street of the Hyacinth, which traverses a Roman quarter whose description opens the story, is of central importance. The street reflects its working-class residents as well as the expanding commerce that has infiltrated even this "narrow, winding, not overclean" corner of "the sacred city of the soul" (170). The sun, obstructed by buildings on either side of the lane, cannot reach the street, so that "looking up from the pavement was like looking up from the bottom of a well"; the well is not only dark but dirty, "owing to the easy custom of throwing from the windows a few ashes or other light trifles for the city refuse-carts, instead of carrying them down the long stairs to the door below" (ibid.).[3] Even the interior of Ettie's residence disappoints the art critic, Noel, who disapproves of a card reading "Miss Ettie F. Macks," which hangs on the front door. Ettie's unselfconscious proclamation of her identity flouts the conventions of Noel's aristocratic social circle: "'Why in the world doesn't she put her mother's card here instead of her own?' he said to himself. 'Or, if her own, why not simply "Miss Macks," without that nickname?'" (171). Cheryl Torsney has usefully pointed out that "Ettie's environment serves to suggest her consciousness in the way women's habitations normally serve as metaphors for states of mind in their writing" (*The Grief of Artistry* 122), yet it may be equally important to see Ettie's environment, both the street she lives on and her own decorative touches, as a very practical manifestation of her class and to recognize this financial status as both a condition determined by cultural forces and a fault held against her by Noel. Caught in a self-perpetuating cycle, Ettie is consigned to poverty because she is a woman and then blamed for a subordinate status beyond her control.

It is noteworthy that the narrator softens his criticism of Ettie's abode when he finds it remodeled into a school—a more appropriate and less threatening space than the studio of a young, female artist. Noel observes, "Even as a school-room it was more attractive than it had been before" (193–94). As Ettie takes on the culturally sanctioned role of schoolteacher,

Noel can comfortably inhabit her space. Ettie's final step toward domestic femininity, her acceptance of Noel's marriage proposal at the end of the story, reflects the fate of the entire street on which she lives. Noel tells her, "They are going to tear down your street of the Hyacinth. The Government has at last awakened to the shame of allowing all those modern accretions to disfigure the magnificent old Pagan temple. All the streets in the rear, up to a certain point, are to be destroyed. And the street of the Hyacinth goes first. You will be driven out" (208). When Ettie agrees to marry Noel soon thereafter, the street's doom resonates not only as a motivating force for Ettie's decision—clearly she is driven to choose Noel as a consequence of being "driven out" of the only home she can afford—but also as a symbol of Ettie's own fate. Her acceptance of Noel is described as "a great downfall," echoing the passage that follows, in which "The street of the Hyacinth experienced a great downfall, also. During the summer it was demolished" (209).

Thus the mythology of "separate spheres" breaks down in Woolson's stories, as the conditions of the home cannot be separated from the commercial and public affairs of men. The confinement of women to feminine roles (schoolteacher, wife) has very real, economic effects on their lives and determines, to a large extent, the kind of home they can inhabit. Taking the implications of this argument further, Aaronna's aunt in "'Miss Grief'" articulates the predatory power by which the narrator maintains his economic superiority: "And as to who has racked and stabbed her, I say you, *you*—YOU literary men!" (265-66). Blaming the narrator for Aaronna's impending death, the aunt makes the accusation both explicit and ghastly: "Vampires! you take her ideas and fatten on them, and leave her to starve" (266). Woolson proves the truth of this analogy in the Roman stories, both of which depict women artists whose careers must be stifled and who cannot attain economic independence. Ettie must marry in order to survive. Aaronna, whose story comes to a more extreme conclusion, dies so that the narrator may live. His "separate" sphere depends upon her submission. In a figurative sense, he needs her pitiful existence as a reminder of his "good fortune." More practically, he keeps her play in a "locked case" and claims, "When I die 'Armor' is to be destroyed unread" (269). Recognizing that Aaronna has a greater talent, the narrator's literary dominance—and the financial success it brings—can only be maintained if Aaronna Moncrief's brilliance is buried.

The narrator's vampiric power also casts him as the monstrous instigator of a perverse heterosexual union. Not surprisingly, during the story it is the narrator who maps heterosexuality onto his relationship with Aaronna, noting after a particularly humble reply on her part, "My chivalry was touched by this: after all, she was a woman" (260). Moved by his own "chivalry" to invite Aaronna to dinner, the narrator makes an offer that Aaronna reads accurately and to which she responds with a warning: "Yes, I will come. I am forty-three: I might have been your mother" (ibid.). Unlike the narrator, Aaronna maintains her professional focus and never conceptualizes their relationship in sexualized terms. Thus the depiction of the narrator as a vampire demonizes his personal relationship to Aaronna by suggesting the predatory implications of heterosexuality and his professional relationship to her as a critic/mentor. Significantly, he stands accused of fattening on her work, deriving his sustenance—blood—from the manuscripts she gives him. This symbolism becomes more gruesome when read against a later passage in which Aaronna asks that her manuscripts be buried with her, telling the narrator, "Don't look at them—my poor dead children!" (268). If Aaronna's offspring have nourished the bloodthirsty narrator, then his hunger has killed them, and the perversity by which he maintains his power and status is compounded.

Woolson's exposure of gender roles as culturally demarcated and separate spheres as economically enforced arises at a historical moment when the dominant culture was busy seeking a physiological basis for the gender hierarchy. Faced with a growing suffrage movement that contested women's subordination and relegation to the "private world," men like paleontologist Edward D. Cope were attempting to establish evidence of a physical weakness that would bar women from effective participation in politics. His 1888 essay, "The Relation of the Sexes to Government," included in *Why Women Do Not Want the Ballot,* asserts, "In women we find that the deficiency of endurance of the rational faculty is associated with a general incapacity for mental strain, and, as her emotional nature is stronger, that strain is more severe than it is in man under similar circumstances. Hence the easy breakdown under stress, which is probably the most distinctive feature of the female mind" (*Women's Rights* 167).

In opposition to Cope's insistence that "we find in man a greater *capacity* for rational processes" (ibid.), Woolson's stories depict women with rational capabilities *exceeding* those of the men they seek as mentors. Both Ettie and Aaronna are intellectual exemplars with astounding powers of memory and insight. When Aaronna recites a favorite passage from one of the narrator's stories, he remarks,

> Her very voice changed, and took, though always sweetly, the different tones required, while no point of meaning, however small, no breath of delicate emphasis which I had meant, but which the dull types could not give, escaped an appreciative and full, almost overfull, recognition which startled me. For she had understood me—understood me almost better than I had

> understood myself. It seemed to me that while I had labored to interpret, partially, a psychological riddle, she, coming after, had comprehended its bearings better than I had, though confining herself strictly to my own words and emphasis. (252–53)

Aaronna's powers of perception seem all the more remarkable because she has recognized the worth of a passage that, though the public "had never noticed the higher purpose of this little shaft," was "secretly [the narrator's] favorite among all the sketches from [his] pen" (252). Not only does Aaronna demonstrate an acute critical eye with regard to the narrator's work, which she knows by heart, but she can also recite her own play in its entirety. To the narrator's surprise, her voice makes the drama perfect: "And she carried me along with her: all the strong passages were doubly strong when spoken, and the faults, which seemed nothing to her, were made by her earnestness to seem nothing to me" (259). Aaronna's ability to emote surpasses more conventional portrayals of feminine "feeling" by successfully convincing a male critic, who is by his own admission conceited and cynical, of her work's value.

Similarly, Ettie can remember and reproduce Noel's discourse on the paintings they visit at a Roman gallery: "There he beheld, written out in her clear handwriting, all he had said of the Doria pictures, page after page of it; she had actually reproduced from memory his entire discourse of an hour" (186). As Noel accompanies Ettie to other galleries, he notes her persistence, dedication, and unwillingness to engage in personal conversation: "It was always very businesslike—they talked of nothing but the pictures; in truth her systematic industry kept him strictly down to the subject in hand. He learned that she made the same manuscript copies of all he said, and, when he was not with her, she went alone, armed with these documents, and worked hard. Her memory was remarkable" (188). Unlike Noel, who often lapses into personal, flirtatious observations about his protégée and her appearance, Ettie never strays from her industrious study of paintings and the critic's analysis of them. Her relentless ambition and integrity contrast with Noel's often flighty attitude toward work.

Critics have not made enough of Woolson's idealized speakers with their superior memories and miraculous voices. Sharon Dean observes that "the most predominant overtone is that Faith is not naive but rather is actively pursuing Noel. Time and again, outsiders acknowledge Faith to be clever or intelligent. She is, at least, smart enough to remember everything Noel has said to her about art" ("The Literary Relationship" 3). In this reading, Ettie's phenomenal memory indicates a cleverness that can only be interpreted as a strategy for catching a husband. The assumption that the intense attention Ettie pays to Noel is a form of romantic pursuit may not be surprising, given the way Woolson utilizes a similar series of events in her 1880 story "A Florentine Experiment." In that story the main character, Margaret Stowe, asks her male companion, Trafford Morgan, to instruct her in art. During the ensuing "lessons," Margaret seeks his opinion of various works of art and never lets his responses veer into the realm of explicit flirtation. As the story eventually makes clear, however, the true motivation for Margaret's "experiment" is to see whether she can form an attachment to Morgan and thereby cure herself of a previous, failed love. In the case of "A Florentine Experiment," the main character's interest in art—and corresponding ability to remain devoted to its contemplation—*is* a strategy with an ulterior, romantic motive.

The case with Ettie is quite different, as the details of Woolson's story attest. In "The Street of the Hyacinth," Ettie's artistic goals and accomplishments are clearly established, and her intellectual ability to absorb and remember Noel's critiques is underscored. Almost miraculously, she can remember details about the vast collections of art that the two visit in the many galleries of Rome: "[S]he soon knew the names and order of all the pictures in all the galleries, and had made herself acquainted with an outline, at least, of the lives of all the artists who had painted them" (188). Indeed the intellectual capabilities of Ettie and Aaronna constitute an important subversion, by which Woolson suggests the power these characters have over their mentors. Recognized by Joan Myers Weimer as a "spokeswoman for the first generation of American women writers, who saw themselves as artists" (ix–x), Woolson has also been discussed quite usefully as a writer whose work depicts "women made silly because no one has shown them how not to be silly: women whose choice is to dote on men or become men because they have not yet found another way" (Dean, "Homeward Bound" 26). Her women artists *do* suffer for their attempts to usurp male creative power, but, in these stories, they come across as anything but silly. Their ability to be dedicated both intellectually and emotionally to their work and to surpass in this respect male mentors who are more interested in chasing women and flirting with high society disputes the rhetoric of men like Cope and indicates the power and potential Woolson saw in the woman artist, even as she recognized an entrenched, patriarchal elitism within the literary and artistic worlds.

Woolson's characters are frustrated by this elitism; having journeyed to Rome, they discover that the artistic criteria held sacred by Rome and their male mentors will not accommodate their work. Noel believes that "Miss Macks, as an artist, would never do anything worth the materials she used" (192). Standing for patriarchal tradition, Noel praises technique; Ettie, on the other hand, insists, "Of course, the subject, the idea is the important thing; the execution is secondary" (190). The narrator of "'Miss Grief'" echoes Noel's aesthetics: "[W]riters are as apt to make much of the 'how,' rather than the 'what,' as painters, who, it is well known, prefer an exquisitely rendered representation of a commonplace theme to an imperfectly executed picture of even the most striking subject" (256). The implication that men stand for form (despite a "commonplace theme") while women endorse ("the most striking") content offers the possibility of a counter-aesthetics that would value art produced by women—or anyone forbidden access to training and prestige. Further, it reveals how economics influences art, as men possess the financial means—as well as the cultural sanction—to study the "execution" they prize and to demonstrate their initiation into a privileged tradition, while women are systematically refused this training. Woolson's investigation of Rome's art culture exposes a closed system that dooms women to exclusion and subordination; at the same time she suggests the inadequacy of this system to gauge a woman's abilities. Thus, although "'Miss Grief'" appears to be the story of a woman artist with "talent" and "The Street of the Hyacinth" the same narrative repeated with a character who lacks talent, the distinction is specious.[4] What matters, what cannot be denied, is the *desire* of these women to create.

In Woolson's stories, the opinion of the male mentors is unreliable, as a suggestive metaphor in "'Miss Grief'" illustrates.[5] Frustrated when she refuses his editorial suggestions, the narrator claims that Aaronna "simply could not see the faults of her own work, any more than a blind man can see the smoke that dims a patch of blue sky" (259). The metaphor reveals the narrator's own lack of vision. The blind man in the analogy, of course, cannot see the sky any more than he can see the smoke. While the outside observer might criticize this lack of discernment, to the blind man himself the distinction would have no use value. As both sky and smoke are denied him, he has no reason to discriminate between the gray and the blue. He finds other ways to negotiate the world. The distinction between colors matters only to the critic and, in this metaphor, appears idle and ridiculous. In "The Street of the Hyacinth," we are similarly confronted with evidence that undermines the definitiveness of the male critic's perspective. Although Noel emphatically points out that Ettie's art is "extremely and essentially bad," he is also forced to acknowledge, to his surprise, that "the most incorruptibly honest teacher in Rome" actually "seemed to think that Miss Macks had talent" (181, 183).

Thus the question of whether Ettie has "talent" becomes a useless inquiry. As "talent" is determined by a closed group in the story and dependent upon access to a particular form of training, the answer is predetermined. The pivotal question that concerned Woolson in her fiction, as Cheryl Torsney has pointed out, is "Where does art lead?" (*The Grief of Artistry* 61). The energy of the stories lies in the drive of Woolson's women to establish artistic careers for themselves, against all odds. Ettie and Aaronna do not want a separate or subordinate artistic domain—domestic arts or crafts—but seek full acceptance into the public (and commercial) art world. This goal necessitates the pilgrimage they make and determines the impressions they receive once there. Art leads them, in a practical sense, to Rome.

"It Is Only the Rich Who Go Away": The Economics of Travel

Like the women artists in her stories, Woolson never returned to the United States after her pilgrimage to Rome in 1879. For her, as for artist-heroines, the journey and its duration were matters of artistic necessity. In the case of Aaronna and Ettie, not only are they required to go to Rome to confront male critics (and criticism) where they live, they are also confined to Rome after they arrive, as they cannot afford to return home. Their lack of mobility makes them, as Joan Myers Weimer has pointed out, exiles rather than travelers. The difference is crucial. The freedom associated with travel is denied the exile, who is compelled for philosophical, political, or practical reasons to remain abroad. More important for my argument are the ways gender and class enforce a state of exile, reserving the status of traveler for the wealthy and privileged. A secondary definition of the term "exile" as "waste or devastation of property; ruin, utter impoverishment" reinforces this reading, as Woolson's characters *are* ruined and impoverished by patriarchal power. If, as Torsney has pointed out, "Woolson lived abroad to economize" (ibid., 33), then her journey would seem to be, at least in part, a forced relocation rather than purely a pleasure trip. Furthermore, if "her hope of meeting Henry James was one factor that impelled her to travel to Europe" (Weimer xxi), Italy became her destination more as a matter of professional and artistic necessity than choice. It is hardly surprising that Rome is depicted in her stories as a hostile city that traps exiled, working-class women. Woolson's Roman scenes seem far removed from the golden idylls of Arcadia invoked in so many American texts of the early- and middle-nineteenth century.

Ettie Macks and Aaronna Moncrief travel to a Rome defined by its affinity with the Western artistic tradition and its hospitality to the male authorities they seek as mentors. Rather than the home of Catholicism and the pope, or of ancient Roman republicanism, Woolson's Rome functions primarily as an embodiment of male artistic values that her characters must negotiate in order to succeed as artists. As a female apprentice, Ettie's relationship to Rome is entirely different from Raymond Noel's. She accepts an impoverished existence there in the service of her larger goal, to become an artist, while Noel emphasizes the more typical, romanticized aspects of travel: "[H]e was very fond of the old streets, and was curious to see whether she would notice the colors and outlines that made their picturesqueness. She noticed nothing but the vegetable stalls, and talked of nothing but her pictures" (180). As a woman responsible for bringing food home to her ailing mother, Ettie must attend to the quality of the produce rather than the city's aesthetics. Yet she shows equal concern for her career, which makes William Vance's observation about this passage surprising: "Neither Rome nor Italy is strange to Woolson, but rather people like Miss Macks who go there wholly blind to its special character (the art critic cannot make Ettie see the beauty of the vegetable markets; all she thinks of are the prices)" (*America's Rome* II:255). The apparent misreading, the substitution of "prices" for "pictures," is striking in light of the story's central conflict. Ettie's sole purpose in coming to Rome is to break the chains that bind her to domesticity and attempt to be taken seriously as an artist, but once there she is read in terms of a typically "feminine" role and then criticized for her failure to conform to the conventions of the (masculine) tourist. She is *not* thinking of the prices, but of her artwork. Yet she is chastised for allowing a stereotypically feminine concern to "blind" her to what a more sensitive (male) observer would notice.

Noel's gender and class enable a certain indulgence in the way he perceives his surroundings: "Noel was . . . an artist—that is, a literary one. But he had been highly successful in his own field, and it was understood, also, that he had an income of his own by inheritance, which, if not opulence, was yet sufficiently large to lift him quite above the *res angusta* of his brethren in the craft" (183). As a man with inherited wealth, Noel would neither have to attend to practical matters nor be obligated to earn his living, leaving him free to browse the city for picturesqueness. A young woman from farm country, Ettie has a different relationship to European travel and to mobility: "It took a good deal to get here in the first place," she tells Noel, "for we are poor" (179). With her twice-widowed mother, Ettie explains, she came from the West: "Tuscolee Falls is the name of our town. We had a farm there, but we did not do well with it after Mr. Spurr's [her stepfather's] death, so we rented it out" (173). Financial pressures follow Ettie throughout the story, constantly informing her decisions and determining her relationship to Rome.[6]

Ettie has struggled to fund her trip to Rome because she sees it as compulsory to her artistic training. In fact, Raymond Noel serves as both the catalyst for the journey and the reward Ettie expects on arrival. As she tells him, she received the imperative to leave America while reading his critical work: "As you seemed to think, Mr. Noel, that no one could do well in painting who had not seen and studied the old pictures over here, I made up my mind to come over at any cost" (174). She underscores this point several times, insisting "it was your writings that brought me here" and declaring emphatically, "Why, Mr. Noel, I came to Europe to see you!" (174, 178). When Noel tries to disentangle himself from her with a stereotypical, tourist's platitude, "I hope you will find Rome all you expected, and I am sure you will; all people of imagination like Rome," she does not let him off so easily: "Rome will not be at all what I expected if *you* desert me" (178). Rome's sole value to Ettie is that it houses Noel; his value is inestimable to her, for he can initiate her into the elite ranks of the art world.

Ettie's dedication to her work allows her to overlook the reality of the Rome she can afford to inhabit: "We get along with it because we must; there seems to be no other way to live in Rome. The idea of having only a story of a house, and not a whole house to ourselves, is dreadful to mother; she cannot get used to it. And with so many families below us—we have a clock-mender, a dress-maker, an engraver, a print-seller, and a cobbler—and only one pair of stairs, it does seem to me dreadfully public" (176). Ettie's Rome is both pragmatic and crowded. She devotes herself to her work even as she is surrounded by residents who must live with theirs. There is no doubt about Ettie's working-class status; she is no tourist. Thus when Noel asserts, "Threads do not break in Rome. He had once said himself that the air was so soft and historic that nothing broke there—not even hearts," it is not Ettie's "air" that he is describing, but the air breathed by the upper classes. Rome is not soft or historic for her; quite the contrary, Rome requires so much work that Ettie's daily cares eclipse the symbolic value of the landmarks around her: "One afternoon in March Miss Macks was coming home from the broad, new, tiresome piazza Indipendenza; the distance was long, and she walked with weariness" (208). The new piazza is notable more for the tedious crossing of it than for the republican promise or historical event it commemorates.

Ettie's heart breaks in Rome under the strain of a twin burden: her obligation to support her sick mother and the discouragement of art teachers whose help she vainly solicits. After her art career collapses, financial obligations again determine her course. The traveler's prerogative—to return home—is unavailable to her: "I doubt if my mother could bear the voyage now. We have no one to call us back but my brother, and he has not been with us for years, and would not be if we should return; he lives in California. We sold the farm, too, before we came. No; for the present, at least, it is better for us to remain here" (197). She remains in Rome to open her school and eventually to marry Noel when the school itself, her home and livelihood, is destroyed. The Pantheon, representative of classical aesthetics and ancient pagan worship, wins the battle against the encroaching streets around it, despite their commercial and residential vitality. The street of the Hyacinth is destroyed so that it will no longer "disfigure" the traditional simplicity of the monument, much as Ettie's artistic flame must be extinguished so that Noel's can continue to blaze.[7]

Rome has a much less obvious presence in "'Miss Grief,'" where it is invoked in name more than in detail or imagery. For the narrator, the city is appealing primarily for the active social life it offers. "I had a large number of acquaintances there," the narrator boasts, "both American and English, and no day passed without its invitation" (248). His wealth essentially isolates him from the country he inhabits, so that he associates with his own compatriots and has little interaction with Italian life and culture.[8] Aaronna, immersed in a "crowded and unclean" Roman neighborhood, experiences no such isolation. Moreover, like Ettie, Aaronna has no option of leaving town, so on her deathbed she must beg the narrator on behalf of her elderly aunt, "Help her to return home—to America: the drama will pay for it. I ought never to have brought her away" (268). The tragic truth is that the drama cannot fund the aunt's travel, for the narrator has lied about having sold it to a publisher. However, the deathbed scene serves Woolson as an opportunity to express a rarely seen and cynical nationalism. Referring to his lie about the drama's supposed publication, the narrator pointedly asks the reader, "What was I to answer? Pray, what would you have answered, puritan?" (266). The context and the label, "puritan," seem to undermine patriotic sentiment by foregrounding a particularly austere tradition in American culture. Such references are few in these two Roman stories, which do not concern themselves much with America's national traits. Here, the question and the cynical form of address underscore the narrator's insecurity about his own behavior. His eagerness to justify his dishonesty by lashing out at the (American, judgmental) reader may suggest his guilt for not having worked harder to see the drama published.

As Torsney points out, "'Miss Grief'" is "the first story [Woolson] published after her mother's death and her own removal abroad" (*The Grief of Artistry* 72), which perhaps explains Rome's minor role in the action. By the time she published "The Street of the Hyacinth" two years later, she had had more opportunity to ponder the city's importance to her narrative themes.[9] As I have argued, the city ultimately represents patriarchal tradition, which complicates Torsney's assertion that for Woolson, as for Elizabeth Barrett Browning, "Italy came to be 'the nurturing matria of a "woman of genius"'" (ibid., 107). Torsney borrows the phrase "nurturing matria" from Sandra Gilbert's essay, "From *Patria* to *Matria:* Elizabeth Barrett Browning's Risorgimento," which explores the construction of Italy as a "woman country" by nineteenth-century women writers. Referring to Italy's "special status as the home, even the womb, of European art," Gilbert contrasts the "natural emotiveness of this mother country" with "the icy artifice of Victorian culture" and refers to "the qualities women writers have sought in Italy—a land that feels, that feeds, that makes art, and that unmakes hierarchies" (197, 207). Motherly though it may be to other nineteenth-century women writers, Italy has none of these characteristics in Woolson's Roman stories, where artist-heroines seek warmth and nurturing but find only the rigid walls of patriarchy manifested in stern mentors and impoverished neighborhoods.

In representing the artistic world of Rome as male, Woolson's work revises the gendered relationship between Italy and the United States as it has traditionally been conceptualized. Nathalia Wright paraphrases Henry James's gendering of nations thus: "In contrast to the 'good married matron' England and the 'magnificent man' Switzerland, Italy was, he promptly reported, 'a beautiful, dishevelled nymph'" (200). With Italy comfortably coded female, literature of the encounter between Italy and the United States could assert American masculinity, a paradigm that informs much nineteenth-century travel writing and also provides Gilbert with a maternal Italy to serve as a nurturing force for women writers.[10] In Woolson's reconceptualization, however, the masculine power structure of both countries ostracizes those women who are dissatisfied with the domesticity prescribed for them. The Rome Ettie flees to is as much a masculine haven as the America she left behind, a city where critics like Noel "lived up with a good deal of determination to [their] own standard of what was manly" (198).

Indeed, Woolson seems to have been unable to feel at home in either country, and even her attempt to deliteralize home by telling Henry James, "Your writings are my country, my real home" (quoted in Weimer xxi), left her with the challenge of accommodating herself to a masculine space. As criticism has established, for James and his American characters, Italy is central to the process of self-realization: "In going to Italy, Anglo-Saxons in James' fiction are thus potentially completing their experience, developing all their faculties" (Wright 219). For Woolson's Aaronna and Ettie, the result is precisely the opposite, as both characters are denied their artistic faculties in Rome and move away from self-realization rather than toward it. If we accept Mary P. Edwards Kitterman's convincing argument that "to James it was clear that the masculine imagination was superior to the feminine" (46), we find that Woolson was left with no sanctuary, no space that would validate both her existence as a woman and her ambition as an artist. Unfortunately, all of the homes—America, Rome, James's texts—Woolson sought to inhabit were controlled by masculine forces, and all were implicated in the cultural imperative that sought to domesticate her.

"Bounded on All Sides": Domesticity as Subjugation

In "'Miss Grief,'" the narrator's description of Isabel as "bounded on all sides" suggests the confinement fundamental to femininity. The distance between "bounded" and "bound" is short, both rhetorically and culturally. Woolson's Roman stories describe a world in which the restrictions advocated by men, the femininity they project onto women to make themselves comfortable, translates into bondage for the woman artist, a position of extreme *dis*-comfort that the characters must accept when they perceive no other options. As a "violet in a garden," the artist is denied her freedom and subjectivity, refused a central component of her identity. The creative energy that the male critic seeks to exorcise or subdue is more than a hobby or sideline for Woolson's artist characters. Art serves as the primary motivator in their lives; they construct themselves around this pivotal desire. Removing it works as a kind of dismemberment, after which, though they may survive, they can never be whole.

For Aaronna, life has no meaning if she is denied the right to be an artist. She tells the narrator, after he has praised her manuscript, "If your sentence had been against me, it would have been my end," then continues, "I should have destroyed myself." The narrator's response, uttered "in a tone of disgust," demonstrates his mainstream sensibility as well as his ignorance of Aaronna's situation: "Then you should have been a weak as well as a wicked woman." She counters, "Oh no, you know nothing about it. I should have destroyed only this poor worn tenement of clay. But I can well understand how you would look upon it. Regarding the desirableness of life, the prince and the beggar may have different opinions" (258). Aaronna recognizes that the narrator's princely rank entitles him not only to social prominence but also to literary success. As a woman artist, she has been relegated to the status of beggar; her economic class confines her to "the most wretched quarters of the city"; furthermore, she has to beg the narrator to read her drama (266). When he resists her request, she asks him, "Look at me, and have pity," then refuses to sit down until he gives his promise. She realizes the tactics she must employ to garner his attention but asserts calmly, "I have no shame in asking. Why should I have? It is my last endeavor; but a calm and well-considered one" (254). There is no question about Aaronna's commitment to her work. She will (and must) risk all for the chance of its success and forfeit life altogether if her work cannot succeed. Indeed, her life is so intimately tied to her work that when the narrator praises her efforts and gives her hope, "her whole frame [is] shaken by the strength of her emotion" (257). When the manuscripts stagnate at the narrator's apartment, she weakens and eventually dies.

Ettie also makes sacrifices toward a similar ambition, which lead Noel to observe, by way of consoling her after they have married and she has given up her artistic career, "But the heights upon which you had placed yourself, my dear, were too superhuman" (290). Ettie, like Aaronna, was empowered by the scale of her ambition to overcome obstacles and arrive in Rome but is ultimately doomed to be silenced through a process of domestication. The threat they pose to the male artists is precisely this willingness to dare, without fear, that stands in opposition to the relative conservatism of men who praise training, form, and tradition—all that gives value to the predictable, "exquisitely rendered representation." Another story Woolson wrote from abroad, "At the Chateau of Corinne" (1886), displays in full detail the attitude of the man who fears a woman's creative "wildness" and needs to contain it.

"At the Chateau" takes place in Switzerland rather than Italy but again explores the trap that imprisons the woman artist. In a frequently quoted passage, John Ford seeks to undermine Mrs. Winthrop's desire to compose poetry by presenting her with a gendered construction of creativity:

> We do not expect great poems from women any more than we expect great pictures; we do not expect strong logic any more than we expect brawny muscle. A woman's poetry is subjective. But what cannot be forgiven—at least in my opinion—is that which I have called the distinguishing feature of [your] volume, a certain sort of daring. This is its essential, unpardonable sin. Not because it is in itself dangerous; it has not force enough for that; but because it comes, and can be recognized at once as coming, from the lips of a woman. For a woman should not dare in that way. (233)

Ford betrays anxiety when he moves from a "natural" order into an invective against women who seek to transgress established boundaries. If, in fact, the natural order is immutable, why must he warn off the woman who dares to do differently? Besides, if it lacks "force," why is this "daring" so threatening? Ford's compulsion to condemn the literary efforts of women like Mrs. Winthrop may suggest his fear that these efforts will not always self-destruct. A "daring" artistic feat that flouts convention and demonstrates precisely what traditional creativity is *not,* perhaps exposes the artistic rigidity (and cowardice) that characterized the mainstream art world of Ford's day. Equally threatening would be the suggestion that the "natural" state of gender roles is, in fact, a cultural construction, one that could be dismantled by a daring woman.

The narrator in "'Miss Grief'" attempts for similar reasons to domesticate Aaronna's work and to make it conform to the masculine parameters that have permitted his success: "I would alter and improve [the drama] myself, without letting her know: the end justifies the means. Surely the sieve of my own good taste, whose mesh had been pronounced so fine and delicate, would serve for two. I began; and utterly failed." Despite his training and insider status—his "sieve" that weeds out bad literary taste—the narrator's powers are useless when applied to Aaronna's work: "I could not succeed in completing anything that satisfied me, or that approached, in truth, Miss Grief's own work just as it stood" (264). Rather than acknowledge a talent so different from his own, the narrator decides to try editing another piece of writing, with similar results. The fruitless endeavors confront the narrator with a quandary, a dichotomy in which he can choose neither option: "I was forced at last to make up my mind that either my own powers were not equal to the task, or else that her perversities were as essential a part of the work as her inspirations, and not to be separated from it" (265). The narrator's rhetoric places on one hand his own weakness and on the other an inspiration that must be vilified as perversity.[11]

His solution is to show the work to Isabel, his "bounded violet," which does nothing to solve the riddle but does reaffirm his masculine power and return him to a universe ordered according to gender.[12] When the narrator tells Isabel, "They were written by a woman," Isabel responds reassuringly, "Her mind must have been disordered, poor thing!" Although Isabel defends her lover's value system by describing the works as "hopelessly mixed and vague," the narrator recognizes that Aaronna's writing is "not so much vague as vast." The vastness is what troubles him, yet he does not share this thought with Isabel: "I knew that I could not make Isabel comprehend it, and (so complex a creature is man) I do not know that I wanted her to comprehend it" (ibid.). Rather than resolve the conflict Aaronna's work forces him to confess, which would require accepting either the inadequacy of his own powers or the strength of Aaronna's "perversities," the narrator buries the whole issue by slipping into the comforting contemplation of Isabel's likeness to a garden flower. Similarly, he buries Aaronna's work, locking it up so that it can never be published. The only solution that allows the narrator to retain his illusions about himself and the prerequisites for "good" writing is the utter and fatal domestication of Aaronna's art.

Ultimately, the "perversity" of her work, its "vast" ambition, is so threatening to the established order that it must be kept "in a locked case" and, after the narrator's death, "destroyed unread" (269).

Domestication is precisely what John Ford advocates, in "At the Chateau of Corinne," as a man's "natural" response to a woman's "daring":

> Thinking to soar, she invariably descends. Her mental realm is not the same as that of man; lower, on the same level, or far above, it is at least different. And to see her leave it, and come in all her white purity, which must inevitably be soiled, to the garish arena where men are contending, where the dust is rising, and the air is tainted and heavy—this is indeed a painful sight. Every honest man feels like going to her, poor mistaken sibyl that she is, closing her lips with gentle hand, and leading her away to some far spot among the quiet fields, where she can learn her error, and begin her life anew. (234)

In Ford's fantasy, romantic love silences a woman and removes her from the sphere in which she wants to contend. Far away from the public (male) realm—where men interact, struggle, and succeed—in the "quiet fields," a woman is safe from influences that might hurt her—or allow her to grow. Ford's analogy serves as a blueprint for what eventually happens to Katharine Winthrop when she accepts the "error" of wanting to be a poet. To Ford's command, "You will write no more," she responds, "I will promise" (246). The story's final scene depicts a chatty John Ford, an unnamed visitor, and a completely silent Katharine, who is addressed by Ford but not permitted to respond.

A similar fate befalls Ettie when the art teacher who tells her to "throw away [her] brushes and take in sewing" (196) ultimately gets his way. By the story's end, Ettie has relinquished artistic study entirely, and the last image shows her completely caged and domesticated, substituting the illusion of freedom for the creative freedom she pursued so passionately when the story began. In the story's final paragraphs, Ettie's desires are completely eclipsed by those of Raymond Noel and her mother, Mrs. Spurr. Noel gets his girl without the inconvenience of her artistic aspirations; Mrs. Spurr gets to enjoy the advantages of Noel's economic class and return (following a brief period of mourning for her son) to her outrageous manner of dress. Ettie exists now as wife and daughter, the identity "artist" erased so completely that she fades silently into the background. This final portrait seems all the more regrettable when contrasted with the talkative and assertive Ettie who arrived hopefully in Rome and struggled valiantly toward her artistic goals through much of the narrative.

In order to assume an appropriately feminine demeanor, Ettie must lose her assertiveness. Fellow travelers on her initial voyage to Europe say of Ettie, "If she was a little more womanly—that is, if she would not look at everything in such a direct, calm, impartial, impersonal sort of way—she would be almost pretty" (176). Later, when she has resigned herself to the role of schoolteacher, Noel remarks how attractive she looks: "The expression of her face had greatly altered. The old direct, wide glance was gone; gone also was what he had called her over-confidence; she looked much older. On the other hand, there was more grace in her bearing, more comprehension of life in her voice and eyes" (194). Ettie's submission to constraining forces means, for Noel, that she becomes "pretty" to the extent that she loses what is "direct" about her character, including her art. She must abandon what Noel reads as "over-confidence" to be domesticated into a graceful, passive acceptance of her station. The irony is that Noel finds her most attractive after the combined forces of poverty and sexism have beaten her down. Ettie's life seems a literalized example of the figurative expression "housebroken."

Katharine Winthrop also becomes more "womanly" in her suitor's eyes when she has been properly harnessed. Indeed, Ford can tender his marriage proposal only after Katharine has become destitute: "I am sorry on your account that your fortune is gone; but on my own, how can I help being glad? It was a barrier between us. . . . I doubt if I should ever have surmounted it. Your loss brings you nearer to me. . . . Now if you are my wife—and a tenderly loved wife you will be—you will in a measure be dependent upon your husband, and that is very sweet to a self-willed man like myself" (246). When Katherine is stripped of her free will (or self-will), she becomes the perfect woman and wife. Only Aaronna escapes incarceration in marriage, but she must sacrifice her life to gain this "freedom." The progression of the stories chronologically, from "'Miss Grief'" to "The Street of the Hyacinth" to "At the Chateau of Corinne" (also a marriage tale) may suggest that Woolson saw less of a way out for her women characters as time passed and she saw more of Europe.[13] Although Aaronna dies without seeing her manuscripts published, she certainly represents the least domesticated of Woolson's artist-heroines; she practices her art for as long as she lives, believes she has succeeded (because the narrator has lied to her), and never has to trade in her art for a husband and economic survival.

Of course, it would be counterproductive to read too much liberatory potential into a character whose success, or subversion, is death. My point is to propose a thematic progression in Woolson's portrayals of women artists. The heroine of Woolson's novel *Anne,* published serially between 1880 and 1882 and written before her European stories, seems to fare better than

Aaronna, Ettie, and Katharine. Cheryl Torsney argues that Anne's "narrative talents grow until, at the climax of the novel, Anne demonstrates her new mastery of narrative form" ("Traditions" 178). Whereas Torsney concedes that "writing her own text of self and arriving at her own identity has not been easy for Anne" (ibid.), this resolution became all but impossible for the characters who succeeded her. From Anne's construction of self to Aaronna's death to the marital self-sacrifice of Ettie and Katharine seems a painful journey that probes ever more deeply into the subjugating potential of the nineteenth-century's rigid gender roles.

Master and Disciple

It seems impossible to talk about Constance Fenimore Woolson without discussing the theme of mentorship, and impossible to talk about mentors in her work without bringing up Henry James. Yet it also seems important to resist falling into the trap of relegating Woolson to a minor status alongside the great James. Torsney points out that Woolson's "life and writing have always been marginalized, have always been read as ancillary to James's" and that "Woolson . . . has been remembered as the journeywoman, the protégée, who relied on James for guidance" (ibid., 170). It is equally important to me to avoid reductive biographical readings that seek only to note parallels between art and life.[14] Critical discussions of Woolson and James as the real-life equivalents of May Bartram and John Marcher in "The Beast in the Jungle" are common enough that no more is needed on the subject. Any discussion of James seems to risk displacing Woolson, yet the thematic correspondence between their works demands attention. Between 1880 and 1888, both writers published stories that take as their central conflict the relationship between mentor and student.

Both James and Woolson were compelled to work out, over and over, the related concepts of apprenticeship and mastery. In the work of both, moreover, the power relationship between master and disciple intersects with the power dynamics of gender. This thematic correspondence is worth pursuing, as the work of each author sheds light upon that of the other. James published "The Lesson of the Master" in 1888, two years after Woolson's "At the Chateau of Corinne" came out. In 1888 James also published his biographical work, *Partial Portraits,* a collection of sketches about selected writers—George Eliot, Anthony Trollope, Ralph Waldo Emerson, Robert Louis Stevenson, Guy de Maupassant—which included an essay titled "Miss Woolson." Clearly, during the 1880s the two writers were much concerned with the mentorship theme and with each other. In contrast to the critical tendency to subordinate Woolson as the apprentice or to offer her historical relationship with James as some magical key to understanding her work, I want to examine how Woolson's stories foreground and develop a theme that remains conveniently uninterrogated in James's work.

James's "Lesson of the Master" portrays Paul Overt, a young, apprentice writer whose life is dramatically altered following a series of encounters with an influential and successful older author, Henry St. George. The master teaches his protégé two crucial lessons, one explicit and the other implied, both betraying the privileges of the male artist. The explicit and intentional lesson, alluded to in the title, is a warning to Overt about the dangers of selling out: "[T]ake my lesson to heart—for it is a lesson. . . . Don't become in your old age what I have in mine—the depressing, the deplorable illustration of the worship of false gods." He defines these "false gods" as material comforts: "money and luxury and 'the world'" (93). Notably, a young *woman* who also harbors literary ambitions, Marian Fancourt, is not taken so seriously by the "master." In her case, the teacher/master St. George assumes the role of "lord and master" and, rather than warning her about the temptations of success, dismisses Miss Fancourt's artistic ambitions and makes her instead into his wife.

This more insidious, gendered lesson underlies the plot and fuels the narrative action for much of the story. In repeated conversations, St. George conveys to Overt and to the reader that artistic prowess and rights are (and must be) transmitted along an all-male line of inheritance. As Overt becomes enamored of Miss Fancourt, St. George cautions him to steer clear of romantic love, insisting that women "interfere with perfection," that they "haven't a conception of such things" as literary works. Resisting his master's argument, Overt objects, "Surely they on occasion work themselves," to which St. George responds, "Yes, very badly indeed. Oh, of course, often they think they understand, they think they sympathize. Then it is they're most dangerous" (116). Overt persists in his questioning: "Are there no women who really understand—who can take part in a sacrifice?" St. George's answer crystallizes the patriarchal view of women's role in artistic production: "How can they take part? They themselves are the sacrifice. They're the idol and the altar and the flame" (119). Relegated to a position of illusory power, Miss Fancourt need not trouble herself about the choice between integrity and greed. Constructed as an object with value only in relation to men, she is cast either as an impediment to artistic creativity or as a harmless image that cannot participate in a man's domain, but never as an artist. As objects rather than subjects, women can be controlled. The James story charts this lesson's impact on

Overt, who, duly inspired by his teacher, goes on to attempt a true work of genius, leaving Miss Fancourt behind to make wedding plans and fawn over other people's writing. In contrast, Woolson's stories pursue the implications of this lesson on the women whom it dismisses, charting the fate of apprentice female artists after they learn the sobering truth from their masters. The implicit lesson, artistic production's sexist underpinnings, becomes explicit in Woolson's work.

Raymond Noel, too cowardly to teach the lesson directly in "The Street of the Hyacinth," sends Ettie the message that she cannot succeed as an artist first by sending her to "the most incorruptibly honest teacher in Rome" (183) and then by mailing her a pointed selection of books. His dirty work is eventually done, not by the teacher, who falls in love with Ettie, but by the cumulative weight of the books and Ettie's own experiences in Rome. "Knowing the world as I now know it," she explains to her ineffectual mentor, "I see that it was all that could have been expected" (196). The lesson Ettie learns from Noel is that she cannot defeat patriarchal power, that she has no choice but to resign herself to the second master who falls in love with her, that male teachers can conceptualize her only as an object of desire. Ettie's role is that outlined by St. George; she shall be the altar at which Noel makes his artistic sacrifices. Similar to the "altar of affection" Nancy Cott locates in the idealized nineteenth-century home, the altar of artistic sacrifice renders women symbols rather than agents. Thus women sacrifice their individuality to become constants against which men can define and strengthen themselves. Even Aaronna, though she manages to escape marriage and the concomitant relinquishing of art, gets appropriated and objectified by her master, who keeps her work "as a memento" and who refers to her in the story's last line as "*my* poor dead, 'unavailable,' unaccepted 'Miss Grief' " (269, emphasis added). The rhetoric casts Aaronna in the same position as the other two women who become wives—as the possession of a man.

Woolson's stories differ from James's by acknowledging a crucial difference between the power structure that keeps women subordinated to men and the subordination of the disciple to the master. The disciple is permitted, even encouraged, to grow artistically and eventually displace his master. Gender constructions, on the other hand, insist that a woman's weakness is essential and unconquerable. Her only option is to accept her subordinate status and occupy the position of humble wife, thus garnering for herself the fictitious power romantic discourse produces. John Ford commands Katharine, "You may not care for me; you may never care. But only let me see you accept for your own sake what I have said, in the right spirit, and I will at least ask you to care, as humbly and devotedly as man ever asked woman. For when she is her true self she is so far above us that we can only be humble" (235). The convolutions of Ford's logic allow him to assert that Katharine's "true self" will appear only after she has accepted his sermon on the weaknesses of her poetry—that is, someone else's construction of her identity. He ascribes to this true self a superiority, which upon examination turns out to be the power to submit. Placed on the altar against her will and forced to relinquish her individuality and her passions, Katharine achieves the hollow victory that exemplifies the fate of the woman artist in Woolson's work.

The theme of the woman artist in Rome occupied Woolson's life and fiction, its complexities both nourishing her art and overpowering her own identity. She recognized how patriarchy deployed its power, and her stories represent her attempt to expose the underside of accepted, nineteenth-century gender roles. However, gender politics were changing in the later decades of the nineteenth century, as Woolson's work indicates. Woolson's fiction took root and grew in the pivotal space between the separate spheres rhetoric of the mid-nineteenth century and talk of a New Woman at the turn of the century. The complexities of her stories contributed to and reflect the turmoil of the era, her struggles as a writer enabling the early phases of a shift in women's conceptions of themselves that would develop over the years up to and after the First World War. Woolson's artist characters argued for a new acknowledgment of women's power and helped pave the way for the modern woman, who would appear in Edith Wharton's short story "Roman Fever."

CHAPTER 6

Roman Fever Revisited

Roman fever, like the city for which it is named, is a shifting literary and historical concept as dependent upon context as the constructions of femininity and nationalism I have investigated in the preceding chapters. Both as historical materialities and as ideological symbols, women and Rome itself—the breeding ground of malaria—have been subject to power structures whose attempts to constrain or domesticate them for economic gain can ultimately prove destructive.

Femininity and fever are central to Edith Wharton's short story "Roman Fever" (1934), which identifies and develops the connection among generations of American women and the danger associated with Rome. Indeed, Wharton goes further to demonstrate that the fever's multiple manifestations and the experiences of women, the public and the private, are inextricably linked. Revealing how American women's experiences abroad determine the fever's literary and mythological contours, the story construes the terms "woman," "disease," and "Italy," often taken as self-evident and constant, as multifaceted and variable. Through the similarities among Rome, Roman fever, and post–World War I American women, the story suggests the subversive potential of American women's travel to Rome and the increasing command with which they negotiated their environments in the twentieth century. The changing significations of the concepts of fever, woman, and Rome ultimately forward the story's theme of women's progress, both potential and achieved.[1]

In the decades between the publication of Constance Fenimore Woolson's short stories, discussed in the previous chapter, and Wharton's drafting of "Roman Fever," roughly the 1880s to the 1920s, American women experienced what Estelle Freedman has called a "transition period" (268).[2]

The United States witnessed large-scale changes in women's activity outside the home, including the birth of the women's-club movement, the founding of women's colleges, a marked increase in the number of women working for pay outside the home, and the successful mobilization of the women's suffrage campaign. Thus the True Woman of the earlier nineteenth century, associated with the home, gave way to a New Woman defined by her increased mobility in the public sphere. As critics like Elizabeth Ammons have demonstrated, Wharton's stories and longer fiction portray variations on this New Woman, whose arrival clearly shapes "Roman Fever" as well.[3] Significantly, Wharton sets this story in postwar Rome, during the rise of a Fascist government in Italy. My argument in this final chapter centers on the implications of this Roman setting in the story's feminist theme and in Wharton's conception of the "New," twentieth-century American woman.

Just as American cultural definitions of women and their mobility changed over the course of the nineteenth century, so the Roman *campagna*—the countryside surrounding the city—experienced degrees of toxicity depending upon governmental and papal policy, agricultural methods, and cultural climate. The history of Roman fever (or malaria, meaning "bad air") in the campagna was primarily a function of Italian economic practice. Giuliano Procacci notes that "in the nineteenth century travellers saw almost deserted stretches of land, devastated by malaria, where in the sixteenth century there had been relatively well-populated farmland" (183). The danger that—to nineteenth-century travelers—became synonymous with Rome resulted from "the increasing tendency of the big landowners of the Roman countryside to turn arable land over to pasturage" because "in the sixteenth century the Romans devoured a great deal of lamb and sheep-cheese and it was more profitable to provide them with those things than to sell cheaper bread to the people" (Procacci 183). As early as 1841, Catharine Maria Sedgwick identified malaria's economic roots in *Letters from Abroad to Kindred at Home,* explaining that "the condition of the land [the campagna], and the misery resulting from it, are owing to a violation of those laws of Providence which, if strictly observed, would secure food and raiment to every member of the human family" (II:215). Ironically, Mussolini's rise to power in the early-twentieth century would facilitate the countryside's restoration, with the land reclamation of the Pontine Marshes beginning in 1928. Meanwhile, nineteenth-century travel texts were littered with references to the deadly campagna and the disease that forced the middle and upper classes to flee the area during the summertime. Wharton herself used the convention in her historical novel *The Valley of Decision* (1902), portraying an eighteenth-century character who shuts up her carriage windows while traversing the marshland and exclaims on the other side, "Thank God, we're rid of that poison and can breathe the air" (33). Playing upon this history of economics and disease in her short story, Wharton picks up the narrative of Roman fever by intertwining it with the story of two twentieth-century American women, veteran travelers, reunited in Rome.

Linked by Roman fever, the female ancestors of the story's main characters, Mrs. Slade and Mrs. Ansley, have all traveled to Italy, where each generation seems to encounter similar events revolving around clandestine romance and the marriage quest. The repeated themes of women's competition and betrayal have led critics to comment on the story's darkness. Dale Bauer argues that the theme of "Roman Fever" is "a daughter's 'dark inheritance' from her mother" (8), while Barbara White asserts, "I would call it a story simultaneously light and bleak about the impossibility of escaping the past" (7). With Roman fever symbolizing the lethal results of a patriarchal insistence upon marriage, I agree with Bauer's assertion that women's "violence to each other belongs . . . to the violence women have engaged in to force a place for themselves in society, a violence resident at the center of Western civilization" (156); yet I suggest that there is more to this story of Roman fever and American women than an endless cycle of repetition.[4] In my reading I hope to highlight the story's sense of movement and change and in so doing offer a more hopeful explication of the Roman presence in the narrative.

The connection between the women, Grace Ansley and Alida Slade, and their locale is established in the story's first line, in which the two women "looked first at each other, and then down on the outspread glories of the Palatine and the Forum, with the same expression of vague but benevolent approval" (3). The rhetoric suggests comfortable contentment, a familiarity (as opposed to "fever") with each other and the city that is borne out by the rest of the story; the travelers have been here before, as have generations of their maternal ancestors. Their ease in this foreign environment pervades the narrative, and when "they both relapsed upon the view, contemplating it in silence, with a sort of diffused serenity which might have been borrowed from the spring effulgence of the Roman skies" (4), the affinity between woman and place almost elides the boundary between them. Such calm confidence, contrasted with the passionate and sometimes frenzied pitch of American women travelers in the nineteenth century, suggests the frequency and familiarity of intercontinental travel for privileged women in the twentieth century. Sophia Peabody Hawthorne scurried about, trying to visit as many Italian galleries as possible in one day—perhaps fearful she would not have a second opportunity—and her travel journal reflects a life packed with detail and activity. Mrs. Slade and Mrs. Ansley, on the other hand, settle into Rome with the composure of women meeting an old friend. They are in no rush to go anywhere, and Mrs. Slade feels justified in saying, "I don't see why we shouldn't just stay here" (ibid.) at the restaurant where they have recently finished lunch.

With its comfortable, commanding, efficient travelers, "Roman Fever" shows us the American woman's mastery of the foreign environment by twice juxtaposing the central characters' grace with the ineptitude of the stereotypical tourist. In the first case, several tour groups at the restaurant who are "gathering up guide-books and fumbling for tips" are also described as "detained by a lingering look at the outspread city" (ibid.). Mrs. Slade and Mrs. Ansley, on the other hand, settle in to savor the view thanks to Mrs. Slade's savvy handling of the waiter: "Signing to the headwaiter, she explained that she and her friend were old lovers of Rome, and would like to spend the end of the afternoon looking down at the view—that is, if it did not disturb the service? The headwaiter, bowing over her gratuity, assured her that the ladies were most welcome, and would still be more so if they would condescend to remain for dinner" (5). The contrast between the tourists' "fumbling for tips" and Mrs. Slade's ample "gratuity" is marked. Whereas the tourists can only cast a longing glance at the view, the accuracy with which Mrs. Slade reads the situation and the poise with which she manipulates circumstances indicate her independence and efficacy and allow her to get what she wants. Her social expertise is the more remarkable when we recall that early in the 1920s the Fascist government had established laws to prohibit tipping.[5] William Vance notes that the stricture "ought to have eliminated a constant bother" but "in fact made for greater confusion" among tourists (*America's Rome* II:320). Wharton's portrait of a woman who can adapt to and control a difficult, shifting environment tempers the story's suggestion elsewhere that these American women are disempowered by their culture's patriarchal values.

The comparison between the crude tourist and the effective traveler arises again as evening falls on the restaurant. The women remain unmolested, chatting in a "shadowy and deserted" corner, when "a stout lady in a dust-coat suddenly appeared, asking in broken Italian if anyone had seen the elastic band which held together her tattered Baedeker. She poked with her stick under the table at which she had lunched" (19). Her sudden appearance and waving stick suggesting irritability, the stout woman (of unknown nationality) highlights the ease with which the American women fade into their surroundings, as though part of the scenery. The tourist's voice disrupts the peaceful scene, and her heavy reliance on a guidebook demonstrates that repeated travel (evidenced by the battered book) has not succeeded in teaching her the manners or the language of Italy. The crass and inappropriate tourist is a familiar trope in travel literature, which Wharton uses here to emphasize her characters' decorum and expertise. Although Mrs. Slade and Mrs. Ansley *are* trapped in a marriage economy that damages their relationship to each other by encouraging competition, they seem to have moved beyond the stereotype of dependent, infantile womanhood that Wharton so despised.[6] We might say they remain hampered by some nineteenth-century ideals even as they lay claim to the advances of the twentieth.

The New Woman of the twentieth century is fully developed in the main characters' daughters, who gaily explore the Roman streets, notably without chaperones. Even more than their mothers, Barbara and Jenny are able to take command of the foreign environment, recognizing in the process the concomitant changes in their mothers' roles and lifestyles. Barbara remarks that "we haven't left our poor parents much else to do" other than knit, because the older women are no longer responsible—as Daisy Miller's mother once was—for escorting their daughters to social functions and monitoring their interactions with the foreign (3). Mrs. Ansley observes that "the collective modern idea of Mothers" has "given us a good deal of time to kill," underscoring that the primary innovation of the "modern idea" is the independence granted to the new generation of women (4). This independence signifies an absence or diminishment of concern for the daughters, left to boldly flirt with the Italian aviators who "invited them to fly to Tarquinia for tea" (5). With the daughters as with the mothers, a woman's independence registers as the ability to travel freely and confidently. Although the daughters certainly take this freedom to a new level, availing themselves of modern technology to demonstrate their liberation, Wharton's story reveals that such subversion extends backward historically, like Roman fever, and pointedly associates it with travel to Rome.

In a central and frequently quoted passage, Mrs. Slade observes the shifting significance of Rome and its fever: "[W]hat different things Rome stands for to each generation of travellers. To our grandmothers, Roman fever; to our mothers, sentimental dangers how we used to be guarded! to our daughters, no more dangers than the middle of Main Street" (10). Foregrounding women's role in defining Rome's significance, the passage moves from distant "travellers" to the contemporary experience of Jenny Slade and Barbara Ansley. The effect is to zoom in on the present moment of the story, while maintaining the connection between the dangers of "the middle of Main Street" and the Roman fever of three generations before, allowing Wharton simultaneously to project progress and continuity. At each historical moment, Rome is associated primarily with danger; its symbolic value to generations of traveling American women inhering in the threat it poses to their health. Of course, the danger only threatens those who flirt with sexual transgression, which underscores Rome's other significance, its availability to American women as a locus of sexual rebellion. Almost every female ancestor of the women in question has transgressed normative marital boundaries in Rome. Such widespread sexual liberty perhaps explains Mrs. Slade's subtle elision of her own generation in a sentence that moves directly from "our mothers" to "our daughters," conveniently dropping herself and Mrs. Ansley out of the list. Yet later in the story Wharton implicates these women, like the generations before them, in sexual risk taking and indicates that women's resistance extends far into the past, in a chain that joins Great-Aunt Harriet to Mrs. Slade and Mrs. Ansley and to Barbara and Jenny.

The circulation of what Dale Bauer calls a "cautionary tale" within the story, often read critically as indicating stagnation or lack of change, I would argue reinforces the theme of movement toward increased women's power and similarly invokes a subversive spirit stretching back as far as Mrs. Slade and Mrs. Ansley can see. The tale originates with Mrs. Ansley's Great-Aunt Harriet, "the one who was supposed to have sent her young sister out to the Forum after sunset to gather a night-blooming flower" (13). The "family tradition," Mrs. Ansley explains, is that Aunt Harriet later confessed to casting her sister intentionally into danger because they both loved the same man (14). After this competitive treachery gets replicated by Mrs. Slade and Mrs. Ansley, the "tradition" has apparently been fortified enough to be mapped onto the younger generation, hence the critical stance that history is doomed to repeat itself.[7] Yet the projection of competitiveness onto the young women seems to happen entirely from within Mrs. Slade's subjective point of view and has little bearing on the interactions we witness between Jenny and Barbara. The story implies that Jenny and Barbara are not necessarily doomed to the same fate as their predecessors.

Mrs. Slade's inner monologue is our only source for the suggestion that her daughter, Jenny, is somehow less vibrant than Barbara Ansley. Inwardly reflecting that "dear Jenny was such a perfect daughter that she needed no excessive mothering," Mrs. Slade considers this eventuality "a little boring" (8). She thinks of Barbara Ansley "half-enviously" and characterizes her as having "rainbow wings" (8, 12). Yet the validity of this contrast is undercut by the opening page's description of Barbara's "girlish voice" that "echoed up gaily" and Jenny's answer in "a voice as fresh"

(3). Similarly, Mrs. Slade projects competition onto the two young women, convincing herself indignantly "If Babs Ansley isn't out to catch that young aviator—the one who's a *Marchese*—then I don't know anything. And Jenny has no chance beside her" (11). Given the absence of signs of competition between Barbara and Jenny—we know only that they "go everywhere together" (ibid.)—Wharton's attribution of the phrase "then I don't know anything" to Mrs. Slade is probably laced with irony. Furthermore, Jenny and Mrs. Ansley are portrayed with similar dispositions: Mrs. Ansley has a "small quiet face" and a "sweetness" while Jenny is described as an "angel." Yet these virtuous exteriors seem to be contradicted by our knowledge that, years ago, Mrs. Ansley trysted with Mrs. Slade's fiancé and gave birth to Mr. Slade's daughter. The story gives us cause to wonder whether a sweet, quiet demeanor necessarily signifies a cowardly or passive interior. Furthermore, might not Barbara's alleged vibrancy come from the ostensibly timid mother whose daring in Rome resulted in both a life-threatening fever and an illegitimate pregnancy? When the story's apparently self-evident statements become suspect, we must wonder whether there is an ironic undercurrent to Mrs. Slade's pronouncements about certain kinds of women, including her own daughter. Indeed, Wharton suggests that the "Museum specimens of old New York . . . good-looking, irreproachable, exemplary," as Mrs. Slade describes Mrs. Ansley and her husband, in fact live scandalous lives (6). Certainly there is ample reason to mistrust Mrs. Slade's observations about the women in her life; even if she is not malicious, her perspective is flawed.

A more hopeful reading of the story, then, foregrounds those moments when things are not as they seem and thus emphasize the changes that occur beneath the surfaces of even the most apparently monolithic concepts such as motherhood, Italy, and the image of the American woman abroad. Indeed, even the Colosseum, perhaps Rome's most lasting and recognizable symbol, metamorphoses over the course of Wharton's narrative. In the noon to dusk of the story, the "outlying immensity of the Colloseum [*sic*]" becomes a divided image, as "its golden flank [is] drowned in purple shadow" until finally the enormous structure is a "dusky secret mass" (11, 13, 20). The different aspects of the Colosseum mirror its diverse significations: by day a symbol of patriarchal conquest and by night a secret hideaway where the women of Wharton's story meet their lovers. Although it is possible to conclude, as Sweeney does, that "Rome and the Roman Colosseum represent in this story the knowledge and power that Wharton's female characters are denied" (316), the story's transferal of this monument's significance from the affairs of men to those of women may suggest otherwise.

The story's setting in the Rome of the 1920s is both crucial and understated. While the title accents the location, details about the calamitous historical moment are few. Still, given Wharton's expatriated life in France during World War I and her extensive knowledge of Europe, she would have been more aware than most Americans of the changes taking place in Fascist Rome. In the years between 1922 and the Second World War, the time during which Wharton wrote and published her story, not only did the Fascists impose severe governmental restrictions on the Italian people—"sacrific[ing]," in Vance's words, the "democratic freedoms of speech, press, and assembly" (*America's Rome* II:322)—but the party also attempted to effect a rebirth of Rome and Italy by starting a new calendar with the year "I" and remodeling the city's familiar profile. Even the Colosseum was deployed in the "reshaping of Rome into an architectural stage set symbolically expressing Fascist ideals" (II:337). Specifically, under the new regime's design the Colosseum served as an endpoint to "the great boulevard created in 1932 to accommodate Fascist parades" (II:316). Throughout the city the Fascist party attempted to claim the signifying power of historical monuments in order to erase past ideologies and political movements and imply that Fascism's presence in Rome had been eternal. Certainly to the inhabitants of Rome in the 1920s, Fascist activity (including the violent murder of Giacomo Matteotti shortly after he spoke out against Fascism) would have been a reminder of how suddenly and drastically life can change.

Additionally, the First World War had shattered many people's faith in order and constancy. A virtual expatriate for the last thirty years of her life, Wharton directly encountered the war in Europe through extensive relief work and several visits to the front lines. The experience changed her drastically. In a 1919 letter to Charles Scribner, she alludes to the irrevocable impact of the war on her writing: "In the first relief from war anxieties I thought it might be possible to shake off the question which is tormenting all novelists at present: 'Did the adventures related in this book happen before the war or did they happen since?' with the resulting difficulty that, if they happened before the war, I seem to have forgotten how people felt and what their point of view was" (*Letters* 425). Later, after completing a war novel in 1923, she considered abandoning her literary career: "After 'A Son at the Front' I intended to take a long holiday—perhaps to cease from writing altogether. It was growing more and more evident that the world I had grown up in and been formed by had been destroyed in 1914, and I felt myself incapable of transmuting the raw material of the after-war world into a work of art" (*A Backward Glance* 369–70). For Wharton, the chasm that opened between pre- and postwar life threatened her faith in literary constancy.

Twelve years after the end of the war, when Wharton returned to Rome, the war continued to affect her perceptions. In 1931 she wrote from the Albergo Palazzo to Margaret Terry Chanler of her unexpected reaction to the city: "In spite of man's havoc Rome has never seemed to me so beautiful, so matchless. Besides, contrary to my expectations (I had not been here since 1914) man has *not* been wholly vile, & nothing that has been done lately has the criminal horror of the Victor Em. monument, wh. of course I knew. On the contrary, the uncovering of the Republican Temples of the Largo Argentina has been beautifully done, & the fairy loggia and gothic windows of the Palace of the Knights of St John, just being disengaged from rubble, were surely worth seeing again" (*Letters* 541).[8] Wharton's fear that World War I and Fascism would have damaged the Rome of her memory gives way first to the relief of seeing Rome's beauty unmarred by human folly and then to the joy of discovering certain improvements due to Mussolini's restorative efforts. The letter suggests the extent to which the First World War had prepared Wharton, like many Americans, for disastrous upheavals; it further offers the surprising revelation that change, even the menacing policies of Fascism, could have a beneficial outcome.

One such outcome, as literary history tells us, was modernism. During the '20s, American writers used innovative discursive strategies as they attempted to make sense of a cold and unsympathetic world where violence could be as ruthless as it was irrational. Although Wharton is not often cited as modernist, her fiction following the war adopts certain "modern" strategies. In her letters she criticized the "raw material" being produced by James Joyce and T. S. Eliot, yet clearly she was attempting, like other modernist writers, to piece together the fragmented world through fictional reconstructions.[9] In her work we can identify certain conventions that have come to be associated with modernist fiction: the quest for meaning in a confused world, a tight narrative frame closely focused on one (or few) characters, a stark tone achieved through minimal, realistic details. Thus the complex, though subtle, valence of the Roman setting in "Roman Fever" can be read as a "modern" discursive strategy.

Given that Wharton uses details about Rome sparingly, it is worth noting that three aspects of Roman life alluded to in "Roman Fever"—the Colosseum, the practice of tipping, and the U.S. Embassy—are also designated by William Vance as evidence of Fascism's attempt to create a new Rome grounded in the present. As I have discussed, Vance notes the Colosseum's incorporation into Fascist public displays and its visibility from the Piazza Venezia, where citizens gathered to hear Mussolini speak from his famous balcony. Similarly, the authoritarian government imposed its will on social life by prohibiting the tipping not only of waiters but also of cabdrivers and other service workers. Vance also comments on the new order's impact on the American embassy, formerly "a sinecure for writers or artists" but now "filled with lawyers, businessmen, and professional diplomats, most of whom had no knowledge of Rome before they arrived" (*America's Rome* II:321–22). In their attention to twentieth-century ideals and concerns, these new embassy visitors represented the modern era, reflecting the perspective that what was most important about Rome—and the world—was what was happening *at that moment*—a perspective that the Fascist party also promoted, though toward different ends.

When Wharton invokes these three icons of Roman life, she performs a revision of her own that emphasizes the modernist present. By defining the Colosseum and the act of tipping in relation to women, the story attempts to reconstruct the postwar wasteland to the advantage of the twentieth-century woman. Vance argues that Mrs. Slade's observation regarding Roman fever's transmutations is ironic because "as the story develops, it appears that the changes both in Rome and in what it 'stands for' have been superficial" (II:318). In Vance's reading no real change happens; the Roman setting, with its "eternal realities of lust and deceit," "serves as ironic comment: these women . . . are small; their lives are small, and their jealousies self-demeaning. The Roman images that surround them . . . can only make them smaller" (II:319). Certainly to the Romans subjected to a Fascist regime, the changes in Italy were more than "superficial." Similarly, many twentieth-century women would not have defined their lives and concerns as "small," but rather would have acknowledged the importance of the struggle and the advancements that had occurred during the rise of the New Woman. The political stakes of a reading that asserts "eternal realities" for Italians and women are profound; the denial of change relegates the powerless to perpetual stagnation. In contrast I would argue for a more politically progressive reading. Rather than serving to diminish the women who are juxtaposed with its hulking and eternal mass, the Roman setting as Wharton portrays it highlights the New Woman and the historical centrality of women's affairs.

The U.S. Embassy, like the other revised symbols in "Roman Fever," operates as a sign of the new times. In the story the embassy signifies as the location where Barbara and Jenny are introduced to the Italian aviators, the men who invite them on a flight to Tarquinia. In addition to indicating the populist spirit of twentieth-century diplomatic offices—

which had opened their doors to American tourists and Italian pilots alike—the embassy's depiction as a romantic meeting place emphasizes young love and the future generation. This auspicious encounter means that Barbara and Jenny will not be forced to risk death in order to pursue romance in the dark recesses of Roman ruins. They will, in fact, soar as far above the site of contaminated history as it is possible to go. Of course, other dangers accompany them there, a fact that the story makes clear and which I do not mean to elide. When Mrs. Slade offers that today's generation will discover in Rome "no more dangers than the middle of Main Street" (10), the reader will likely recognize (although Mrs. Slade may not) that the dangers of Main Street, USA, are real and present to a young woman in a patriarchal culture. Yet the story gives us the sense that American women have moved past some dangers, even if new dangers lurk around Main Street's next corner.

"Roman Fever" is often singled out in criticism as a landmark story for Wharton. Bauer calls it "one of her most biting stories" (147). White identifies it as "one of Wharton's most widely anthologized stories" (7), and Wolff names it as "perhaps Wharton's single most popular short story" (xiv). Clearly one factor in the fiction's popularity is its effective surprise ending, which gives the reader both a jolt and a sense of appropriate closure. A surprise ending alone, however, cannot account for a story's endurance, and "Roman Fever" must offer something more to its readers. For me, the story's memorable attribute is its portrayal of strong women on the cusp of a new era. By story's end, Mrs. Slade and Mrs. Ansley have achieved a new level of honesty with their confession of past sins, Barbara and Jenny have been set free to pursue what earth and sky can offer them, and—in a story that significantly offers only women as characters—all four have demonstrated a self-determination that contrasts with the forced dependence inflicted upon many characters from earlier decades. Daisy Miller dies for attempting independence, whereas Grace Ansley survives to raise a daughter whose independence exceeds her own.

The concept of change over time, within literary texts and in the critical approaches that surround them, energizes both artistic creation and political action. Lack of change is death, and nostalgia is often the privilege of the elite. Those who hearken back to a golden past, who would return to the "good old days" and have time stand still, are often those who enjoyed a superior social position. I speak to, for instance, our early-twenty-first-century penchant for mourning the lost days when life was "simple" and "wholesome," when families had "values." Who would really benefit from a return to the past? Many subgroups of the American population stand to gain nothing by turning back the clocks and in fact would lose ground. Go back about sixty years, and Japanese Americans would be found in internment camps; eighty-five years and women cannot vote; one hundred and fifty brings us back to the days when Black Americans were enslaved. For oppressed groups, the belief in future change has been and continues to be a crucial component of political action. In contrast to those who idealize the past or yearn for an unchanging present, the women in this study wrote, as a group, toward the future.

My intention is not to overstate feminism's advances or to sugarcoat the political present, but certainly the distance between the bronze wings of Florence Nightingale's archangel and the "rainbow wings" of Wharton's Barbara Ansley suggests that change does happen and testifies to the women who have fought the status quo. Many of the changes that nineteenth-century women dreamed of have come to pass. Many of the issues women wrote about came to the public's attention precisely because of that writing. The women of my study who blurred the public/private boundary on behalf of their politics took that risk because they believed change could rectify social problems if enough people were informed and involved. They also believed in their capacity to contribute to political activism through literature.

Catharine Maria Sedgwick's *Letters from Abroad to Kindred at Home* became letters to a country full of her kin, as her personal experiences became proposals for how a nation ravaged by internal conflict might ease its citizens' pain. When her servant, for example, is denied permission to enter a Venetian arsenal, Sedgwick makes the bridge to politics and then across the ocean to her own country's injustices: "These gentry refused entrance to our courier; service being a disqualifier for such privilege here, as colour is in our own *enlightened* country. We trust these shadows will, ere long, pass quite off the civilized world" (II:106). Though shadows remain to darken the twenty-first century, Sedgwick's faith in the future has been in some measure justified.

Margaret Fuller recognized, perhaps more than any of the women included here, that concern for human welfare must transcend boundaries of race, gender, class, and nation. Her dispatches reveal her belief that private happiness and the public good are inseparable; thus her insistence that "voluntary association for improvement . . . will be the grand means for my nation to grow and give a nobler harmony to the coming age. But it is of only a small minority that I can say they *as yet* seriously take to heart these things; that they earnestly meditate on what is wanted for their country,—for mankind,—for our cause is, indeed, the cause of all mankind at present" (165; emphasis added). The phrase "as yet" conveys the faith that fueled Fuller's dispatches. Like Sedgwick, Fuller writes of and to a future nation that will remedy social ills, creating that future in the act of writing it.

It is interesting that Harriet Beecher Stowe reconstructed the Italian fifteenth century to write her country's future, setting in motion narrative ripples that reached her present day and interjecting narrative reminders about nineteenth-century political "reality." The historical moment she chose for *Agnes of Sorrento* was ripe with import for her American audience because Italy in the late-fifteenth century was on the verge of change: "All through Italy at this time there was the restless throbbing and pulsating, the aimless outreach of the popular heart, which marks the decline of one cycle of religious faith and calls for some great awakening and renewal" (118). Writing to the "popular heart" of her own era, Stowe sought to instigate a similar "awakening and renewal" that would signal the end of slavery and the other human rights violations that plagued nineteenth-century America.

Alluding to her agenda in her preface, Sophia Peabody Hawthorne asserts that she will be "well repaid for the pain it has cost [her] to appear before the public" if *Notes in England and Italy* encourages her readers to "enjoy" the Italian religious masterpieces whose message she viewed as crucial. Hawthorne's text exposes the term "enjoy" as a euphemism for a more complicated process that involves a personal investment on each reader's part: a voyage in search of great artworks, the devotion of time to artistic study, and a mode of apprehension that emphasizes art's humanist message. Her goals were communal, though her means were personal, and her cautious optimism about both appears in the text's final paragraph: "That prophecy of Christian love and peace has not yet been fulfilled; but the genius of Domenichino presents it hourly here for consideration and imitation. It is amazing how slow we are, though the divinest forms, in marble and color, forever speak to the eye, in all degrees of beauty and truth" (548). To Hawthorne the potential and the guides were available, if only people would recognize them. Itself a representation of artistic genius, her own text constituted one more opportunity for Americans to receive the message that would redeem the future.

Although hope for the future is scarce in Constance Fenimore Woolson's work, her commitment to social change is central. She published time and again the story of a woman with artistic genius and in so doing made this woman believable and acceptable, even though the acceptance came too late to save Woolson herself. Miss Grief has "the greater power," as her critic is forced to admit, and Ettie Macks shows the "dilettante" Raymond Noel what it is to be "true and sincere." Though the narratives depict only dead ends for their women artists, Woolson's return to this narrative theme implies her desire for a positive ending, even as her endings indicate the inescapability of her era's sexism.

Wharton concludes her autobiography, suggestively titled *A Backward Glance,* with the following observation about the future: "Life is the saddest thing there is, next to death; yet there are always new countries to see, new books to read (and, I hope, to write), a thousand little daily wonders to marvel at and rejoice in, and those magical moments when the mere discovery that 'the woodspurge has a cup of three' brings not despair but delight" (379). While she recognizes the early-twentieth-century world as an "old floundering monster" that "all the cranks and the theorists cannot master," she can still locate the occasional "little ray through the fog" that "helps humanity to stumble on, and perhaps up" (ibid.). Her faith in new beginnings tempers her knowledge of life's pain, and this perspective informs "Roman Fever" with its young women characters rising out of a diseased world and into a new era.

The possibility of change allowed Sedgwick and Fuller to dream of a more benevolent nation, catalyzed Stowe's political activism, and bolstered Sophia Hawthorne's artistic agenda. Woolson's fiction calls for change, and Wharton's capitalizes on it. Likewise, changes in the critical study of American literature enable a project such as this one by emphasizing the heterogeneity of American experience and advocating a more inclusive canon. The variable and complex ways that White American women apprehended, navigated, and created the foreign world around them in the texts I have explored contribute, I hope, to a broadened understanding of how educated, middle-class women negotiated public and private spheres in the nineteenth and early-twentieth centuries. Ultimately, I would hope this study fortifies feminist studies in American literature and reaffirms faith in ongoing change both in the texts we read and in the way we read them. In deference to the women writers included here, the question I would call upon us to ask of the future is, how can we continue to expand our understanding of the diverse ways that countless and varied people have contributed to the construction of America?

NOTES

Notes to Introduction

1. An insightful study that groups women's texts to investigate specifically the impact of gender on travel and travel writing, Mary Suzanne Schriber's *Writing Home: American Women Abroad, 1830–1920* examines American women's experiences abroad in a range of countries, rather than focusing specifically on Italy as I do here.

2. Some left temporarily; others, for extended periods of time. I am struck by how many of the women in my study died abroad—Hawthorne in England, Woolson in Venice, Wharton in France—or without reaching the American shore, as in the case of Margaret Fuller.

3. See, for example, Nancy Cott's *Bonds of Womanhood* and Gillian Brown's *Domestic Individualism,* both of which treat the nineteenth-century's demarcation of the domestic sphere extensively. For a discussion of "the tension between the values of domesticity and the opposing values of independence and equality," see Beverly Voloshin's "Limits of Domesticity: The Female *Bildungsroman* in America, 1820–1870." Susan Coultrap-McQuin explores how women writers negotiated their careers within a dominant culture that championed domesticity in *Doing Literary Business: American Women Writers in the Nineteenth Century.* A provocative recent discussion of the shortcomings of separate spheres rhetoric, Cathy N. Davidson and Jessamyn Hatcher's *No More Separate Spheres!* pushes beyond the familiar binarisms to argue that "we have run the gamut of what the separate spheres model can tell us about nineteenth-century America and beyond" (11).

4. Sophia Hawthorne actually predicted dire consequences for Rome and invested malaria with a worldwide symbolic meaning, observing, "What a strange and mysterious retribution upon the Empress of the World is the malaria! It is said to be encroaching, so that Rome will finally be left desolate, a sign and a portent to the nations" (281).

5. In "The Female Woman: Fanny Fern and the Form of Sentiment," Lauren Berlant aligns women's exclusion from language with their exclusion from the rhetoric of patriotism when she speaks of "Two disembodied and objective patriarchal forms that define the negativity of women's experience: the dictionary and the nation" (274).

6. Reinforcing Margaret Fuller's contention that "the American in Europe, if a thinking mind, can only become more American," the hero of William Dean Howells's *Indian Summer* remarks of American artists in Florence, "They all, whether they were ever going back or not, were fervent Americans, and their ineffaceable nationality

marked them, perhaps, all the more strongly for the patches of something alien that overlaid it in places" (83).

7. Caroline Gebhard argues persuasively in "The Spinster in the House of American Literature" that women writers continue to be defined by their personal lives: "[T]he woman writer of the last century has come down to us in the dominant literary histories as either a sentimental creature given to extravagant emotions and equally extravagant fictions—the schoolgirl as sentimental novelist—or else as a sterile creature whose passionless gentility renders her art equally sterile—the spinster turned writer" (87).

8. Recent works such as Karen Lawrence's *Penelope Voyages* (1994) and Schriber's *Writing Home* are notable exceptions to the norm, offering illuminating approaches to women's travel writing that go beyond the biographical.

9. For a thorough discussion of the evolution of modern travel to Europe, see James Buzard's *Beaten Track*.

10. Regrettably, Lewis's accomplishments have been elided by many historians, and it is only now that the work of scholars like Marilyn Richardson promises to restore her to her rightful place in the history of American sculpture. For more information on Lewis, see Richardson's "Edmonia Lewis' The Death of Cleopatra: Myth and Identity" or Charlotte Streifer Rubinstein's biographical entry on Lewis in *American Women Sculptors*.

Notes to Chapter 1

1. As Sedgwick's text was published in two volumes, parenthetical citations throughout will indicate the volume number, followed by the page number. I observe the same convention in references to William Vance's *America's Rome,* also published in two volumes.

Sedgwick's admission seems the more surprising, given the nationalistic bias she exhibited early in her career. In 1821 she wrote that American writers should "venture to put our cheerful dwellings, and fruitful fields, and blooming gardens against the ivy-mantled towers and blasted oaks of older regions, and busy hands and active minds against the 'spectres that sit and sigh' amid their ruins" (quoted in Spencer 85).

2. It is interesting to note that, according to Vance, these comparisons were approaching the height of their popularity at the time Sedgwick's travel text was published: "Literary responses to the Forum by which Americans identified themselves with the people of ancient Rome reached the greatest intensity and variety in the 1840's" (I:7).

3. In response to the outrage many Americans expressed on seeing a statue that depicted their political father nude from the waist up, Greenough explained that his intention was not to represent a common man: "Greenough expected that viewers, coming to his image with their own prior knowledge of the man, would be glad to find in it the idealization of that 'complex of qualities' that set him apart, not those accidents he shared 'with other gentlemen of his day' " (ibid., 344).

4. A central distinction in Buzard's study is made between the terms "traveler" and "tourist." He describes a historical tendency, evident as early as the late eighteenth century, to differentiate between the two, with "tourist" carrying a distinctly negative and vulgar connotation. The aim of nineteenth-century visitors to Europe, then, was to establish, through certain culturally determined signs, their identity as travelers. A complex and sometimes ambiguous term, "traveler" came to imply "a loosely defined set of inner personal qualities that amounts to a superior emotional-aesthetic sensitivity" (Buzard 6). In contrast, tourists were identifiable primarily by their tendency to follow the crowd and

experience a foreign location in a prepackaged, mass-produced, and completely predictable way. See the introduction to Buzard's *Beaten Track*. It is interesting to note Sedgwick's conception of herself as a "traveler" seeking more than the average "tourist" experience: "I like, of all things, to stop at these inns which are not the regular stopping-places. The people are social and frank, and you get some insight into the national modes of getting on" (II:132).

5. Of course, Sedgwick would have reconstructed this scene in a letter after all of the events had transpired and may have grafted the reference to Radcliffe onto the narrative from a later vantage point, knowing already how the scene would work itself out. Still, the narrative order suggests a connection between preconceived gothic notions of Italy and Sedgwick's actual experience there.

6. Buzard identifies George Putnam's *Tourist in Europe* (1838) as the first American guidebook to Europe, published only a year before Sedgwick embarked on her trip (195). Sedgwick may have consulted this guide, or she may have had access to one of the British guidebooks already in print. John Murray, for example, published the first of his famous handbooks in 1836. Several passages in *Letters* indicate that Sedgwick herself made use of a guidebook on her trip; remembering a stop she made on the French border before crossing the Alps into Italy, Sedgwick writes, "Our guidebook had promised us 'a tolerable inn,' and a regale of trout from the lake" (II:16). Unfortunately, the inn proves memorable more for the refuse piled on the kitchen floor than for its hospitality, casting the credibility of the guidebook into question.

7. For a discussion of the picturesque in travel writing and the ways American writers manipulated its conventions in the service of domestic excursions, see Beth L. Lueck's *American Writers and the Picturesque Tour: The Search for National Identity, 1790–1860*.

8. Eaton's text is a favorite source for textual borrowings in *Letters*. *Rome in the Nineteenth-Century*, published in 1820, is noteworthy both as one of the earliest nineteenth-century guides to Rome and as an early book of art criticism written by a woman.

9. In contrast, men often made the Grand Tour as bachelors, taking the time to "see the world" independently before settling down at home with a family. See Buzard, 130–54.

10. American travelers and consumers of travel narratives justified glorification in their search for the "authentic" experience, the vision that would provide escape from the realities of domestic life. The travel writer who acknowledged squalid conditions abroad risked rupturing the escapist fantasy that supported both the travel industry and the business of travel writing. For Americans, the stereotype of the Italian lifestyle as sweet, indolent, passionate, and impractical proved an irresistible lure. Nathalia Wright notes in *American Novelists in Italy* that the "chief aspects of the ideal life which [nineteenth-century American writers] projected in Italian terms were intellectual stimulation and freedom from commercial pressures" (32). Sedgwick herself articulates the fundamental dichotomy between American and Italian culture when she reflects, in Milan, that "the opera, with all its accessories, is the study of this nation, as 'financial systems' are the study of England and the United States" (II:40). In Sedgwick's text the contrast between the artistic quality of Italian life and U.S. pragmatism often serves her political project.

11. After observing a group of Milanese Catholic girls in an orphanage, she writes, "beautiful girls they were—and each, as she passed, saluted us with a graceful bow and a sweet smile. I wish teaching could give such manners, and our stiff-jointed girls could be taught them!" (II:48).

12. In Kelley's chronology, this tradition is inaugurated by Dame Julian of Norwich in the fourteenth century and continues through the work of Margery Kempe in the fifteenth

century and Anne Bradstreet, writing in the American colonies in the seventeenth century.

13. This is not to say that Sedgwick advocated an unmarried life for all women or that she did not have doubts about her decision to remain single. Her journal reflects her confusion and occasional loneliness, especially as her brothers married and her childhood family fractured and scattered: "From my own experience I would not advise any one to remain unmarried—for my experience has been a singularly happy one. . . . I have always felt myself to be an object of attention, respect and regard—though not first to any" (*Power* 123). The journal entries often show Sedgwick's vacillating feelings about her own lifestyle decisions but nonetheless continually return to a constant theme: that not marrying was a viable option for women, and that even married women needed to maintain an existence, financial and psychological, separate from their husbands.

14. First named in Barbara Welter's 1966 essay "Cult of True Womanhood, 1800–1860," this prescribed code of conduct for nineteenth-century women is frequently cited in critical works, including Cott's *Bonds of Womanhood,* Brown's *Domestic Individualism,* and Joyce Warren's *The (Other) American Traditions.* Based on the fundamental tenet that the home functioned as a sanctuary from an increasingly competitive and corrupt world, the cult devolved upon women the responsibility of maintaining a morally and emotionally sound domestic environment.

15. Vance observes that Sedgwick was unique in her praise of the papal practice allowing non-Catholic worship; other Americans "considered that being driven to worship with the English in an improvised chapel outside the Porta del Popolo constituted a form of persecution" (II:268).

Notes to Chapter 2

1. In the foreword to the revised edition of *The Woman and the Myth: Margaret Fuller's Life and Writings,* Bell Gale Chevigny provides a comprehensive and invaluable survey of recent Fuller criticism and other relevant secondary sources.

2. For a useful discussion of how and why the "Fuller myth" was constructed and is perpetuated, see Marie Urbanski's "Margaret Fuller's *Woman in the Nineteenth Century:* The Feminist Manifesto" in *Nineteenth-Century Women Writers of the English-Speaking World.*

3. Citations from Fuller's dispatches are taken from Larry J. Reynolds and Susan Belasco Smith's *"These Sad but Glorious Days": Dispatches from Europe, 1846–1850,* the most complete collection of Fuller's journalism. Other collections, like *The Essential Margaret Fuller* and Perry Miller's *Margaret Fuller: An American Romantic,* excerpt only selections from the dispatches. The original publication of the collected dispatches, *At Home and Abroad* (1856), is no longer in print.

4. The newspaper is not a private document attributable to one author, but rather the result of a network of forces. Fuller's involvement in such a network both contributed to her literary reputation and testified to the stature she had attained as a writer.

5. Anderson connects the communal consumption of the newspaper with the creation of imagined community: "Each communicant is well aware that the ceremony he performs [that of reading the daily paper] is being replicated simultaneously by thousands (or millions) of others of whose existence he is confident, yet of whose identity he has not the slightest notion. Furthermore, this ceremony is incessantly repeated at daily or half-daily intervals throughout the calendar. What more vivid figure for the secular,

historically clocked, imagined community can be envisioned?" (35). Printed and consumed on a national scale, the newspaper becomes the common link for a republican nation that accepts any given issue as a coherent whole, despite the fortuitous common denominator (time) that determines its contours. Likewise, citizens accept the nation as an organic whole, its inhabitants bound together in some essential and meaningful way, despite their merely coincidental cohabitation and general ignorance of each other's lives.

In addition, Anderson distinguishes between a medieval belief in time infused with religious predestination, "a simultaneity of past and future in an instantaneous present" in which "Christ's second coming could occur at any moment," and, on the other hand, a modern apprehension of time that has lost its religious inflection (23–24). Whereas "the mediaeval Christian mind had no conception of history as an endless chain of cause and effect or of radical separations between past and present," in the modern era "what has come to take the place of the mediaeval conception of simultaneity-along-time is . . . an idea of 'homogenous empty time,' in which simultaneity is, as it were, transverse, cross-time, marked not by prefiguring and fulfilment [*sic*], but by temporal coincidence, and measured by clock and calendar" (23–24). This understanding of time as a simultaneity connecting the various members of an imagined community is both a result and a precondition of the modern newspaper.

6. Not only did Fuller work as director of the Fate Bene Fratelli hospital for the wounded in Rome, but she also became intimately involved in friendships with two key revolutionaries, Giuseppe Mazzini and Adam Mickiewicz, and involved romantically with a rebel fighter, Giovanni Ossoli.

7. Demonstrating the extent of the populist sentiment in Europe, Polish revolutionary Adam Mickiewicz, Fuller's close friend, made the following demand of his country: "To the companion of life, Woman, brotherhood, citizenship, entire equality of rights" (222). It is not surprising that Fuller included this "declaration of faith" in one of her dispatches, or that Mickiewicz and his humanitarianism appealed so greatly to an American woman whose own "democratic" nation made no such provisions for women or non-White Americans.

8. It is interesting to consider how *Godey's Lady's Book* and sentimental literature enabled different kinds of imagined group consciousness. Of *Godey's*, Isabelle Lehuu writes, "women's pictorial representations shared in the construction of sentimentality and domestic femininity" (90), and Berlant argues that "sentimental ideology served as a structure of consent in which domestically atomized women found in the consumption of popular texts the experience of intimate collective identity" (270). Such forms of "women's" writing contributed primarily to an imagined community based on the home and traditional values, while the newspaper constructed the public community, the "nation" in its most conventional and masculinized sense. Much critical work remains to be done on the intersection of these two imagined (gendered) communities, specifically on women's "collective identity" as a central component of nation formation and conception.

9. Both key figures in the rise of transcendentalism, Emerson and Fuller are often compared by critics, with Emerson's individualist philosophy often placed in opposition to Fuller's wider, communal perspective. Dorothy Berkson writes, for example, "[Fuller's] vision, though not so fully and often articulated as Emerson's is, I would argue, a larger and more complex vision than his in that it recognizes and attempts to accommodate human weakness, the existence of evil, and the potential for failure and despair" (26).

Notes to Chapter 3

1. For discussions of the domestic in Stowe's fiction, see, for example, Elizabeth Ammons's essay "Heroines in Uncle Tom's Cabin" in *Critical Essays on Harriet Beecher Stowe,* Brown's "Domestic Politics in *Uncle Tom's Cabin*" in her book *Domestic Individualism,* Eric Sundquist's introduction to *New Essays on Uncle Tom's Cabin,* and Jane Tompkins's "Sentimental Power: *Uncle Tom's Cabin* and the Politics of Literary History," reprinted in the Norton Critical Edition of *Uncle Tom's Cabin.*

2. For an examination of the novel's relation to nineteenth-century constructions of a Catholic "other," see Jenny Franchot's critical study of American Protestant textual responses to Catholicism, *Roads to Rome.* The novel is also briefly mentioned in Susan Griffin's "Women, Anti-Catholicism, and Narrative in Nineteenth-Century America."

3. This is not to say that Agnes is not Christlike, but to assert that the text posits a more primary affinity to Mary, the invocation and worship of whom represents a fundamental distinction between Catholicism and Protestantism. Vance notes in *America's Rome* the three issues that preoccupied American visitors to Rome in the nineteenth century: "miraculous icons and relics, the Virgin Mary and above all the power and infallibility of the pope" (II:4). That Agnes-as-Mary triumphs in this text suggests Stowe's powerful attraction to Catholicism and the extent to which the novel challenged prevailing nineteenth-century American notions regarding Catholicism. For a discussion of Eva as a type of Christ, see Ammons's "Heroines in *Uncle Tom's Cabin.*"

4. Franchot also reads this dichotomy in gendered terms, describing Stowe's portrayal of "Catholicism as a force of gendered excess, its (feminine) ardent piety and (masculine) unprincipled power yoked in a union that disrupts the gendered, separated spheres of American middle-class domesticity" (248). Thus Agnes redeems Catholicism's feminine features while Father Francesco emblematizes the worst aspects of the church patriarchy. This is only one manifestation of the text's ambivalent portrayal of Catholicism, as both potentially salvific and potentially damning.

5. Agostino's fantasy of Agnes's role in his life codifies this reversal of power: "You should be my wife," he tells her, "my queen, my empress. You should lead me where you would; your word should be my law" (165). The text validates Agostino's vision, as Agnes does, in fact, lead and save him.

6. For a thorough discussion of gender roles in *Uncle Tom's Cabin,* see Ammons's "Heroines in *Uncle Tom's Cabin.*"

7. Franchot's argument proposes that Catholicism, for Stowe, was "an aesthetic and psychological region that enabled [her] literary production" (197). Like the idea of Italy, which provides a certain narrative freedom, Catholicism functions as a liberatory thematics as much because of its exotic and "otherized" valence for nineteenth-century America as because of its "real" doctrines or tenets.

8. Perhaps in anticipation of objections from readers who would resist Catholicism, who would presume its history of idolatry and misplaced emphasis, Stowe's narrator asks, "And for that matter, who is enlightened? who carries to God's throne a trouble or a temptation in which there is not somewhere a misconception or a mistake?" (346). The question reminds readers that human fallibility, despite prevailing beliefs about "enlightenment," can affect, or infect, any form of organized or individual worship.

9. Albert Gelpi acknowledges that certain nineteenth-century American writers *did* celebrate selected aspects of Catholicism, as Franchot argues, but usefully reminds us that what they were attracted to was "Catholic Europe, especially the Catholicism of Italy,

explicitly *not* the unwashed and uncultured Irish and Italians crowded into the slums of their cities to operate the mills and factories that ensured the wealth and social status of the Protestant upper class" (199).

10. For a lengthy, although dated, discussion of the construction by Americans of Italy as Arcadia, see Van Wyck Brooks's *Dream of Arcadia*.

11. It is interesting to consider the relevance of this date in its proximity to 1492, the year Columbus reached the Americas. In her historical regression, Stowe returns to the infancy of European expansionism, to a time when potential can retrospectively be constructed as unlimited and the evils of imperialism have yet to materialize.

12. Significantly, Stowe locates her story in Italy, and specifically Rome, the central historical nexus of one of the world's largest and most influential religious communities, that of Catholicism.

13. The text's repeated celebration of visual art's communicative power may imply a critique of textual efficacy. Stowe's narrator defends pretextual sign systems when she asserts, "The rosary, the crucifix, the shrine, the banner, the procession, were catechisms and tracts invented for those who could not read, wherein the substance of pages was condensed and gave itself to the eye and to the touch" (112). Often the narrator's tone, in passages such as this, suggests that more immediate and effective transmissions can result from apprehension of nonverbal symbols.

14. The novel romanticizes both the viewer's experience and the artist's creative process: Pictures such as Fra Angelico's *Crucifixion* "were painted by the simple artist on his knees, weeping and praying as he worked, and the sight of them was accepted by like simple-hearted Christians as a perpetual sacrament of the eye, by which they received Christ into their souls" (291). For both the artist and the spectator, the interaction with the image occurs passionately and powerfully, more intensely, it would seem, than the corresponding aesthetic experiences of Stowe's fellow Americans.

15. The fantasized, prenational religious community may be read as an extension of the project begun in *Uncle Tom's Cabin* with the depiction of an idealized Quaker community that shelters George and Eliza. Within that novel, however, the community can serve only as a stopping place on George and Eliza's flight across national borders to Canada. The context of *Agnes* frees Stowe from the crisis of slavery, thereby permitting her to project the community on a grander scale, temporally and geographically.

Notes to Chapter 4

1. Because using the name "Hawthorne" would create confusion as to which writer I mean, I will refer to Sophia by her first name throughout.

2. The controversy that surrounds Sophia as a literary figure, indicated in Badaracco's statement, arises from the editorial cuts she made in Nathaniel's journals before publishing *Passages from the English Notebooks* (1870) and *Passages from the French and Italian Notebooks* (1871) after his death. Divided on the issue of Mrs. Hawthorne's effectiveness as an editor, some critics share Sterling Eisiminger's view that "those portions of *The French and Italian Notebooks* that Sophia Hawthorne omitted are of great interest to us for they support the idea that Hawthorne was a cigar-loving, sensual man who had a fine sense of humor" (89). Others endorse a more favorable view of Sophia's editorship, like Warren, who notes that the deleted passages, namely those that allude to alcohol or sex, chronicle what might have been seen as indecorous behavior on the part of the author, and that Sophia "was acting as Hawthorne would have desired," recognizing her husband

as a man to whom propriety was of signal importance (*American Narcissus* 205–6). Carol Hanbery MacKay defines Sophia's intervention as "preserving privacy, exercising prudery, insisting on grammatical correctness and social decorum—in short, cleaning up Hawthorne for the public eye" (190). The critical debate over her editorship continues, unlikely to be resolved and serving mostly to obscure Sophia's other, independent achievements. Indeed, she is remembered in much criticism for what she did *not* produce. Amid all the speculation about Sophia's editorial talents, Thomas Woodson reminds us that, in addition to references to her husband's questionable behavior, Sophia also removed descriptions of "minor mishaps and illnesses" and, in an apparent effort to focus attention on her husband's extrafamilial life, made it her policy "to suppress references to herself" (*The French and Italian Notebooks* 925–26).

3. Exhibiting a tendency toward hyperbole, some criticism endows Sophia with inspirational powers beyond the mere suggestion of characters. Leland Person reads Nathaniel's fiction against his love letters to Sophia and concludes that Nathaniel's intense feelings for his wife created and shaped his literary career. "Not only did Hawthorne admit Sophia's power to make him 'be,' in other words," Person asserts in his reading of a representative love letter, "but in this passage he granted her an ability to make him write." More particularly, Person continues, "in identifying himself with her, he might be able to bring a newly creative self into being and so achieve a new verbal power" (223). Similarly, Julie M. Norko extols Sophia as "the source of [Nathaniel's] salvation, his identity, his perception of the sacred, and his art" (127). Faced with such a body of criticism, the reader rightly begins to wonder, who was this woman, capable of simultaneously performing the functions of model, wife, muse, critic, and priest?

4. As a convention, self-effacement had been established in travel writing by the time Sophia Hawthorne published her text. That is, we need not take too seriously her dismissive preface, for it represents a trope familiar to readers and writers of travel literature. For further discussion of the tropes of travel writing in the nineteenth century, see chapter 2, on Catharine Maria Sedgwick, and Buzard's *Beaten Track*.

5. Sophia Peabody Hawthorne's art is on public display in the New York Public Library, the Concord Antiquarian Society, the Essex Institute, the House of the Seven Gables, the Pierpont Morgan Library, and the Ralph Waldo Emerson House. For more specific information, see Patricia Valenti's "Sophia Peabody Hawthorne: A Study of Artistic Influence."

6. In addition to Sophia's rhetorical style, this passage documents an anti-Semitism that remains uninterrogated in the text and which I do not mean to dismiss. Although an isolated moment in the text, it points up the potential for Christianity, even that preached by the most avowedly humanitarian writers, to be exclusionary and prejudiced.

7. For a discussion of how this aesthetic influenced Nathaniel Hawthorne's apprehension of art as well as his fiction, see Valenti's article, "Sophia Peabody Hawthorne: A Study of Artistic Influence."

8. Even Emerson's meditation in "Nature" on European "originals" suggests how slippery the distinction between original and copy can become: "The American who has been confined, in his own country, to the sight of buildings designed after foreign models, is surprised on entering York Minster or St. Peter's at Rome, by the feeling that these structures are imitations also—faint copies of an invisible archetype" (40). His logic serves a nationalistic project in which anxiety that American architecture is derivative can be allayed by the belief that even Old World originals are reproductions of some originary model that exists beyond time and space.

9. Sophia Hawthorne's editorial activities are explored at length in Claire Badaracco's essay, "Pitfalls and Rewards of the Solo Editor: Sophia Peabody Hawthorne," and, from a more traditional point of view, in Eisiminger's "Mrs. Hawthorne's Editing of *The French and Italian Notebooks*."

10. James's phrase stuck, and contemporary critics continue to refer to these women as "the white marmorean flock." The irony of using the term "white" to describe Lewis points up the disparity between the strict, marble ideals of classical sculpture and the heterogeneous reality of the U.S. population in the nineteenth century.

11. Rubinstein indicates how ambitious Lewis's undertaking would have been, arguing that "few of the American neo-classical sculptors attempted two-figure compositions even though they had skilled carvers to put their works into marble" (54).

12. For a detailed discussion of how the White feminist movement has historically excluded Black women, see Hazel Carby's essay, " 'Woman's Era': Rethinking Black Feminist Theory," in her book, *Reconstructing Womanhood: The Emergence of the Afro-American Woman Novelist.* Carby argues that Black women were denied a political voice in organized feminist events and further "had to confront the dominant domestic ideologies and literary conventions of womanhood which excluded them from the definition 'woman' " (6).

13. Unfortunately, despite her pioneering role in American art history, much of Lewis's biography remains obscure, and many of her artworks have not been located. Critic Marilyn Richardson, who has devoted years to researching Lewis, discovered one of Lewis's major works, a sculpture titled *The Death of Cleopatra,* in a Midwestern shopping mall. Revived critical attention to Lewis's life and work promises to remedy such gross oversights.

14. A sign of her dedication to art, Hosmer's decision not to marry further indicates the extent to which she foiled gender expectations. Explaining her philosophy in an 1855 letter to Wayman Crow, she writes, "I am the only faithful worshipper of celibacy and her service becomes more fascinating the longer I remain in it—even if so inclined an artist has no business to be married—for a man it is all well enough, but for a woman on whom matrimonial duties and cares weigh more heavily, it is a great moral wrong, I think, for she must either neglect her profession or her family, becoming neither a good wife and mother or a good artist. My ambition is to become the latter so I wage eternal feud with the consolidating knot" (quoted in Sherwood 124). Of course, as critics have observed, Hosmer's decision to resist normative heterosexual marriage has other motivations as well, namely the strong attachments she formed with other women during her lifetime. Still, in her letters and writing it is the fear of losing her artistic passion that she underscores when expressing concerns about marriage.

15. Representative examples of this discourse of "mysterious power" can be found in Nathaniel Hawthorne's *Marble Faun,* "when we have left Rome in such a mood as this, we are astonished by the discovery, by and by, that our heartstrings have mysteriously attached themselves to the Eternal City, and are drawing us thitherward again, as if it were more familiar, more intimately our home, than even the spot where we were born" (236), and in Edith Wharton's *Backward Glance:* "I rank Compostela not far behind Rome in the mysterious power of drawing back the traveller who has once seen it" (371).

Notes to Chapter 5

1. Two useful discussions of how the conflict between a woman's domestic responsibilities and her artistic ambitions informs Woolson's work are Sharon Dean's "Homeward

Bound: The Novels of Constance Fenimore Woolson" and Cheryl Torsney's *Constance Fenimore Woolson: The Grief of Artistry.* See also chapter 9, "The Challenge of Art," in Dean's book-length study of Woolson, *Constance Fenimore Woolson: Homeward Bound.*

2. In his article, "Cultural Ambivalence in Constance Fenimore Woolson's Italian Tales," Robert L. White observes that Woolson published a total of eleven stories set in Italy. His discussion highlights six of these stories and, ironically, despite his insistence throughout the article on Woolson's lack of literary talent, presents a useful argument regarding Woolson's varying responses to Italy and Italians. Interestingly, White does not include either of the stories I focus on here, most likely because "The Street of the Hyacinth" and "'Miss Grief'" emphasize the artist-heroine and her American mentor, leaving the Italians for the most part out of the plot. A more insightful—and less disparaging—reading of Woolson's expatriate fiction is available in Peter Caccavari's "Exile, Depatriation, and Constance Fenimore Woolson's Traveling Regionalism."

3. Depictions of residences in Rome often suggest that the artist's economic class determines the number of stairs she must climb. Poor artists, like Woolson's Ettie Macks and Hawthorne's Hilda in *The Marble Faun,* were often relegated to the top floor of apartment buildings, leaving visitors to lament the weariness of "climbing those staircases, which ascend from a ground floor of cookshops, cobblers' stalls, stables, and regiments of cavalry, to a middle region of princes, cardinals and ambassadors, and an upper tier of artists, just beneath the unattainable sky" (*The Marble Faun* 235).

4. Surprisingly, criticism often takes at face value Noel's pronouncements, casting "poor Ettie" in the position of a misguided and talentless girl doomed to fail in Rome. Vance's gloss in *America's Rome* assumes Ettie's incompetence: "Ironies arising from ill-founded hopes are compounded here by the fact that 'Ettie' has come to Rome, dragging her 'uncultivated' old mother with her, not for the sake of Rome or the Romans, but to impose herself on another American, an art critic whose writings have inspired her" (II:254–55). If anything, Woolson's stories seem to undermine the reliability of traditional yardsticks for measuring talent. Dean insightfully articulates this underlying theme in Woolson's work, arguing that "[Woolson] makes the implications about the quality of Ettie Mack's art even more obscure [than her treatment of the theme in "'Miss Grief'"] because she wants to raise questions about how we judge art" (*Constance Fenimore Woolson and Edith Wharton* 209).

5. The fact that Woolson's heroines study and memorize the critical opinions of these male "experts"—despite harboring a basic disagreement with their sexist premises—might suggest the pragmatism that underlies their pilgrimages. Sharp enough to recognize who holds the power, Ettie and Aaronna seek to manipulate dominant theories without necessarily endorsing the aesthetics that go along with them.

6. Dean insightfully points out the difficulties posed for the reader by Ettie's eventual marriage to Noel: "If we read the marriage as a conventional happy ending, the story is unsatisfying because Noel never engages the sympathy of most readers." Dean goes on to propose that "the best way out of the problem is to admit that Ettie loses our admiration and that Woolson intended this and also gained her own authorial revenge by foreshadowing that the marriage will become a trial to Noel" (*Homeward Bound* 183). Certainly one way out of this quandary is to interpret the marriage in light of Ettie's material circumstances, that is, to see it as a matter of economic necessity.

7. Describing the Pantheon as the "best-preserved and noblest of ancient Roman temples," Vance asserts that "the great simplicity of its beauty was preferred to the baroque elaboration in form and decoration of St. Peter's" (I:156, 157). As a structure, it

was aligned with the manly ideals of simplicity and dignity, as opposed to the ornamentation of a Catholic cathedral, which was often coded feminine.

8. Although the narrator's social life seems evidence for Vance's observation that "Woolson's Rome is thus the separate and peripheral foreigners' city" (II:255), I maintain that this "separatism" is a sign of male economic privilege. The female artist characters' lives are *not* separate from or peripheral to the daily workings of Rome.

9. Torsney argues that "the longer Woolson lived in Europe, a continent where the margins of time are blurred, the more she came to examine the universality of the conflict between a woman's artistic vocation and the life that society dictates she live" (*The Grief of Artistry* 87).

10. For a discussion of how gender inflects travel, including the gendering of nations, see chapter 2 of Buzard's *Beaten Track*.

11. For a further discussion of the implications of the "perversity" of Aaronna's work, see Kristin Comment's "Lesbian Impossibilities of 'Miss Grief.' "

12. The name of this character has had a somewhat erratic history. When the story was originally published in 1880 in *Lippincott's,* Woolson used the character name "Ethelind." When the story was reprinted in *Stories by American Authors,* the name was changed to "Isabel." Although the edition of the story published in Joan Myers Weimer's collection uses "Isabel," more recent reprints of the story (like that included in, for instance, the 2002 *Norton Anthology of American Literature*) have reverted to the earlier name.

13. Anne E. Boyd speculates usefully that the differences among the three stories may be due to Woolson's increasing familiarity with Henry James and his negative feelings about women artists. "'Miss Grief'" was written before Woolson had actually met James and portrays a narrator who can, at least, recognize Aaronna's talent, whereas the other two stories depict male critics "who convince women artists they have no talent and no right to pursue careers" and who are "modeled on the man [James] with whom she had developed an intense relationship, and who, she learned, had a more inflexible position on women writers than she had imagined" (193).

14. Torsney credits Leon Edel's biography of James with establishing the stereotype of Woolson as "a desperate, lovesick writer, no longer a cub, nipping at the heels and thereby embarrassing the exalted lion" ("The Traditions of Gender" 164). Torsney also locates origins of "the legend of the spinster chasing the lion over a continent" in Edel's work. Both of these mythologies influence criticism of Woolson's work too heavily, making James often the central figure and Woolson an eccentric, lesser presence in the American literary tradition.

Notes to Chapter 6

1. Italian influences on Wharton's writing were profound and pervasive, with Italy figuring prominently in her novel *The Valley of Decision* (1902); her travel narratives, *Italian Villas and Their Gardens* (1904) and *Italian Backgrounds* (1905); and her autobiography, *A Backward Glance* (1934). Although all of these texts reward study, my purpose in this concluding chapter is to indicate the movement into the modern era and to focus on Wharton's "Roman Fever" as a useful indication of the changing roles of American women. For a broader treatment of Wharton's work set in Italy, see Sharon Dean's *Constance Fenimore Woolson and Edith Wharton: Perspectives on Landscape and Art* and Sarah Bird Wright's *Edith Wharton's Travel Writing.*

2. Ammons identifies the 1920s as the decade during which Wharton composed "Roman Fever" (*Argument* 169). Between the 1920s and the story's publication in 1934, Wharton visited Italy twice. In 1926, Wharton drove with Walter Berry across northern Italy, and in 1930 her Italian tour included a stop in Rome (*Letters* 420, 541).

3. For a full discussion of the New Woman as depicted in Wharton's work, see Ammons's *Edith Wharton's Argument with America*.

4. Susan Elizabeth Sweeney, for example, argues that " 'Roman Fever' offers its female characters little opportunity for change. Indeed, the rivalry of Grace's and Alida's daughters Barbara and Jenny, who are actually half-sisters—a sibling relationship which recalls Grace's great aunts—suggests that another generation of women will enact the story once again" (315). Beyond the sibling connection, however, the story offers no evidence that Jenny and Barbara will resort to the sabotage their matriarchal ancestors exhibited.

5. According to Joseph Warren Beach's *Meek Americans* (published in 1925), tipping must have been an early concern of the Fascist government. Beach, who traveled to Italy in 1923 (year two of the Fascist era), comments on tipping regulations that were already in effect (Vance, *America's Rome* II:319–20).

6. For a thorough discussion of Wharton's "conviction that America, rhetoric and world's fairs aside, continued to prefer infantile females" (11), see Ammons's *Edith Wharton's Argument with America*.

7. Cynthia Griffin Wolff notes, for example, that "Mrs. Slade and Mrs. Ansley have been competing with each other for more than twenty years; now their daughters, Babs and Jenny, are continuing the competition" (xiv).

8. Wharton refers here to the monument erected in honor of Victor Emmanuel II, an enormous white structure built in 1911 to commemorate the first king of a unified Italy, which has been criticized for its ostentatious size and its placement in the heart of the Roman Forum and is known derisively as "The Wedding Cake."

9. In 1923 Wharton wrote to long-time friend Bernard Berenson that Joyce's *Ulysses* was "a turgid welter of pornography (the rudest schoolboy kind) & unformed & unimportant drivel; & until the raw ingredients of a pudding *make* a pudding, I shall never believe that the raw material of sensation & thought can make a work of art without the cook's intervening. The same applies to Eliot" (*Letters* 461).

BIBLIOGRAPHY

Adams, Henry. *The Education of Henry Adams.* Boston: Houghton Mifflin, 1974.

Adams, Percy. *Travel Literature and the Evolution of the Novel.* Lexington: University Press of Kentucky, 1983.

———, ed. *Critical Essays on Harriet Beecher Stowe.* Boston: G. K. Hall, 1980.

Ammons, Elizabeth. *Edith Wharton's Argument with America.* Athens: University of Georgia Press, 1980.

———. "Heroines in *Uncle Tom's Cabin.*" *Critical Essays on Harriet Beecher Stowe.* Boston: G. K. Hall, 1980.

———. "Stowe's Dream of the Mother-Savior: *Uncle Tom's Cabin* and American Women Writers before the 1920s." In *New Essays on Uncle Tom's Cabin,* ed. Eric Sundquist. Cambridge: Cambridge University Press, 1986.

Anderson, Benedict. *Imagined Communities.* London: Verso, 1983.

Badaracco, Claire M. "Pitfalls and Rewards of the Solo Editor: Sophia Peabody Hawthorne." *Resources for American Literary Study* 11 (1) (Spring 1981): 91–100.

Bailey, Brigitte. "Gender, Nation, and the Tourist Gaze in the European 'Year of Revolutions': Kirkland's *Holidays Abroad.*" *American Literary History* 14 (1) (Spring 2002): 60–82.

Bauer, Dale M. *Edith Wharton's Brave New Politics.* Madison: University of Wisconsin Press, 1994.

Baym, Nina. *Woman's Fiction: A Guide to Novels by and about Women in America.* Urbana: University of Illinois Press, 1993.

Berkson, Dorothy. " 'Born and Bred in Different Nations': Margaret Fuller and Ralph Waldo Emerson." In *Patrons and Protégés: Gender, Friendship, and Writing in Nineteenth-Century America,* ed. Shirley Marchalonis. New Brunswick, N.J.: Rutgers University Press, 1988.

Berlant, Lauren. "The Female Woman: Fanny Fern and the Form of Sentiment." In *The Culture of Sentiment: Race, Gender, and Sentimentality in Nineteenth-Century America,* ed. Shirley Samuels. Oxford: Oxford University Press, 1992.

Bhabha, Homi K., ed. *Nation and Narration.* New York: Routledge, 1993.

Boyd, Anne E. "Anticipating James, Anticipating Grief." In *Constance Fenimore Woolson's Nineteenth Century: Essays,* ed. Victoria Brehm. Detroit: Wayne State University Press, 2001.

Brooks, Van Wyck. *The Dream of Arcadia.* New York: E. P. Dutton, 1958.

Brown, Gillian. *Domestic Individualism: Imagining Self in Nineteenth-Century America.* Berkeley: University of California Press, 1990.

Buonomo, Leonardo. *Backward Glances: Exploring Italy, Reinterpreting America (1831–1866).* Madison: Fairleigh Dickinson University Press, 1996.

Burgard, Timothy Anglin. *Edmonia Lewis and Henry Wadsworth Longfellow: Images and Identities.* Brochure for exhibit at Fogg Art Museum, February 18–May 3, 1995. Cambridge: Harvard University Art Museums, 1995.

Butler's Lives of the Saints, ed. Herbert Thurston and Donald Attwater. New York: P. J. Kenedy & Sons, 1956.

Buzard, James. *The Beaten Track: European Tourism, Literature, and the Ways to Culture, 1800–1918.* Oxford: Clarendon, 1993.

Caccavari, Peter. "Exile, Depatriation, and Constance Fenimore Woolson's Traveling Regionalism." In *Women, America, and Movement: Narratives of Relocation,* ed. Susan L. Roberson. Columbia: University of Missouri Press, 1998.

Carby, Hazel. *Reconstructing Womanhood: The Emergence of the Afro-American Woman Novelist.* New York: Oxford University Press, 1987.

Castiglia, Christopher. "In Praise of Extra-Vagant Women: *Hope Leslie* and the Captivity Romance." *Legacy* 6 (2) (Fall 1989): 3–16.

Chevigny, Bell Gale. *The Woman and the Myth: Margaret Fuller's Life and Writings.* Boston: Northeastern University Press, 1994.

Comment, Kristin. "Lesbian Impossibilities of 'Miss Grief.' " In *Constance Fenimore Woolson's Nineteenth Century: Essays,* ed. Victoria Brehm. Detroit: Wayne State University Press, 2001.

Cott, Nancy. *The Bonds of Womanhood.* New Haven, Conn.: Yale University Press, 1977.

Coultrap-McQuin, Susan. *Doing Literary Business: American Women Writers in the Nineteenth Century.* Chapel Hill: University of North Carolina Press, 1990.

Davidson, Cathy N., and Jessamyn Hatcher, eds. *No More Separate Spheres!* Durham: Duke University Press, 2002.

Dean, Sharon. *Constance Fenimore Woolson and Edith Wharton: Perspectives on Landscape and Art.* Knoxville: University of Tennessee Press, 2002.

———. "Constance Fenimore Woolson and Henry James: The Literary Relationship." *Massachusetts Studies in English* 71 (3) (1980): 1–9.

———. *Constance Fenimore Woolson: Homeward Bound.* Knoxville: University of Tennessee Press, 1995.

———. "Homeward Bound: The Novels of Constance Fenimore Woolson." *Legacy* 6 (2) (Fall 1989): 17–28.

Deiss, Joseph Jay. *The Roman Years of Margaret Fuller.* New York: Thomas Y. Crowell, 1969.

Douglas, Ann. "Feminine Sentimentalism: The Bitterness of Harriet Beecher Stowe." In *Critical Essays on Harriet Beecher Stowe,* ed. Elizabeth Ammons. Boston: G. K. Hall, 1980.

———. *The Feminization of American Culture.* New York: Avon, 1977.

Eaton, Charlotte. *Rome in the Nineteenth Century.* London: Henry G. Bohn, 1852.

Eisiminger, Sterling. "Mrs. Hawthorne's Editing of *The French and Italian Notebooks.*" *Nathaniel Hawthorne Journal* (1978): 89–92.

Emerson, Ralph Waldo. *Selected Prose and Poetry.* New York: Rhinehart, 1954.

Erlich, Gloria. *Family Themes and Hawthorne's Fiction.* New Brunswick, N.J.: Rutgers University Press, 1984.

Fetterley, Judith. "Only a Story, Not a Romance: Harriet Beecher Stowe's *The Pearl of Orr's*

Island." In *The (Other) American Traditions*, ed. Joyce Warren. New Brunswick, N.J.: Rutgers University Press, 1993.

Franchot, Jenny. *Roads to Rome: The Antebellum Protestant Encounter with Catholicism*. Berkeley: University of California Press, 1994.

Freedman, Estelle. "The Benefits of Separate Female Organizations." In *Major Problems in American Women's History*, ed. Mary Beth Norton. Lexington, Mass.: D. C. Heath, 1989.

Fuller, Margaret (Ossoli). *"These Sad but Glorious Days": Dispatches from Europe, 1846–1850*, ed. Larry J. Reynolds and Susan Belasco Smith. New Haven, Conn.: Yale University Press, 1992.

Gebhard, Caroline. "The Spinster in the House of American Criticism." *Tulsa Studies in Women's Literature* 10 (1991): 79–91.

Gelpi, Albert. "The Catholic Presence in American Culture." *American Literary History* 11 (1) (Spring 1999): 196–212.

Gilbert, Sandra M. "From *Patria* to *Matria:* Elizabeth Barrett Browning's Risorgimento." *PMLA* 99 (2) (March 1984): 194–211.

Giles, Paul. *American Catholic Arts and Fictions: Culture, Ideology, Aesthetics*. Cambridge: Cambridge University Press, 1992.

Gossett, Suzanne, and Barbara Ann Bardes. "Women and Political Power in the Republic: Two Early American Novels." *Legacy* 2 (2) (Fall 1985): 13–30.

Griffin, Susan. "Women, Anti-Catholicism, and Narrative in Nineteenth-Century America." In *The Cambridge Companion to Nineteenth-Century American Women's Writing*, ed. Dale Bauer and Philip Gould. Cambridge: Cambridge University Press, 2001.

Hawthorne, Nathaniel. *The Marble Faun*. New York: Signet, 1961.

Hawthorne, Sophia Peabody. *Notes in England and Italy*. New York: G. P. Putnam, 1869.

Hearder, Harry. *Italy during the Age of the Risorgimento 1790–1870*. New York: Longman, 1983.

Hedrick, Joan. *Harriet Beecher Stowe: A Life*. New York: Oxford University Press, 1994.

Hennessy, Rosemary. *Materialist Feminism and the Politics of Discourse*. New York: Routledge, 1993.

Howells, William Dean. *Indian Summer*. New York: Vintage, 1990.

Hoyt, Edwin. *The Peabody Influence: How a Great New England Family Helped to Build America*. New York: Dodd, Mead, 1968.

James, Henry. "The Beast in the Jungle." *The Turn of the Screw and Other Short Fiction*. New York: Bantam, 1981.

———. "The Lesson of the Master." *Daisy Miller and Other Stories*. New York: Penguin, 1963.

———. *Partial Portraits*. Ann Arbor: University of Michigan Press, 1970.

———. *The Portrait of a Lady*. New York: Signet, 1979.

Kelley, Mary. "Legacy Profile: Catharine Maria Sedgwick." *Legacy* 6 (2) (Fall 1989): 43–49.

———, ed. *The Power of Her Sympathy: The Autobiography and Journal of Catharine Maria Sedgwick*. Boston: Massachusetts Historical Society, 1993.

Kitterman, Mary P. Edwards. "Henry James and the Artist-Heroine in the Tales of Constance Fenimore Woolson." In *Nineteenth-Century Women Writers of the English-Speaking World*, ed. Rhoda B. Nathan. New York: Greenwood, 1986.

Kolodny, Annette. *The Land before Her: Fantasy and Experience of the American Frontiers, 1630–1860*. Chapel Hill: University of North Carolina Press, 1984.

Lawrence, Karen R. *Penelope Voyages: Women and Travel in the British Literary Tradition.* Ithaca, N.Y.: Cornell University Press, 1994.

Lehuu, Isabelle. "Sentimental Figures: Reading *Godey's Lady's Book* in Antebellum America." In *The Culture of Sentiment: Race, Gender, and Sentimentality in Nineteenth-Century America,* ed. Shirley Samuels. Oxford: Oxford University Press, 1992.

Lueck, Beth L. *American Writers and the Picturesque Tour: The Search for National Identity, 1790–1860.* New York: Garland, 1997.

Lukens, Margaret A. "Columnist of Conscience: Margaret Fuller's New York Years." In *Margaret Fuller: Visionary of the New Age,* ed. Marie Mitchell Olesen Urbanski. Orono, Maine: Northern Lights, 1994.

MacKay, Carol Hanbery. "Hawthorne, Sophia and Hilda as Copyists: Duplication and Transformation in *The Marble Faun.*" *Browning Institute Studies* 12 (1984): 93–120.

Martin, Robert K., and Leland S. Person, eds. *Roman Holidays: American Writers and Artists in Nineteenth-Century Italy.* Iowa City: University of Iowa Press, 2002.

Melton, Jeffrey Alan. "Touring Decay: Nineteenth-Century American Travel Writers in Europe." *Papers on Language and Literature* 35 (2) (Spring 1999): 206–22.

Miller, Edwin Haviland. "A Calendar of the Letters of Sophia Peabody Hawthorne." *Studies in the American Renaissance* (1986): 199–281.

Miller, Perry, ed. *Margaret Fuller: American Romantic.* Garden City, N.Y.: Anchor, 1963.

Mulvey, Christopher. *Anglo-American Landscapes: A Study of Nineteenth-Century Anglo-American Travel Literature.* Cambridge: Cambridge University Press, 1983.

Nathan, Rhoda B., ed. *Nineteenth-Century Women Writers of the English-Speaking World.* New York: Greenwood, 1986.

Nightingale, Florence. *Cassandra: An Essay.* Old Westbury, N.Y.: Feminist Press, 1979.

Norko, Julie M. "Hawthorne's Love Letters: The Threshold World of Sophia Peabody." *American Transcendental Quarterly* 7 (2) (June 1993): 127–39.

Perosa, Sergio. *American Theories of the Novel: 1793-1903.* New York: New York University Press, 1985.

Person, Leland, Jr. "Hawthorne's Love Letters: Writing and Relationship." *American Literature* 59 (2) (May 1987): 211–27.

Pfister, Joel. *The Production of Personal Life: Class, Gender, and the Psychological in Hawthorne's Fiction.* Stanford: Stanford University Press, 1991.

The Power of Her Sympathy: The Autobiography and Journal of Catharine Maria Sedgwick, ed. Mary Kelley. Boston: Massachusetts Historical Society, 1993.

Pratt, Mary Louise. *Imperial Eyes: Travel Writing and Transculturation.* New York: Routledge, 1992.

Procacci, Giuliano. *History of the Italian People,* trans. Anthony Paul. New York: Penguin, 1970.

Renan, Ernest. "What Is a Nation?" In *Nation and Narration,* ed. Homi Bhabha. New York: Routledge, 1990.

"Review of *Letters from Abroad to Kindred at Home.*" *The Eclectic Review* 10 (September 1841): 265–77.

Richardson, Marilyn. "Edmonia Lewis' The Death of Cleopatra: Myth and Identity." *The International Review of African American Art* 12 (2) (1995): 36–52.

Romines, Ann. *The Home Plot: Women, Writing and Domestic Ritual.* Amherst: University of Massachusetts Press, 1992.

Ronda, Bruce, ed. *Letters of Elizabeth Palmer Peabody.* Middletown, Conn.: Wesleyan University Press, 1984.

Rubinstein, Charlotte Streifer. *American Women Sculptors.* Boston: G. K. Hall, 1990.

Schriber, Mary Suzanne. *Telling Travels: Selected Writings by Nineteenth-Century American Women Abroad.* DeKalb: Northern Illinois University Press, 1995.

———. *Writing Home: American Women Abroad, 1830–1920.* Charlottesville: University Press of Virginia, 1997.

Sedgwick, Catharine Maria. *Hope Leslie; Or, Early Times in the Massachusetts.* New Brunswick, N.J.: Rutgers University Press, 1987.

———. *Letters from Abroad to Kindred at Home.* 2 vols. New York: Harper & Brothers, 1841.

———. *The Power of Her Sympathy: The Autobiography and Journal of Catharine Maria Sedgwick,* ed. Mary Kelley. Boston: Massachusetts Historical Society, 1993.

Shapiro, Ann. *Unlikely Heroines: Nineteenth-Century American Women Writers and the Woman Question.* New York: Greenwood, 1987.

Sherwood, Dolly. *Harriet Hosmer, American Sculptor, 1830–1908.* Columbia: University of Missouri Press, 1991.

Spencer, Benjamin. *The Quest for Nationality.* Syracuse: Syracuse University Press, 1957.

Stebbins, Theodore, Jr. *The Lure of Italy: American Artists and the Italian Experience, 1760–1914.* New York: Harry N. Abrams, 1992.

Stowe, Harriet Beecher. *Agnes of Sorrento.* St. Clair Shores, Mich.: Scholarly Press, 1970.

———. *Uncle Tom's Cabin: A Norton Critical Edition,* ed. Elizabeth Ammons. New York: W. W. Norton, 1994.

Stowe, William W. *Going Abroad: European Travel in Nineteenth-Century American Culture.* Princeton, N.J.: Princeton University Press, 1994.

Sundquist, Eric, ed. *New Essays on Uncle Tom's Cabin.* Cambridge: Cambridge University Press, 1986.

Sweeney, Susan Elizabeth. "Edith Wharton's Case of Roman Fever." *Wretched Exotic: Essays on Edith Wharton in Europe.* New York: Peter Lang, 1993.

Thoreau, Henry David. *Walden and Civil Disobedience.* New York: Penguin, 1986.

Torsney, Cheryl B. *Constance Fenimore Woolson: The Grief of Artistry.* Athens: University of Georgia Press, 1989.

———. "The Traditions of Gender: Constance Fenimore Woolson and Henry James." In *Patrons and Protégées: Gender, Friendship, and Writing in Nineteenth-Century America,* ed. Shirley Marchalonis. New Brunswick, N.J.: Rutgers University Press, 1988.

Urbanski, Marie. "Margaret Fuller's *Woman in the Nineteenth Century:* The Feminist Manifesto." In *Nineteenth-Century Women Writers of the English-Speaking World,* ed. Rhoda B. Nathan. New York: Greenwood, 1986.

Valenti, Patricia Dunlavy. "Sophia Peabody Hawthorne: A Study of Artistic Influence." *Studies in the American Renaissance* (1990): 1–21.

Vance, William. *America's Rome.* 2 vols. New Haven: Yale University Press, 1989.

———. "Seeing Italy: The Realistic Rediscovery by Twain, Howells, and James." In *The Lure of Italy: American Artists and the Italian Experience, 1760–1914,* ed. Theodore Stebbins Jr. New York: Harry N. Abrams, 1992.

Voloshin, Beverly R. "The Limits of Domesticity: The Female *Bildungsroman* in America, 1820–1870." *Women's Studies* 10 (1984): 283–302.

Von Mehren, Joan. *Minerva and the Muse: A Life of Margaret Fuller.* Amherst: University of Massachusetts Press, 1994.

Warren, Joyce. *The American Narcissus: Individualism and Women in Nineteenth-Century American Fiction.* New Brunswick, N.J.: Rutgers University Press, 1984.

———. "Introduction: Canons and Canon Fodder." *The (Other) American Traditions.* New Brunswick, N.J.: Rutgers University Press, 1993.

Weimer, Joan Myers. "Introduction." *Women Artists, Women Exiles: "Miss Grief" and Other Stories.* New Brunswick, N.J.: Rutgers University Press, 1988.

Wharton, Edith. *A Backward Glance.* New York: Charles Scribner's Sons, 1964.

———. *The Letters of Edith Wharton,* ed. R. W. B. Lewis and Nancy Lewis. New York: Charles Scribner's Sons, 1988.

———. *"Roman Fever" and Other Stories.* New York: Collier, 1987.

———. *The Valley of Decision.* New York: Charles Scribner's Sons, 1902.

White, Barbara. *Edith Wharton: A Study of the Short Fiction.* New York: Twayne, 1991.

White, Robert L. "Cultural Ambivalence in Constance Fenimore Woolson's Italian Tales." *Tennessee Studies in Literature* 12 (1967): 121–29.

Wolff, Cynthia Griffin. "Introduction." *"Roman Fever" and Other Stories.* New York: Collier, 1987.

Women's Rights in the United States: A Documentary History, ed. Winston E. Langley and Vivian C. Fox. Westport, Conn.: Greenwood, 1994.

Woodson, Thomas, ed. *The French and Italian Notebooks.* Columbus: Ohio State University Press, 1980.

———, ed. "Sophia Hawthorne's Diary for June 1861." *The Nathaniel Hawthorne Review* 15 (2) (Fall 1989): 3–5.

———, James A. Rubino, and Jamie Barlowe Kayes. "With Hawthorne in Wartime Concord: Sophia Hawthorne's 1862 Diary." *Studies in the American Renaissance* (1988): 281–359.

Woolson, Constance Fenimore. "A Florentine Experiment." *The Atlantic Monthly* 46 (October 1880): 502–30.

———. *Women Artists, Women Exiles: "Miss Grief" and Other Stories.* New Brunswick, N.J.: Rutgers University Press, 1988.

Wright, Nathalia. *American Novelists in Italy.* Philadelphia: University of Pennsylvania Press, 1965.

Wright, Sarah Bird. *Edith Wharton's Travel Writing: The Making of a Connoisseur.* New York: St. Martin's Press, 1997.

INDEX